Getting New Mexico

Rhenna St. Clair

Pace Press
Fresno, California

Published by Pace Press
An imprint of Linden Publishing
2006 South Mary Street, Fresno, California 93721
(559) 233-6633 / (800) 345-4447
QuillDriverBooks.com

Pace Press and Colophon are trademarks of
Linden Publishing, Inc.

ISBN 978-1-61035-344-1

135798642

Printed in the United States of America
on acid-free paper.

This is a work of fiction. The names, places, characters, and incidents
in this book are used fictitiously, and any resemblance to actual people,
places, or events is coincidental. Whenever real celebrities, places, or
businesses have been mentioned or appear in this novel, they have been
used fictitiously.

Library of Congress Cataloging-in-Publication Data

Names: St. Clair, Rhenna, author.
Title: Getting New Mexico / Rhenna St. Clair.
Description: Fresno, California : Pace Press, [2019]
Identifiers: LCCN 2019039228 (print) | LCCN 2019039229 (ebook) |
ISBN
   9781610353441 (trade paperback ; acid-free paper) | ISBN
9781610353632
   (kindle edition) | ISBN 9781610353632 (epub)
Subjects: LCSH: Redemption--Fiction | New Mexico--Fiction
Classification: LCC PS3619.T2329 G38 2019 (print) | LCC PS3619.
T2329
   (ebook) | DDC 813/.6--dc23
LC record available at https://lccn.loc.gov/2019039228
LC ebook record available at https://lccn.loc.gov/2019039229

Contents

This book is dedicated to all the employees of
Sam's Club New Mexico

CHAPTER 1

Clementine Atwater

"Should I bail him out one last time, Winston? Just once more?"

Clementine Atwater knew any answer to her simple question would be complex. That was a given. Anything concerning her son, Aaron Schuyler, was complicated because his personal history resembled a cesspool. Schuyler had been unfaithful to his wife, neglected his children, cheated his business clients, slept with his partner's wife, and was now living like a bum.

Only an unorthodox solution could resolve such a knotty problem—the question of whether Aaron deserved another bailout—but Clementine was confident such a solution existed. Her deity was no novice at cleaning up messes, and his advice was ever flawless. Clasping her hands in expectation, she shifted on her knees and waited. Winston had never yet failed her, and he did not now.

"Make the effort," came the forceful response of a male voice with an upper-class British accent. "As do you, I recognize his latent goodness. But that weighty core of character and virtue are useless if he does not recognize what virtue lies within himself."

"We agree, then?" Clementine whispered. "We'll give him one more chance. Just one. I have a plan in mind."

"Then trust yourself. Press on, for you know best what to do."

Crossing herself, pushing a silvered strand off her forehead, Clementine rose from where she knelt beside her bed. "Thank you, Winston. Thank you."

When it came to beseeching favors from divinity, Clementine Atwater had no use for a disembodied spirit supported by clouds. Her god was a real person, the hero of her childhood during the dark days of World War II. Her hero was the most important person of the twentieth century. This was the man who saved

England from destruction, Europe from tyranny, and brought peace to a war-torn and devastated world.

Oh, how she adored him.

Born in Leeds, England, in 1940, Clementine Neville was christened in honor of Winston Churchill's beloved wife. Her parents, Mary and Francis Neville, ardent admirers of the Churchills, doted on their tiny daughter. They were delighted when the first word she spoke wasn't "mama" or "dada" but "Chuh-Chuh." No childhood idiosyncrasy could have pleased them more than her infant version of the name ever on her father's lips.

Even as a toddler in nappies, little Clementine observed how her mother's anxious brow relaxed and softened when the family listened to the prime minister's bracing radio broadcasts. Mary Neville would be painting another of the many watercolors displayed within their home. Francis would be furiously copying as many of the PM's words as he could into his broadcast diary. Yet both were listening keenly for, in those dark days, Churchill was the one to whom the island nation's citizens looked to for guidance, leadership, hope, and salvation. Churchill, endangering his personal safety to roam London's streets during the horrors of the Blitz, was everything, to every Briton.

Or, at least, most of them.

Little Clementine Neville was a deep thinker, even at an early age. When only five years old she pointed out to her parents that god was dog spelled backward. Mary and Francis were somewhat taken aback, but pleased by their daughter's precocity. They indulged her with a smile. And, when she thereafter poured out her prayers by rote each night to the great man they said nothing, confident she would outgrow her youthful spiritual perspective and embrace the tenets of the Anglican Church.

Not so.

Throughout her early childhood, her teenage years, and into adulthood, Clementine remained the prime minister's faithful petitioner. When asked what sort of gift she would like for birthdays, Christmas, and Boxing Day, her parents guessed her answer before she gave it. Her inevitable choice was whatever new biography of Churchill they could find, or books about British military action during the Second World War. In this she was like her younger brother, Harry, also an aficionado of British history.

January 24, 1965, was the saddest day of Clementine's young life. Winston Churchill died, and his wife for whom she was named was by his side. Now Mrs. Daniel Schuyler, married to an American citizen and living in New York City, Clementine, heavy with child, flew to Heathrow from LaGuardia. She was among the thousands who traveled to London and lined the streets leading to St. Paul's Cathedral on January 30th, the day of Churchill's funeral.

Her sorrow as the solemn cortege passed by on that frigid London day was almost beyond containment. She pulled her plaid woolen coat as tightly closed as possible, patted her swollen belly, and assured its occupant they were still in good hands. Churchill's spirit would prevail. It would guide her through the struggles of marriage and motherhood, and mold her into the valiant and stalwart woman she was meant to be. Of that, she was convinced.

Winston Churchill was the rock upon which Clementine built her church.

Her son, Aaron Schuyler, then nestled safely within her womb, was the cross upon which she hung herself, time after time, for more than fifty years. He was her living altar of self-sacrifice.

Clementine Atwater was a vigorous and sturdy seventy-seven years old, determined to rectify her middle-aged son's ways and fix his footsteps on a nobler path, when she received Winston's answer to her latest prayer.

CHAPTER 2

Akron, Ohio

Aaron Schuyler was only too happy to admit he owed everything to his mother and, in so saying, he didn't mean a smooth glide down the birth canal into the big wide world. His mother, Clementine Atwater, hadn't just given him life. She deserved far more credit than that. In an endless round-robin of give-and-take, when he needed bailing out from debt, she was the one who granted him salvation and restored his credibility. She gave, and he took.

Schuyler was now fifty-two years old. His temples were graying and there were flecks of white visible in his head of thick brown hair. There were creases around his eyes and deep lines traversed the gap between his nose and mouth. Daily, he checked out the slight sag in the skin covering his jaw. Not too bad. No double chin. *So far.*

Considering his dissolute lifestyle, he was far better-looking than he had any right to be.

"Mom, I promise. I'll never ask again." Shameless, he had knelt before his mother during their last encounter in her New York City high-rise flat, just after her most recent marriage. All the while, conscious of the stress to his knees, he wondered why Clementine had sold her lush Axminster carpet. The highly polished hardwood floors now in vogue had their drawbacks.

"This is the last time, Mom. Please help me out. I'm so sorry."

Clementine had promised to consider his request. "I'll get back to you, Aaron. Truly, I will, but I need a few days to consider this. Right now, I'm focused on helping poor Harry. He's failing fast, you know."

Schuyler did know. The agony of his Uncle Harry's struggle with cancer had them both in a holding pattern, wondering when Harry might breathe his last. Clementine's anguish at her brother's losing battle was all-consuming. Schuyler knew further wheedling on his part would be counterproductive, and only serve to irritate his mother. All he could do was wait.

When Harry's health took a slight turn for the better, Clementine felt it safe to leave New York and return to Akron, Ohio, the home of her new bridegroom. The steely verbiage of the text she soon sent her son, requesting he join her there and outlining her terms of financial assistance, was an unexpected game changer.

Schuyler sat up and took notice. Forewarned, is forearmed.

Heretofore, Clementine had dispensed forgiveness and cash in equal measure whenever her son declared repentance. And, although she never asked for much in return, Schuyler hadn't missed the fact that her recent bailouts demanded greater amounts of penance from him. The things she now expected him to do, however, were more like revenge, in his book. But—who was he to quibble? His mother had again girded her loins and come to his rescue even if, this time, her quid-pro-quo requirement was ridiculous. *Excessive.* Painful.

Had she finally wised up?

"You're making this really hard, Mom," Schuyler argued, having phoned her at once to see if he could negotiate a better deal. "What you're asking me to do is intolerable. I don't know how you justify yourself. Why do I have to move to New Mexico?"

This strange injunction alarmed him. Live in the desert? *Really?* He put up a half-hearted fuss, hoping to secure more agreeable terms. "This was Winston's idea, wasn't it?" he challenged, aware of his mother's fantasy fixation.

On meeting Clementine's rigid resistance, however, Schuyler gave in. He acquiesced to his mother's demands—wishes, as she referred to them—for one reason only: To receive the first payment of the amount she agreed to pay him each month if, and only if, he removed himself to the Southwest. What she offered wasn't that hard to take. She was saving his skin again and that's what mattered. Wasn't it?

It behooved him to appear grateful and repentant, although, this time, the realization her threats weren't idle was a nasty wake-up call. Clementine had belatedly developed a stiff backbone and he was being carted off to Santa Fe. Not even Santa Fe, but to some place north of that city called Nambé.

A savage wilderness.

Thus resigned, he packed up his few belongings, snuck out of his Bronx apartment, and drove his battered Ford Fiesta toward Akron where Clementine was, at least temporarily, installed in her new husband's home.

So what if his mother wanted him gone and out of her life, Schuyler reasoned. He could worm his way back into her good graces later. Her second motive for insisting he visit Akron was pretty obvious. Clementine wanted him to meet her new husband, Stan—*Atwater?* Was that it? Her list of surnames, including one remarriage to the same man, was a blur to him but this new guy, the Midwest jerk, deserved some respect. Atwater had managed to detach his mother from New York City and remove her to what Schuyler considered a backwater. Akron. That was no simple task. Must have taken some sweet argument.

The more Schuyler considered it, the more the goodly distance between her home in Akron and his exile in New Mexico seemed like a fine idea. She wouldn't always be in his face.

This was Schuyler's thought process only until he arrived in Fairlawn Heights, Akron, and stopped the Fiesta in front of an iron-fenced and gated compound covering about two acres. *Holy buckaroos.* Atwater had done all right for himself, and so had his mother in snagging him. It was obvious Atwater wasn't a fortune hunter, and Clementine didn't need a penny of his money. A marriage made in heaven.

Schuyler exited the car and pressed the buzzer. When the gate opened he steered along the curves of a chestnut tree-lined drive until he reached the mansion's entrance, where he parked the Fiesta. A woman dressed in jeans and a T-shirt opened the door and greeted him with, "Hi there. I'm Sally, the estate manager.

You must be Clementine's son. Make yourself at home. We're casual here."

So I see, was Schuyler's unspoken thought as he followed Sally's denim backside into the house. And what did Clementine think of Miss Casual, Miss Not-New-York-By-a-Longshot? Since his mother at once emerged into the foyer wearing slacks and a pullover sweater, he guessed she'd adjusted just fine to the culture shock. Schuyler had never seen her wearing such a getup.

No pearls.

"Hello, Mom." He greeted her with a peck on the cheek. "Good to see you." And, for some reason he meant it. He'd never seen her looking better. Her long gray hair was dressed in a bun and the effect was smashing. Her skin looked good. Glowing. Better than he'd ever seen it, and he knew she'd given up face-lifts years ago. He even admired the ruby-red cashmere pullover, a startling addition to his mother's wardrobe, as he'd previously known it.

"Good to see you, too, Aaron." Clementine's expression was stony, but to him her fierce hug felt like it would never terminate. This told him, despite her quirky and dictatorial demands, just how much she loved him.

"I have everything ready for you in the library," Clementine pronounced as she took off down the hallway with a purposeful stride.

His mother might love him, and she might be needy, but she was anxious to get down to business. As they passed through what would have been termed a "drawing room" in the good old days, Schuyler quickly assessed what its Louis Quinze furnishings were worth. The huge library they next entered was just as impressive, with bookshelf-lined walls, comfortable chairs with footstools, and massive desks. Two of them. *His and hers?* Anyway, their classic Hepplewhite styling took his breath away. Schuyler knew quality when he saw it, and these desks were authentic. With provenance, to boot. Atwater knew how to spend the bucks.

"I'm making a fresh start with Stan." Clementine wasted no time on small talk. She sat down behind one of the desks and motioned her son to sit opposite her. "I've had it up to here with you, Aaron. It's taken quite a while for me to make these arrangements, so take note. I mean everything I say. This time, there aren't any loopholes for you to take advantage of. You're not getting this check for nothing."

She slapped a leather-bound executive-sized checkbook down on the top of her desk, opened it, filled in the blanks on a check, and, with care, freed it along its lines of perforation. This was placed in a Vuitton briefcase along with several other documents.

"Now, we're going to the bank. Together," she finished with a grim set to her lips and a firmer grip on the negotiables. "You'll sign these papers in front of a notary."

More or less sign my life away, was Schuyler's take. He followed his mother through the library, the drawing room, down the hallway and into the foyer, then out onto the porch just as a chauffeured vintage Jaguar, pale yellow in color, slowed to a stop in front of the steps. A willowy older man a little more than six feet tall emerged from the back seat. Schuyler, who had expected an entirely different personage—some flabby, cigar-smoking rubber tire magnate, but not this suave but menacing gentleman in a hand-tailored suit—was surprised.

"Darling!" Clementine hailed the newcomer. "You're just in time. We're leaving for the bank. Stan, this is my son, Aaron. Aaron, I'd like you to meet my husband, Stan."

"How do you do?"

As Atwater extended his hand, Schuyler hesitated. His new stepfather's terse greeting was laden with frost. Schuyler could only conclude his mother had given her husband an earful about her wayward son. Said husband had, thereupon, drawn his own erroneous conclusions. The last thing in the world he'd want to do was meet his wife's wayward son.

Uh-oh.

Schuyler seethed. Oh, yeah. Atwater's rigid smile said it all. The man was no doubt thinking he'd rather deal with a rambunctious teenager than this mooching reprobate who, according to Clementine, had broken his mother's heart many times over.

Beyond that, Atwater must be wondering, based on Clementine's revelations, why his middle-aged stepson had made nothing of himself in life and hadn't a cent to his name.

"I'm well. And, yourself?" he responded, startled by his new stepfather's crushing grip. To judge by Atwater's lined face, thin hair, and stooped shoulders he must be near Clementine's age, in his seventies, yet the animal power he radiated was downright scary. Something Schuyler had only experienced with bad people. Very bad people. Atwater's steel-gray eyes burned a hole right through Aaron. The set of his chin said, "Go ahead. Try to land one."

"I also am well," Atwater replied, then turned toward Clementine. "My dear, let me help you." He guided her into the back seat of the Jaguar, shut the car door, then turned again to face Schuyler.

"Son, let us understand each other from the get-go," he said in a quieter voice. "If your mother appears at any point in the future—meaning from this moment in time, right now, as we stand here—to be at all upset by your shenanigans, you'll hear from me. Are we clear?"

"How dare you speak to me like that?" hissed Schuyler in the same suppressed tone, as surprised as he was outraged. "How dare you interfere in our family affairs!"

"Act like a man, fucker, and I won't have to. Your mother's happiness is now my affair. Good day to you." Atwater knocked on the car window, blew a kiss to his wife as she waved him goodbye, then headed into the house.

Schuyler glanced toward Clementine, whose nose was pressed against the car door window. His mother looked radiant. Could he even say, blissful? *Unreal.* She was no doubt assuming the two men in her life had exchanged pleasantries and were thrilled to meet each other. Grimacing, he climbed into the car but abruptly raised his palm to forestall any conversation. His face felt hot to his touch and must look beet-red. It would be her fault if a blood vessel exploded.

With a confused look, Clementine turned away from her son and addressed the chauffeur. "Please, Tim, take us to United Capital Bank."

Neither party in the back seat broke the weighty silence during their drive to downtown Akron.

⤿

"How do you do, Mr. Schuyler," exclaimed the man who scurried to meet them at the door of United Capital Bank. Clementine had introduced her son to James Matthews, the bank manager. "What a pleasure to meet you!"

His black mood no lighter, Schuyler gave only a curt nod, ignoring the manager's extended hand and effusive greeting. It was obvious his mother was a valued client here.

"Well, then," continued Matthews, unruffled and still smiling as he ushered them through the massive carved front door then into a spacious conference room, "I'll alert Mr. Chang, our notary, that you have arrived, and he will be with you in a tick!"

Schuyler said nothing to Clementine as they awaited the notary. He glanced around the room paneled in dark walnut and decorated with portraits of men whom he assumed to be bank owners, bank executives, or other big shots. A long rectangular table claiming the center of the thick carpet was also made of walnut, and the chairs surrounding it were upholstered in a rich, brown leather. This was no small-time bank.

The conference room door opened, then closed with a *shush* over the carpet. The man who entered was tall, about Schuyler's height, but slighter in build. The fact that he was Asian surprised Schuyler. Maybe because all the employees he'd seen so far at United Capital Bank were pasty white? Maybe because he'd been making snarky assumptions. Wrong assumptions. Par for the course.

The newcomer offered the seated pair a skeptical smile as he hoisted a heavy briefcase onto the table. "I'm Alan Chang." He smiled as he reached for Clementine's hand. "How are you today, Mrs. Atwater? I'm here to help you in whatever way I can."

When his handshake was received in silence, and he appeared somewhat daunted by Clementine's pursed lips, Chang proceeded to take a seat. "Mr. Schuyler, I presume?" He glanced in Schuyler's direction as he opened his briefcase, but the rigid glower he met didn't encourage conversation.

"I have some documents for you to sign, sir. Let's start with this one." Chang extended a pen toward Schuyler, who proceeded to read the first paper.

Puzzled, he stared at the page. Why would Clementine feel this required his notarized signature? The page stated he must attend his Uncle Harry Neville's upcoming funeral in New York. *As if he'd miss it.* Of course, he'd attend Harry's funeral. Looking for a bone to pick, he frowned at the wording. Why did it say "upcoming funeral"? After all, his uncle was still alive.

"When will the funeral take place, Mom?" Schuyler asked in an innocent tone, directing his anger at Atwater's crude dismissal toward his mother, hoping to irritate her. "This paper says 'upcoming.'"

"Don't be an arse," Clementine snapped. "You know Harry isn't dead. Just be ready. And don't skive off when the time comes!" Her brother Harry was slipping fast. After fighting prostate cancer for years, he was now in hospice, and prepared to depart this world at any moment. "I expect you to show up. You're a bloody loser if you don't appreciate how much you owe him."

"Too right, Mom," Schuyler agreed, looking down at the document. He struggled to maintain his cool, but her barb had gone deep and hurt more than his self-esteem. It didn't help that Alan Chang was staring at him, goggle-eyed. "But you'll have to try harder if you want to hurt me. I have the skin of a rhino."

Clementine had no call to label him a loser. Schuyler knew what he was. He had turned taking advantage of other people into an art form. Besides himself and his mother, the only other person he cared for was Uncle Harry Neville. Harry had always been more a father to him than Daniel Schuyler, producer of the procreative seed, ever was. The notion he might not show up for Harry's funeral was unthinkable.

He swallowed hard, scribbled his signature, and slid paper number one back across the table to Chang, who affixed his seal and signature to it.

"Thank you, Mr. Schuyler." Chang shot a wary glance toward Clementine. Upon her curt nod to proceed, he handed a second document to Schuyler. "And don't we have a lovely spring day today, sir?"

Still stinging from Clementine's angry rejoinder, Schuyler stared at the outline of her specific requirements for his bailout. Beyond an agreement to stop smoking, this piece of nonsense required, in no uncertain terms, his relocation to New Mexico—he already knew that—and his procurement of a job. But not just any job. Her terms stipulated he must find employment with Sam's Club in Santa Fe and agree never to start another business of his own. Schuyler realized this latter article was meant to minimize his opportunities for preying upon his fellow men.

"Are you enjoying this, Mom? Grinding that stiletto heel into my face." His mother's collection of Manolo Blahnik footwear was notorious.

"Sign the paper, if you want your check each month." She ignored the provocation.

Schuyler shrugged his shoulders and signed. Well, why not? Clementine had guaranteed him a small monthly stipend to supplement the lower wages he would, no doubt, receive in New Mexico. She would also pay rent for six months on the house north of Santa Fe destined to be his new home. Not a bad deal.

"Keep that job at Sam's Club, Aaron. I'm warning you. Don't quit. Otherwise, all bargains are off."

When Schuyler scribbled next to the red X, the notary's gaze shifted from Clementine to Schuyler, then back to Clementine.

"Um—" He squirmed in his chair as he notarized this second document. "Should I continue, Mrs. Atwater?"

"Please do, Mr. Chang," she said sweetly, glaring at her son.

"Here you are, sir." The third paper Chang urged across the table toward Schuyler concerned aspects of Clementine's final bequest.

This article stated Schuyler must never return to New York, the scene of his many downfalls, the one exception being his required presence at Uncle Harry's funeral. If he failed, the trust providing for him after Clementine's death would be nullified. Schuyler wasn't sure this was legal since the New York City streets weren't his mother's private property, but there was no point in arguing. It wouldn't hurt to humor her.

"And I don't want you ever to return to Akron while I'm living." Clementine retrieved a tissue from her handbag.

"Fat chance. Why would I do that?"

"I mean it, Aaron," she stated with dignity. To Alan Chang's alarm, she swiped at the tears escaping down her cheek. "Don't come back. My end-of-life arrangements are settled. You are welcome to attend my funeral, but I don't expect you'll choose to do so."

Schuyler slammed his pen down on the table and pushed his chair away from the table. *What a petty business.* Clementine's last sappy comment was just a further slap in the face. Reclaiming the pen, he signed the third document, his hand shaking with fury, but avoided her eye. He could never bear to see his mother cry. As he shoved the paper toward Chang he wondered what the notary was thinking. The man's sympathies obviously lay with Clementine. Schuyler ground his teeth. Somehow, he always emerged from these encounters with a teary-eyed Clementine looking like a louse.

"Is there anything further I might assist you with today, Mrs. Atwater?" Chang whispered to Clementine.

She shook her head, sniffed, and again daubed at the corner of her eye. "No, thank you. How very kind. You have been a great help."

Chang bowed to her, offered a stiff nod to Schuyler, gathered the documents into his briefcase, and made good his retreat. As the heavy door closed behind him, Schuyler sounded a harsh grating laugh. There was nothing his mother enjoyed more than her role of long-suffering parent. And, he had to admit, in seeking to be fair, he'd given her a lot of practice. He stood up and helped her put on her jacket. They left the bank together, in silence, and walked toward the yellow Jaguar awaiting them.

⌐

Arrived back at the Atwater mansion, Clementine and Schuyler entered the foyer, passed through the drawing room, and returned to the library. Lost in the seething sea of his murky thoughts, reviewing all the unsaid comebacks that would have quashed his mother's high-handed ways once and for all, Schuyler hadn't realized Clementine was speaking to him.

"I most often order these from Amazon," she said. "But knowing you would be here, Aaron, I went ahead and bought these at Best Buy. This gives you a good supply."

Schuyler wasn't surprised by the contents of the plastic bag she thrust at him. The cassette player-recorder, two clamshells of size D batteries, and three packs of cassette tapes inside it were the extent of Clementine Atwater's foray into the Information Age. *Oh, well.* The cassette player would not only be useful on the drive to New Mexico but would replace the one he was currently using when it no longer functioned. *That could be any day now.*

The plastic bag also contained two recorded tapes secured with a rubber band and these, along with the other contents of this bag, represented far more than what their physical appearance implied. A special agreement of long duration, beyond anything monetary or material, existed between Schuyler and his mother. An agreement unspoken and unwritten. An agreement based upon a mutual, deep-seated love that neither one ever verbally acknowledged to the other. Schuyler would continue listening to Clementine's periodic tape-recorded health reports. This commitment demanded from him, in his considered opinion, an ongoing repulsive task, yet it was a duty he neither questioned nor neglected, and never hesitated to fulfill.

Although certain of the contents of the two recorded tapes, Schuyler glanced at the writing on the tape cases. One was dated "Week of March 26." The second advised, "Week of April 2."

"Thanks, Mom." He sighed in audible disgust and, resigned to his duty, accepted the bag. Schuyler had been in the trenches of life for a long time now and was, at last, at the age of fifty-two, learning to pick his battles. A show of humility wasn't a bad trade-off for the check he'd stuffed into his pocket.

"I'll review the tapes while I'm driving to Santa Fe. I'll mail my responses back to you as soon as I locate a post office. If there is one in New Mexico."

Despite his best efforts to prevent it, Schuyler's heart softened. His mother was a generous soul who'd spent most of her life lamenting her son's chosen life path and picking up the pieces when he smacked headfirst onto the pavement of that path. She didn't ask for much. Since her generosity included giving him a vehicle to replace the aged Ford Fiesta, he would restrain himself, and refrain from calling her a hypochondriac to her face.

As far as he could tell, from here on out his worst problem would be the truck Clementine had chosen. The twenty-year-old Toyota pickup, almost as old as the Ford Fiesta, was parked outside the mansion's front door.

"Couldn't you have bought a sedan?" he whined. "Something newer. I've never driven anything like this junk heap."

"That truck is special. You don't appreciate it now, but someday you will. Believe me."

Schuyler would drive this clunker with a stick shift, no less, to New Mexico. He, a lifelong New York City resident who had only learned to drive later in life, was being forced to do this. On his first road trip. He hoped his backside would survive the ordeal.

"Well, Aaron, what would you like to eat? Are you hungry?"

"Huh?" Schuyler realized Clementine was offering to fix him some lunch.

"I have cream cheese and bagels, if you want something more like breakfast." His mother's tone was eager. With the moment of parting now at hand she had checked her temper and quelled her hard feelings, not wishing to say goodbye to the bane of her existence.

"Or, you could have a tuna sandwich. I chopped hard-cooked eggs into the tuna, the way you like it." Her moist eyes pleaded with a look forlorn, yet hopeful.

Schuyler averted his glance. It was always like this. They might bitch and gripe at each other, ad nauseam, for hours. But, at the core of their relationship was a bond neither one would ever sever, although they tested its strength to the breaking point. The crux of that bond was the acknowledgment that they were both alive and Daniel Schuyler, husband and father, their mutual nemesis, was dead.

Amen to that.

"Thanks, Mom, but—no time. I'd better get a start on this fantastic great new life you've mapped out for me," Schuyler answered.

He would have liked the sandwich—she mixed up the tuna to perfection, with a touch of brine from the dill pickle bottle added in, but he always felt more comfortable with the armor of sarcasm wrapped around his heart. That rebuffed his mother, kept her in her place, and saved him the embarrassment of indulging her with the hug she longed for. The tight hug he longed to give her.

"You could stay the night," Clementine suggested, tugging at his jacket sleeve. "Spend some time with Stan after he finishes his golf game. Get going early tomorrow. We have seven guest rooms."

Spend time with Stan? Endure that old buzzard's steely glare? Oh, yeah.

"I'm going, Mom."

The sight of her tears welling up once more almost changed his mind, but even thinking about an evening of strained small talk with Atwater and his mother left Schuyler weary.

"I appreciate what you've done for me," he added in a softer tone, realizing he meant what he said. *Fancy that.* He wasn't feeding her a line of bullshit. "I'll mail your tapes back to you as soon as I get to Santa Fe. Thanks for the truck."

He retreated out the front door, opened the Toyota's creaking door, and placed the envelope with his copies of the legal documents on the passenger seat. There, it joined his faithful diary and a pack of Orbit gum. When he inserted the key in the ignition the old truck jerked, then grumbled, then swayed gently from side to side. It resisted his first attempt to shift into first gear with a grind and a shriek.

As he steered jerkily toward the estate gates, Schuyler looked back several times at Clementine standing in the open doorway of her new home, waving at him. He sometimes pitied the woman, took advantage of her at every possible opportunity, and found her prayerful devotion to Winston Churchill ridiculous.

What the hell was wrong with him? Why did he prey upon the only human being who loved him? One of the only two human beings he loved in return. Despite his mooching and his unfilial attitude, his mother held the foremost place in his heart, and she deserved it.

No—she deserved better.

He glanced through the rear-view mirror as he rounded the first curve of the drive, when he entered the stand of chestnut trees, and when he reached the closed gate. As it swung open and he departed the Atwater property, he honked twice and looked back for the last time.

Clementine was still standing there. Waving.

CHAPTER 3

Funerals

Schuyler spent a week on the road to New Mexico, his emotions alternating between a seething sense of wrongful mistreatment about his ejection from the civilized world, a craving for the amenities of big city life forbidden to him, an unanticipated eagerness to discover what lay ahead, and a fear that life in New Mexico would be even worse than he expected. He took frequent breaks to ease what he termed "driving compression of the old bumster." His sore rear end. The seats of the old truck were merely boards upholstered in an old Naugahyde that had split and cracked many times over and tortured his gluteus muscles.

He listened to Clementine's two taped health reports, groaning as the week of April 2nd started with a familiar complaint that was almost a repetition of the tape of March 27th.

As you know, son, I've never been the same since my surgery for a deviated septum two years ago. My sinus congestion wasn't resolved then, and now may even be worse. I don't know if it's the move to Akron, or what. Here, there's no breeze blowing in off the Atlantic. Since I arrived here the nasal discharge seems thicker. It's also a darker shade of yellow. I can't get rid of it and seem to run through a box of Kleenex every day. There's more drainage, too. Sometimes I wake up at night coughing and can't hawk up the mucous . . .

On, the message ran. On to April third, on to the fourth, the fifth. On and on . . . Schuyler switched off the tape and manipulated the radio dial, searching for a local station with sounds more agreeable than his mother's voice. Whenever he got a clear signal, whether it was AM or FM, he was forced to choose between tinny, twanging country-western tunes or strident, revival-type preaching. Abomination of abominations.

Saaa-ve me, Jesus!

He'd already had it up the wazoo with cultural deprivation, meaning the bland fare he'd been forced to consume along interstate highways—Indiana, Illinois, Missouri, Kansas. This meant chicken-fried steak, an endless string of hamburgers, or various versions of spaghetti.

Schuyler referred to his craving for culinary subtlety as "the prosciutto effect." In other words, decent comestibles. One more mouthful of truck stop food and he was going to barf. Honest to God. One diner he stopped at for breakfast listed "croissants" on the menu and his spirits soared. The item on the plate before him, however, was not something to salivate over. Or, digest. It was a greasy fried doughnut, burnt on the edges.

He settled on breakfast as being his meal of choice, three times daily. He could have fried eggs, or he could have scrambled eggs, or he could have an overcooked omelet. He could have bacon, or ham, or sausage. And there were always hash browns.

Schuyler had suffered from IBS—Irritable Bowel Syndrome— even during childhood, and this ailment beset him more times on this road trip than he could count. Realizing restrooms might be hard to find, he resorted to buying senior pads that stuck to his underwear by a clever adhesive system. This saved him many changes of clothing.

It could have been worse, although he couldn't imagine how. And would he ever get out of Kansas with its endless rows of corn and amber waves of grain?

Saaa-ve me, Jesus!

⌐

Despite his jerky shifting and trouble mastering the rusty clutch, Schuyler at last put the long drive behind him. As he crossed the Colorado state line into northeastern New Mexico on a Tuesday evening, he searched his jacket pocket for Clementine's note with the name of his landlord. *Hugh Leigh.* She had written down a phone number and asked him to phone Mr. Leigh as soon as possible. Leigh would provide him with pertinent information about garbage, electricity, plumbing, the well, etc.

Will do, Mom, although he felt uneasy about what this "well" might involve. People in New Mexico had wells?

He still had a way to go but when he finally reached Santa Fe, he figured out how to proceed north on I-25, heading toward his rental home. When he, at last, turned onto County Road 503, he found this was a pleasant drive flanked on either side by houses of an architectural type he'd never encountered. These were all variations on a theme—flat roofed with logs protruding from beneath the roofline and stucco siding. *Weird.* And, in the twilight, they looked even weirder.

On arriving at his rental home, built just like all these others, the old Toyota collapsed with a sigh as he parked in the carport. Schuyler himself nearly collapsed when he climbed out of the truck. *Enough is enough.* His legs were shaking as he peered at his unfamiliar surroundings. He didn't care what the place looked like, all he wanted was a hot shower and a good long sleep.

To his relief, he found a house key hidden beneath a potted cactus that looked half-dead, exactly as described to him. But even as he fumbled with the back door lock, his cell phone chimed. "Mom" flashed across the screen.

Give me a break, Clementine.

"Aaron, dear boy," his mother choked through a flood of tears. "I'm sorry to tell you Harry passed last night." She blew her nose loudly. "Sorry, it's these damned sinuses. Stan and I are driving to the city straight away and the funeral will be Thursday. Fly into Newark. Let us know your arrival time and we'll pick you up. You can stay at our flat. Bring a suit."

That was all she said before hanging up. No goodbye. No inquiry as to his mental or emotional well-being after hustling cross-country into the oblivion of New Mexico. *Bring a suit.* Schuyler, benumbed, turned off his cell phone.

Uncle Harry was dead.

How was he supposed to deal with this swamp of shock, sorrow, and self-indicting disgust? Schuyler had thought he'd have at least one chance, if not more, to visit his uncle in the hospital. His game plan was to follow Clementine's orders, get settled in New Mexico, and then fly back to New York. Plenty of time to contemplate the final goodbye that would be so hard to say. The final goodbye postponed for so long, he'd now never get to say it.

Oh, my God.

Harry was dead, and the news weighed upon his heart like an anvil. Why had he waited? What the hell had he been thinking? It would have been so easy to stop by the hospital as he left New York and visit with his uncle before driving on to Akron.

Schuyler pulled a Camel, no filter, from the pack he'd bought on the road despite having sworn to Clementine he'd quit the filthy habit. If ever he'd needed to light up, he needed to now. Without a fag how could he even begin to manage the emotions assaulting him?

Harry was dead, and Schuyler himself was no longer breathing. Oxygen entered his lungs in plunges that hurt like hell. Once inside his chest they took their time in leaving. The exiting poison sucked his lungs dry, making it ever harder to take the next breath. *And the pain.* Not just his lungs and not just his chest, but his heart. His heart was about to burst.

This wasn't his fault, though. He would have visited his uncle if Clementine hadn't made him so angry with her catalog of demands. In a pet, he'd decided to bypass the hospital and drive straight to Akron. He'd thought that would teach her a thing or two. He'd been sure she'd grill him. Want to know if he'd visited Harry. His satisfaction would have come from his own acid comeback. "No, not enough time to visit. I was too busy fulfilling your rigid expectations."

Well, wasn't it true? This was all her fault.

The only way she ever addressed him was to give orders—like he was a seven-year-old kid. Even now, had she bothered to say hello? *No.* Asked him how the drive to New Mexico had gone?

No. Expressed solicitude for the long miles he'd driven, or the hardships he'd endured?

No.

All Clementine had said was, "Bring a suit." Was he now a mere trained dog she and Atwater would boss around as they saw fit? Want a Milk-Bone, Aaron? His mother would voice a command and he'd sit up, lie down, play dead. *Arf. Arf.* Like a dog.

And why was she always calling him "boy"?

A bit more whining wasn't out of order. He'd arrived at a very strange-looking, dilapidated house in a state he would never have chosen to visit, let alone live in. He hadn't yet retrieved his diary and suitcase from the truck. Tomorrow, Tuesday, he must drive south to Albuquerque, he guessed, since it was the only New Mexico city of any size, and hop a plane to Newark.

Leaving his luggage in the pickup, Schuyler brought only his overnight bag, his diary, the cassette player, and the few groceries he'd purchased into the house. He rummaged in the sack containing the housewarming gift he'd bought for himself and from it extracted a fifth of Jack Daniels.

"Here's to a new life," he muttered. "Here's to New Mexico, Land of Enchantment." *Figure that one out.* Finding no glassware in the kitchen cupboards, he took a long pull from the bottle. "Here's to the state of Derangement!"

He also had no chair to sit on. The only furniture he discovered was a twin bed in the bedroom closest to the carport entrance door. Left behind by the landlord? This Hugh Leigh guy?

Picking up his diary, Schuyler slunk into the bedroom and flopped onto the mattress. He cringed as his ribs met the springs. The ceiling he stared upward at was the oddest he'd ever seen. It was made of logs and smaller pieces of wood. He didn't want to think about what was living behind that debris. He took another swig from the bottle and opened the diary. Harry had educated his nephew on the value of consistent, if not daily journal entries. He'd encouraged Aaron to be faithful in recording his thoughts and doings, and Aaron had complied. Not every day, no, but several times weekly.

Now, more than ever, the diary would be Schuyler's anchor, his only remaining connection to Harry. No one, however, not even his uncle, was ever permitted to browse the diary. Those pages were sacred. He recalled those times, years ago, when the diary was a bone of contention between Schuyler and his ex-wife, Natalie.

"Why can't I just take a peek?" she would query.

"Because you can't. That's all there is to it," was Schuyler's unvarying response. "Keep your nose out of my business." He protected the diary with his life and carried it to work in his brief-case. Because he'd loved his uncle with a fierce loyalty and was grateful for his stand-in parental guidance, diary-keeping under Harry's guidance had often been his only link to sanity. But, even though his love for his uncle was closely akin to worship, he didn't agree with every one of Harry's singular views.

"Those of English extraction . . ." His uncle's diction was always crisp and clean, like Clementine's. His Eton accent was never extinguished by life in America, ". . . owe much of our history as we know it, much of our military history, to the men and women who were faithful diarists and letter writers. Take the officers of the Sepoy Mutiny, for example . . ."

Schuyler didn't give a shit about the Sepoy Mutiny. He could have cared less about Marlborough, Nelson, impressment of American sailors, the Boer War, and any other of Harry's interests. The study of history was a waste of time. Only his deep respect for Harry and for Harry's habits, tethered him to the habit of diary-keeping. Now, lying on that mattress of torture in the cold house north of Santa Fe, on this the darkest night of his life, he flipped through the diary pages littered with his sprawling handwriting and found the date he was searching for.

This entry concerned funerals. Schuyler hated funerals as much as he hated history and admitted to a twinge of guilt when he recalled how often he had abused those solemn events.

Yes, abused. There was no other word for it.

A shameful incident from his not so distant past, about seven years ago, crawled out of the hole he'd buried it in, that hole being the chronicle contained within the diary's pages. Schuyler was then as down on his luck as he'd ever been. Clementine was furious with him and she had every right to be. Oh, how he hated the validity of hindsight.

Useless, useless, useless.

Yet he couldn't stop himself from reading, once more, what he had written.

Dear Diary,

Someone who is most definitely not a friend, spilled the beans to my mother about funeral crashing and she read me the riot act. *Again.*

"You're worse than a disgrace to the family name," she shrieked. "I'm glad Natalie left you. You were a rotten husband. And you're still a lousy father!"

Blah. Blah. Blah. That was last night, but I've heard it all before.

"Why do you keep up this blasphemous practice?" she harangued me.

Well, here's the answer, Mom. I started the *blasphemous practice* of crashing funerals as a lark. Yet, it wasn't just a lark. It was more of a necessity. I needed to eat. I crashed funerals to stretch my measly food budget. Later on it became something of a hobby. A challenge. A means of entertaining myself. I also crashed wedding receptions, museum fundraisers and art gallery openings every chance I got. I've been crashing NYC social events for a year now.

The Crash, to me, is a means of expression, something I can sculpt and mold any way I wish depending on the circumstances. It proves to me I would have been a *very* good actor if I'd been allowed to follow that occupation. My all-knowing parents, (*that means you, Mom*) in the oh-so-long ago had other ideas. Clementine and Daniel sent me to Phillips Exeter Academy and then to Yale. Not what I wanted by a long shot.

Now I hone my acting skills by crashing three or four times a week, and most often come away satisfied. I admit this might sound smug, but I don't give a shit what anyone else thinks. Least of all, *her*. I get a good meal. I drink a bit of alcohol. I'm putting something over on a lot of people who should know better and I'm getting away with it. I like that.

The thrill of it all is in not getting caught.

Since I was born with the proverbial silver spoon in my mouth I should be grateful, shouldn't I? But who knew that spoon would dissolve in the crucible of fate? *Hah.* Who knew funeral crashing would become my economic prop in middle age? Who knew I'd lose almost everything but my best tux when things *fell apart* in November of '08? Not me. I didn't see *that* coming. That debacle sure wasn't my fault. But when I recall some of the shady financial deals Bert and I concocted and sold to our clients—suckers—in those years, I count myself lucky I didn't end up in the slammer. I got off easy—if you can call my crappy way of life easy.

Maybe I deserve the squalor I live in. Maybe I deserve Clementine's disdain. I don't know. Maybe I am a worthless louse like she keeps telling me. But, back in the day, life was good. I owned a Lexus. Had a driver and a four-bathroom apartment with maid service. After Natalie kicked me out and I lost everything, I took it like a man, *didn't I?* Moved into this stinking motel in the Bronx. Pay 250 a week for this sleazy rat hole. Either ride the bus or drive that flippin' falling-apart 1978 Ford Fiesta.

How far have the mighty fallen.

As far as crashing goes, *The Times'* society pages are filled with helpful info. The obits name prospective memorial gardens, as well as churches. All I need to do is follow the directions, pretty explicit, about when and where an event will be held. Does my mother think it's fun riding the bus, wearing my tux to evening events? Or driving the Fiesta wearing a threadbare suit to *funerals?* Gotta go. Gallery opening. Finish tomorrow.

January 29, 2010

Dear Diary,

Where was I? Oh, yeah. Crashing. I'm picky. I choose funerals that attract a large attendance. The beauty of a sizable group is that mourners are less likely to know each other. *And me.* All I need do is keep an eye on the ritzy crowd arriving at a church or funeral home. (These used to be *my* people, by the way!) I stand at the back. Lay low. My own well-groomed self looks like all the other well-groomed selves. In their eyes, clothes make the man. *Amen to that.* You dress the part, you are the part. On rare occasions if I run into a former acquaintance— some jerk itching to snub me, social pariah that I am—I offer a cool nod and they do the same. Back at ya, buddy!

After the rites I turn on my headlights and follow along to the burial site. That is, if I even bother to attend a burial. It's not always necessary. That's helpful in sizing up the overall situation if the obit didn't specify a location for the reception.

I park at a discreet distance from the burial site and most often don't get out of my car. I seldom go graveside but tag along behind the motorcade, following the crowd to the inevitable wake. Once I'm there, again I park a fair distance away, then swing into action, sallying into the wake like I own the place. I *love* this part! I love the hypocrisy of the whole scene. Once inside I almost can't stop myself from laughing. It's that hilarious. That easy.

Of course, the deceased isn't *totally* forgotten by attendees, but these fake mourners are focused more on the spread they're about to consume than on sorrow. They don't pay any attention to who's behind them in queue. Let the party begin!

As for me, I assume a sober frown and wait my turn. I've tucked a handkerchief soaked in onion juice into the breast pocket of my suit jacket. By sniffing the handkerchief, I keep my eyes in a swollen condition. That's desirable. *Brilliant, in fact.* The rancid odor deters anyone seeking to commiserate about the sad occasion. My fellow mourners could care less about me, and I have zero interest in them. Not even the chicks with their Gucci handbags. It's all about survival. I keep my eyes downcast, my expression grave. I'm all business. I'm a bereaved man who wants *no part* of idle pleasantries. And, that's true. My grief is monumental.

I have only one goal. I solace myself by focusing on the food. I heap my plate with prime rib, seafood, cheeses, pate, cold cuts, hard rolls. With grace I balance a second plate of luscious pastries. Stuff the leftovers into my pockets. There's no trick to it. You only need to concentrate on what you're doing.

One careful step at a time.

The liquor flowing like water at these events reminds me of my salad days living on Park Avenue. I relish each swallow. *Oh, yeah.* Only twice have I been so lacking in couth that the security guards eighty-sixed me for getting tipsy. Most often, out of respect for family members, security ignores minor disturbances. Making a fuss might disturb the grief of attendees who are busy drowning their sorrows in drink.

Personally? I feel nothing but gratitude toward the deceased. There have even been times, at some funerals, when I discarded my onion-scented handkerchief, and shed real tears. Most often, at the funeral of a child.

Death. Mourning. It's all so very sad. *Hiccup.* May the departed rest in peace.

January 30, 2010

Schuyler stared at the last few words of the diary entry. *Hiccup.* The enormity of his inappropriate behavior overwhelmed him. Had he been so crass, so coarse, so lost to all feeling and sensibility that he glorified in writing his inebriation, his depredations, his trespassing upon a sorrow-filled rite devastating to those closest to the beloved deceased?

Yes. He had been.

Glancing through the diary again, he noticed the preponderance of the word "I."

I.I.I.

Sickening. He closed the diary. Were those shameful days worthy of the ink or time it had taken to write about them? Did he want to live the rest of his life with a buzz on, in an alcoholic haze, inhaling the fumes of his own debauchery?

Lying on the lumpy mattress in his Nambé home north of Santa Fe, Schuyler pondered how his personal disgrace had spilled over onto Natalie, his ex-wife. Onto Nora and Sandy, his daughters. Onto Nathan, his son. Not to mention Clementine. He had tainted all of them and it wasn't a pretty sight.

He sat up on the bed and reached for his cell phone. Every time he tried to sort out why he had so dishonored himself, and everyone close to him, he gave up the sorting effort because he could only stand to look at his own crap for a brief time.

Enough. This was no time to wallow in self-loathing and regret. This was no time to kick himself in the ass for what was over and done with. He had a plane reservation to make.

He had Uncle Harry to mourn, and that was a real tragedy.

Schuyler downed another swig of Jack.

CHAPTER 4

Uncle Harry's Memorial

Standing on the curb outside the arrivals exit at EWR, the Newark, New Jersey, airport, Schuyler's attention was claimed by a voice he knew all too well. "There he is! Pull over, Stan," he heard his mother cry. "Aaron! Over here!" He watched her crawl out of the vintage yellow Jaguar, waving to him and shouting as he wheeled his bag toward her.

He flung the bag to the pavement and wrapped his arms around her, the ferocity of his grip startling him. *What's this, Schuyler? A guilt trip?* His mother's expression as she exclaimed, "Lovely! It's good to see you, too, Aaron!" told him his fierce hug had surprised her even more.

Schuyler kept hold of her hand as she steered him toward the Jaguar's trunk. It automatically swung open and he stowed his bag inside. As he climbed into the back seat, he saw his mother fix her husband with a meaningful stare. *So.* He wasn't the only one on his mother's shit list. It was good to know Atwater at least occasionally lapsed from her good graces.

"Good to see you, Schuyler. Please, accept my sympathies. Harry Neville was a fine man." The asshole, Stan, was rewarded by Clementine's gratified smile when Schuyler grasped the hand he extended over the back of the front seat.

"Thank you! Thanks for coming to pick me up," Schuyler answered as he buckled his seat belt. Atwater's cordial handshake and friendly greeting were unexpected. Confusing. Especially since the older man had called him a fucker at their first encounter. Schuyler wasn't sure what Atwater's game was, but he'd play along. For his mother's sake. After all, he'd only be in New York for two days.

"Good flight?" continued Atwater.

"Not bad. I changed planes in Kansas City."

"The International is a nice airport," Atwater commented.

Schuyler had not anticipated this second encounter with his newest stepfather would be at all pleasant. Or, chatty. In fact, he'd dreaded it. Atwater's cordiality was a puzzling surprise until he glanced toward his mother, then his confusion blossomed into understanding. Her face was, quite literally, wreathed in smiles. A true nephew of his Uncle Harry, Schuyler hated trite expressions unworthy of the august English language, but there was no other way to describe Clementine's delight at this civil interchange between Atwater and himself.

Beaming. She was beaming.

Schuyler admitted a grudging respect for Atwater. This stern man had stifled animosity in order to please his new wife. He must really love her. And, if his mother was happy with Atwater, so be it. He was happy for her, although he winced from a twinge of regret as he recalled how pleasing his ex-wife, Natalie, was never a prime motivation for him. Neither was loving her. This was more than a twinge. It was a gouging bite.

"Mom, please accept my sympathies. You and Harry were so close. Two peas in a pod. I know he meant the world to you, as he did to me."

He loosened his seat belt and leaned forward to peck his mother's cheek. Clementine nodded in response but made no reply as she raised a handkerchief to her eyes. They drove on in silence for a while as Atwater headed into the city. Then, heaving a deep sigh, Clementine turned toward Schuyler in the back seat.

"I prayed to Winston, of course." She swallowed hard. "I never asked him to prevent Harry's passing, but to make it quite easy. I'm confident he heard my prayer, because Harry seemed at peace. I was holding his hand, you know, and at the final moment he did his best to apply a little pressure on mine. That was his goodbye." She lapsed into tears.

"Winston said it's normal to suffer such agony on having one's younger brother predecease oneself. Not at all self-indulgent. Harry should have survived me! It's all so tragic, Aaron. He was still a young chap." Clementine reached for her husband's hand. "I don't know how I would have managed, if it hadn't been for Stan."

In the rear-view mirror Schuyler watched Atwater bite his lip hard, and do his best to keep a straight face. The dour frown and determined grimace could be interpreted as grief or empathy with his wife's suffering, but Schuyler wasn't fooled. Atwater was trying not to laugh. His nonjudgmental acceptance of Clementine's devotion to Winston, this show of love for her, raised him another notch in Schuyler's estimation. That ominous entity, his deceased father, Daniel Schuyler, was always critical of Churchill's deity, never demonstrated a like forbearance, and often cruelly derided Clementine's belief.

Was Stan Atwater shocked when he learned his bride prayed to Winston Churchill, Schuyler wondered. Had he thought Clementine was a bit off her rocker? Well, if he'd come to such a conclusion, it apparently did not taint his regard for her. As for Schuyler, he admitted there were times during his youth and, indeed, throughout his adult life, when he'd entertained that very doubt.

On occasion, he still pondered the oddities associated with Clementine's relationship to her god. Foremost among these was how often Winston answered her prayers. Next, was her unflinching and stupefying assurance that *he* would never fail her. Number three was the fact his mother's English accent became more pronounced whenever she spoke of Churchill. At the bottom of the pile, was his own uncharacteristic restraint in never mocking her singular belief.

⌒

It turned out Stan Atwater was as generous as his new wife. He managed all aspects of the final arrangements for Harry Neville's cremation, interment, and memorial brunch. Based on information supplied by Clementine, he sent appropriate notices to *The Times*, the *Boston Herald*, and the *Philadelphia Tribune*:

Harold Guy Michael Neville, noted authority on English military history, contributor to *The New Yorker* magazine, and owner of the bookstore Novel Ideas in New York City, passed away on April 9 at the age of 75. Mr. Neville was born in Leeds, England, in 1942, where he attended public school. His undergraduate studies in history were begun at Oxford University and completed at Yale, where he later received a master's degree in comparative religions and a doctorate in English history in 1967. His well-regarded thesis, *Victorian Military Strategies*, published by Brooks, Barnes, and Chambers in 1970, was a nonfiction best seller.

In 1970, Neville achieved United States citizenship. He resided in New York City, in the Catskills, where he built his own cabin, and elsewhere.

Neville's charitable pursuits included scholarship funding for minority New York youth, as well as establishing and funding a food bank located in the Bronx. The entire contents of his bookstore, Novel Ideas, are bequeathed to the New York City Library. Neville's most treasured pastime was hiking in the Catskills and the Adirondacks, in India, and Eastern Europe with his nephew, Aaron Peter Schuyler, and elsewhere.

Mr. Neville is survived by his sister Clementine Neville Atwater, by Stanley Oakes Atwater of Akron, Ohio, by Aaron Peter Schuyler of Santa Fe, New Mexico, and by loving friends elsewhere.

It is requested that remembrances be donated to New York City food banks or Memorial Sloan-Kettering Cancer Institute. Interment at Raw Island Memorial Park will be private. A memorial reception will be hosted at 11:00 a.m. on Thursday April 14 at Brookwater Country Club.

RSVP: atwaterindustries@atwaterinternational.net

After rereading this notice, a pensive Clementine stared out at the Hudson River from the window of their thirty-first floor apartment. Her gratitude to Stan was boundless. He supported her fully. He was as much a rock for her as Winston was since, upon her brother Harry's demise, her worries about Aaron became crippling. Nearly crushed her. Knowing the day of the funeral reception would soon be upon them, she had prayed for one favor more than anything. She besought Winston's guarantee of smooth sailing throughout the treacherous waters of Aaron's two-day stay in New York. Her son would never know.

⏝

"Come over here, dear." Stan beckoned to her from where he sat. "Help us out."

She claimed a chair near Atwater and listened as he and Sally reserved a Brookwater Country Club banquet room, planned a lavish brunch, and chose a color theme for the flowers.

"What would you like to do about a memorial board for Harry?" Stan asked, kissing her hand as he did so. "If you feel up to choosing the photos you want to display, someone in advertising at Atwater Industries will do the rest. It won't take more than a couple of hours, and will be a professional piece of work you can be proud of. A true testimony to Harry's worth."

Grateful for an occupation that relieved her maternal worries, Clementine set about the task. Earlier that morning her son, refusing to be chauffeured, had taken a taxi downtown to Harry Neville's bookstore, Novel Ideas, where he would, no doubt, remain for several hours.

Please, Winston, don't let those hours include popping in at any nearby bars.

⏝

Schuyler grinned when he opened the door into Novel Ideas Bookshop and heard the ancient set of chimes announce his arrival. Many were the hours he'd spent here when his uncle was in New York, not visiting one of his summer homes or traveling abroad. The two of them would browse the stacks and Harry would point out to his nephew the books he'd enjoyed or found useful. He allowed the young man to take books from the used-book section home with him, and, thus, Novel Ideas functioned as a lending library for young Aaron.

Ahh . . . The potpourri now greeting Schuyler was a familiar and beloved mix of ever- present, never-changing odors peculiar to this bookstore. Inhaling this mélange, the fragrance of musty old books, the pine plank flooring, the faint but lingering scent of pipe tobacco, and the very dust itself was a pleasing and reassuring reminder of how, as a boy, he was enfolded and protected by this second and most beloved home, a refuge from the tyrannies of his unpredictable father.

Was Harry still here? Schuyler was ready to bet on it. It wouldn't have surprised him to find the old sod asleep in the stacks on the lower level, reclining in one of the bookstore chairs and hiding out from his employees. If not, if Harry had truly passed out of the earthly realm of his bookshop—and Schuyler doubted it— these mingled layers of scent would remain in memory of him.

He took another deep breath in honor of the past. He relished the fragile pages of aged volumes, the fine layer of dust coating every plane and surface, the stillness of an atmosphere seldom disturbed by a hint of fresh air, and the exotic fragrance of the thick sticks of Tibetan incense Harry Neville favored. All were redolent of Harry's presence, subtle reminders meaningless to anyone but himself, but more potent than any photo or other tangible memento of his uncle.

Harry had bequeathed to his nephew whatever number of books he might wish to add to his own library, before the remainder was transported to the city library. One by one, the Novel Ideas staff, busy boxing up thousands of volumes, greeted Schuyler as they encountered him roaming the aisles and expressed their sympathies. He, of course, coveted the shop's entire mouthwatering collection, but since he had no shelving in his new abode, nor even chairs and a table, he restrained his greed in the interests of economy. The cost of shipping vast numbers of books to New Mexico was beyond his means.

He wandered long among the teetering shelves of the three-story shop. He cherished the creak and groan from every step he took, either ascending or descending the ancient staircases. He took his time saying goodbye to Novel Ideas, stopping often to peruse an unsold volume he had enjoyed as a youth, or to admire one of the fine oil paintings sequestered in obscure corners. A subtle depiction of three mustangs nuzzling a dry creek bed, searching for water, beckoned to him. He peered at the signature "L.G." Initials only. Here was an artist with minimal ego.

Schuyler settled, at last, for another copy of his uncle's doctoral thesis, some books on wilderness trekking, and a battered but curious volume in the shop's travel section entitled *The Ultimate Journey*. This was written in 1982, and the authors were identified as Huey Lee and Micah Neuville. Described as lifelong Tibetan Buddhist practitioners, these two men had circumambulated Mount Kailash and had the photos to prove it. Someone with the initials U.C. was credited with photography.

Huh. A photographer with a minimal ego.

Schuyler remembered the many hikes, camping trips, and treks he and Harry had shared, including some in the hill country of India. This was, indeed, a book to treasure. He flipped through the pages until he found the section devoted to photos of that pilgrimage. These were black-and-white and grainy. A series of three shots depicted consecutive actions. In the first, two men were bowing to each other; in the second they held aloft a banner displaying the Tibetan Buddhist Eight Auspicious Symbols; in the third, they kissed each other on the mouth while locked in a passionate embrace.

That last photo left Schuyler breathless. Stunned. The volume slipped from his hands and onto the floor. Scooping it up again, he riffled through the pages to again find the flaming-hot photo and read the brief caption beneath it. *We finish our pilgrimage in the best of health, after three weeks spent circling the mountain on our knees, with full prostrations.*

The man on the right in these photos was Schuyler's uncle, Harold Guy Michael Neville.

Uncle Harry? Micah Neuville?

The other man, the one on the left, must be Huey Lee. Wasn't Lee often a Chinese name? Well, this man wasn't Chinese. Huey Lee was black, shorter than Harry by a mere inch, but of a very dissimilar build. Slender and wiry, as opposed to Harry's substantial paunch, his air of peace, inner calm, and strength was as powerful as a punch even in the photo. What the hell.

Harry was gay?

How many other things did he not know about his uncle? How had he spent weeks at a time with Harry, from the age of five on through college, and had no inkling of his uncle's sexual preference? Schuyler had no memory, during their times together, of Harry ever looking at any man with something even approaching sexual interest. Why had Harry never shared this vital part of himself with his nephew? After all, they weren't just uncle and nephew. They were good friends. Buddies. On the other hand, he'd never seen his uncle look at any woman in that way. Clementine had never, not even once, hinted that her beloved brother was gay. Wouldn't she have said something? On at least one occasion?

What the hell, indeed. Schuyler was beyond shock and unable to describe his own emotions.

⤙

When her subdued son arrived back at the apartment, declined joining his mother and Atwater for dinner at Eleven Madison Park, and said he was going straight to bed, Clementine wrung her hands.

"Oh, Aaron, have you been drinking?" she blurted out.

"No!" was Schuyler's curt reply. "Why do you always think that? I've been over at Novel Ideas. These are the books I'm taking with me to New Mexico." He held up his shopping bag but was relieved when Clementine showed no interest in viewing his choices. "I have a headache, Mom. Tomorrow will be a hell of a long day, and I'm tired."

⤙

At seven thirty the following morning Clementine was surprised to find her son dressed and awaiting her and Stan in the apartment foyer. A morose Aaron was glaring out the front window that gave onto a street with traffic backed up, as usual. He was wearing a dark gray suit, white shirt, navy blue tie, and well-polished black oxfords that had seen better days. She might have stretched the point and described his attire as impeccable, were it not for his jacket's worn cuffs and the shiny backside of his trousers. She refrained from saying anything, however, and hoped Stan would not object to his son-in-law's somewhat seedy attire.

For herself she had chosen a knee-length dove-gray dress with a tissue-wool three-quarters-length coat in black. This ensemble was accompanied by very high-heeled pumps, and her antique pearl necklace and earrings, once the property of her maternal grandmother, Agnes Guy. The Guy name had been bestowed on Harry at his christening. Oh dear, best not to let her thoughts drift in that direction.

"Let's go," Atwater said as he hastened to join them. He herded them out the door, in and out of the elevator, through the building's double front doors, and into the waiting Jaguar. "Traffic could be a bitch," he added, taking a seat next to the chauffeur.

He said nothing about Schuyler's appearance, perhaps didn't notice, but seemed distracted—no doubt worried—Clementine decided, about their tight time frame. The private interment of Harry's ashes was scheduled for eight thirty, and the memorial brunch guests might start arriving at the club around 10:00 a.m. Hopefully, the open bar would keep them occupied.

Atwater's old college friend, Anglican bishop Martin Euless, met them at Raw Island Memorial and offered a brief, heartwarming eulogy for Harry, whom he had never met. Clementine's tears flowed nonstop as she watched the vault door close forever upon her beloved brother's remains. Thus shattered by grief, she failed to see Stan offer a thick envelope to the prelate. Schuyler, however, witnessed the bishop, with a discreet nod, stow the envelope in his breast pocket.

"You'll join us, of course, won't you, Marty?" Atwater asked, shaking hands with the bishop. "It'll be quite a spread. And don't forget, we've got a game on tomorrow afternoon."

"My schedule's light today, Stan. It will be my pleasure to join you and Clementine. And," the Bishop added with a smile in Schuyler's direction, "your stepson, as well."

Schuyler knew how to pick up a cue. He smiled and nodded in reply, then stepped aside.

"Here's my driver. He's been circling the block," stated the bishop as he headed for the building exit. "We'll follow you to the club. God bless you."

"There goes one fine man," commented Atwater as he escorted Clementine to the Jaguar. "And he shoots a pretty low score. Great golf partner. Drinks Macallan."

Schuyler shoved his hands in his pockets, tucked his tongue behind his teeth, and climbed into the back seat.

When Clementine saw how many guests were gathered in the bar, she was appalled. Not that she wasn't glad to see all these people eager to mourn Harry, but each one would want to pay their respects before converging on the banquet room and queuing up for the buffet. Their numbers meant a fatiguing stint at the head of the receiving line in her dove-gray Choo stilettos.

Winston, why didn't I wear my trainers?

She was relieved to see her son so quiet and circumspect, although his grave expression and air of distraction puzzled her. This trend of thought transformed itself into the supposition that Aaron was doing his best to contain his grief. That must be it. Aaron's devoted attachment to his uncle was of long standing. Her brother was Aaron's second father and spent time with his nephew in a way Daniel never had. A flood of gratitude for the deceased Harry overwhelmed her.

"Don't worry, Aaron. Harry will always be with us," she whispered to her son, squeezing his hand. "Don't forget that. He'll be with you, even though he's in heaven with Winston."

"I won't forget, Mom," Schuyler answered through clenched teeth.

Clenching his teeth was one of Schuyler's several responses to not only the tedium of his mother's prayers to Churchill, but also her addiction to platitudes. It was better than biting off his tongue. At times, he scoffed at such confidences. At other times, he mocked her. Today, he would keep his mouth shut, be a model of decorum, and remain immune to the stultifying effect of triteness. He relaxed his shoulders, straightened his hunched posture, and began to breathe more normally.

He had a lot more on his mind than Harry's demise. He'd been forced to admit just how little his family trusted him. Why, oh why, had Clementine never mentioned Harry's sexual orientation? Did she feel she was protecting her brother? Is that why she had never told her son his beloved uncle was gay? Here was the kicker: Schuyler couldn't recall one single instance when he had deserved her trust. When had he deserved Harry's?

With a gracious but somewhat vacant smile, he greeted the woman now clutching his hand. "We will so miss Harry, Aaron," she said in earnest. "And I still remember you as a boy, you know. Such a rascal!"

Schuyler not only held up quite well through the next forty-five minutes of heartfelt condolences, but began to enjoy the black humor of his ordeal. This was acting, wasn't it?

He was good at that.

Harry, why did you never tell me?

"Mr. Dumphreys, how are you, sir?" He could play a part. "Do you and Mrs. Dumphreys still summer at Wilmington? Thank you for coming." He could be as phony as the rest of them.

"Janice Jones! Good to see you again. Thank you for coming." That's what acculturation was all about, wasn't it? Role-playing? Faking what you couldn't feel or didn't understand.

"My uncle was a great admirer of your writing, Mrs. Markham. I believe he carried all your titles in his shop." Covered with dust because they never sold. "Thank you for coming."

He hated the bullshit. The posing. But, why?

Take a look in the mirror, Schuyler. Is it that hard to figure out? He was an expert at posturing. At faking. *Are you proud of yourself?* Here he was, assuming all these people passing through the reception line were as phony as himself. Here he was, assuming all these people were as heedless of the needs of others as he had proven himself to be. More and more he loathed the reckless damage he'd done to almost everyone he'd ever come in contact with. What recourse is there when you find yourself so nauseating?

If he now regretted the injury he'd caused others, did that mean, by corollary, he was tired of playing the old game? Was he fed up with A-list life? Of the life he'd lived up until the past few years? *No way.* Schuyler's response was almost violent. He craved that lost lifestyle and was only fed up with being a bum, utterly dependent upon his mother's generosity. And, in no way did he look forward to leaving New York and returning to New Mexico.

Harry, why did you never tell me?

Shaking off these ruminations, Schuyler realized he hadn't paid attention to the last few guests who had condoled with him. Glancing up and down the receiving line, he was a bit shocked by some of the people who'd already passed by him. *Wow.* Who knew Harry's friends included so many African Americans, Native Americans, and persons from India?

On the other hand, why was he surprised? Harry was a well-travelled man with a wide acquaintance. What was this revelation compared with his discovery that Harry's significant other was an African-American male?

Harry, why did you never tell me?

As the last guest passed through the line with a sorrowful shake of the head, and as Stan Atwater turned toward him with unexpected warmth, the primary object occupying Schuyler's mind was the mellow taste of a double Jack. *No ice.* His primary objective was gaining the solace of oblivion as fast as possible. Forget the events of today and the past two days.

"Well done, my boy." Atwater beamed, shaking Schuyler's hand. "I knew you had the right stuff." With that, he gripped Clementine's elbow and steered her into the banquet room.

What the fuck—*boy?* How much of his tainted personal history had Clementine spilled to her new husband?

More than ever, Schuyler thirsted for the cushioned comfort of a bar stool.

CHAPTER 5

Aftermath

With tears streaming down her cheeks, Clementine Atwater stood looking down at a taxi idling thirty-one floors beneath her high-rise window. She watched her son climb into the back seat, and the driver jerk away from the curb. He would weave his way toward Penn Station, where Aaron would catch a train to EWR and return to his banishment in New Mexico.

The anguish strangling her was nothing new. Again, neither mother nor son had introduced the devastating topics of their past—her marriage to Daniel Schuyler, and Aaron's childhood. The shared sorrows estranging them should have brought them closer, but it never did. How many more chances would she have to suss out how Aaron viewed her as a mother? Where he felt she'd gone wrong as a parent.

Clementine was feeling her age and considering the efficacy of another face-lift. Harry's death had dealt her a nasty blow. Closure on her issues with Aaron, no matter how painful the feedback he'd throw at her, was vital, would make it easier for her to move on.

Before Aaron had arrived in New York on Tuesday, Clementine had no idea what to expect during his funerary visit. She hesitated to broach the topic with Stan, who put a good face on the matter for her sake, but felt his new son-in-law was a good-for-nothing bag of shit.

"Any man over fifty years of age who hasn't made his mark in the world, isn't worth the time of day," was Atwater's avowed perspective. He saw no sense in sugarcoating the truth.

More than anything, what puzzled her was how Aaron had been a model of deportment for the two days preceding the morning of the memorial. Unlike his usual hard-boiled yet overly sensitive self, he was affable, even chatty, after she and Stan picked him up at EWR. She knew her son, she knew his unexpected openness was a pose, and she suspected, during the drive to their upper West Side condo, he was taking Stan's measure as much as Stan was taking his.

Aaron's cordial posture was short-lived. After dinner that evening he retreated to the guest room and closed the door, once again shutting her out, and did not appear until the following morning.

Clementine tried to reconstruct a time line for her son's movements prior to the memorial. The day after his arrival—that would be Wednesday—he'd taken a taxi to Harry's Novel Ideas bookshop. Later that afternoon he returned to the apartment with a few keepsake books, a morose expression, and a curt refusal of her invitation to dine at Eleven Madison Park.

"Sorry, Mom. Headache. Can't do. Count me out."

Clementine had made the reservation with a specific view to pleasing him, knowing he appreciated that elegant restaurant. She was at a loss to explain why he preferred solitary exile in the guest room. To be sure he was saddened by Harry's death, quite overcome, but why had a visit to the bookshop exacerbated his sorrows?

At the interment Aaron was meticulously polite to Bishop Euless, as well as to every brunch guest passing through the long reception line. Despite his slick but appealing veneer, however, she recognized warning signs she was all too familiar with. Helpless, she watched him withdraw into the private world where he was seduced by perilous thoughts and wrestled with many devils. A mother knows these things, doesn't she?

Am I not correct, Winston?

After the last guest had shuffled through the line, she and Stan took their seats in the dining room. They were both famished, and Clementine was ready to kick off her Jimmy Choos under the table. Drawn into conversation with friends and acquaintances, she failed to notice Aaron hadn't accompanied them. His seat, reserved with a place card, was empty.

Not until she and Stan watched their guests trickle out of the banquet room and began to relax after the fatiguing day, did she realize Aaron was not in the banquet room. Was he waiting for them outside the club? Had their chauffeur already brought the Jaguar to the door?

When the muffled sound of someone singing an off-key version of the "Star-Spangled Banner" reached her ear, she glanced, wide-eyed with horror, at Stan, then jerked her head toward the murky interior of the lounge. Aaron's torso was draped across a bar stool, his head supported by the massive Fall River granite counter. Several memorial guests stood in the lounge doorway, staring, murmuring, speculating how the Neville–Schuyler heir could have fallen so low.

"Oh, no!" Clementine cried, tugging at her husband's sleeve and pointing toward Aaron.

"What the—?" hissed Stan, tensed like a tiger ready to spring. Shrugging off her grip and straightening his tie, he strode toward the bar. He shook Schuyler's shoulder but received only a weak salute and a slurred reply.

"At—at—at your servisss—oh, say can you see—!"

"Schuyler! You friggin' idiot!"

Stan turned toward the bartender. "How much has he had?"

"I don't know, sir. I just came on shift and was counting my drawer."

"Quick! Get my chauffeur. Yellow Jaguar. It'll take two of us to get him into the car."

Clementine stood frozen in the doorway of the lounge, in her bare feet, a high-heeled shoe held in each hand. Her wayward son had again disgraced the family, and Stan's frequent glances away from the befuddled Aaron and toward her brimmed with anguish for his wife.

Oh, Winston—I feared this might happen! Aaron—drunk again! She knew Stan's worst expectation had been fulfilled, his fear that Aaron might cause a scandal, humiliate his mother and bring shame upon Harry's memory on this solemn occasion.

A mix of emotions claimed Clementine's face—and not just the disappointed expression she knew Stan was fast becoming accustomed to and always dreaded seeing whenever their conversation veered toward the unwelcome subject of Aaron. No, no. There was much more than that.

She felt anger, frustration, and a copious despair. How could Aaron revel in such weakness in front of her new husband? *Forget the sodding guests enjoying the spectacle!* How sad it was that Stan should have his early opinion of Aaron, a conviction based solely upon her own disclosures, receive such patent confirmation.

"Aaron!" she had shrieked, tripping toward him, a stiletto clutched in each fist. "How could you! What a bloody cock-up!"

Now, as she stared out the high-rise window at the departing cab, Clementine wondered if she was glad, or sad, that her son was departing for New Mexico at 9:15 a.m. this morning.

CHAPTER 6

Tom Jannssen

An exhausted Schuyler drove into his carport in Nambé, the area north of Santa Fe where he now lived, at 3:00 a.m. on Saturday morning. The two flights of his journey had been brutal. Too bumpy, too crowded, no toilet paper in the restroom cubbyhole, screaming kids, barfing kids, and a four-hour delay in Kansas City.

He could have waited until Tuesday to leave the East Coast—midweek flying conditions might have been more tolerable—but after sobering up the thought of spending more time with his mother and Stan Atwater seemed a godawful penance. Even before Atwater's scorching reproof nearly flayed him alive, Schuyler was mortified by his own inexcusable behavior. Atwater was silent but steaming with unuttered reproaches during the drive to the condo. Certain things couldn't be said in front of a chauffeur. Once returned home, all hell broke loose.

"How could you treat your mother to such an appalling scene?" ranted Stan, rolling up a convenient newspaper as if he was about to swat a fly. Or a dog. "Humiliate her. Did you stop to think how she'd feel seeing you wallow in a stupor like a common drunk!"

"I am a common drunk!" Schuyler shouted back. "And I have a stinking headache! I'm sorry—*okay*?"

"My lack of restraint was unforgivable!" he added, squelching the indecent response to Atwater's well-deserved upbraiding that hovered on the tip of his tongue. He gestured toward Clementine, her face blanched white. "She has the right to ream me out! You don't!"

He gripped his aching temples after that semi-apology. Out of the corner of his eye he saw his mother squeeze Atwater's hand. It was meant to be a shushing gesture but her husband glanced down at her almost as if, in the heat of battle, he'd forgotten she stood by his side.

"I have every right you've given me due to your disgraceful behavior!" Atwater was relentless. "The insult to your mother is intolerable. The embarrassment to me—!"

"That's it, isn't it? You! That's what this comes down to!" Schuyler's tone was laden with sarcasm. "*You!*"

Until her son's last retort, Clementine had said nary a word. Now she grabbed a tissue from a nearby box and burst into tears as she fled the room, "I can't take this any longer! Where did I go wrong, Winston?"

"Darling—!" Startled by her outburst, Atwater abandoned his adversary and rushed out after her, still wielding the newspaper.

Schuyler retreated to the guest room. If he'd had the where-withal he would have left the condo and booked himself into a Motel 6. That was not possible. Clementine had spotted him only enough cash to pay to get his truck out of hock at the Albuquerque airport and buy gas for the drive back to Santa Fe.

⌐

The next morning neither Clementine nor Atwater had emerged from their bedroom to say goodbye. Unaware that his mother, wearing an expression both sorrowful and resigned, stood at her bedroom window looking down at the waiting taxi, Schuyler hauled his bag onto the elevator and out through the building exit. A helpful doorman smiled and touched his cap. "Have a nice day, sir." Then, he was into the taxi and off to Penn Station.

Throughout that night of alcohol-interrupted sleep preceding his departure, during the flights west, and during his drive from Albuquerque to Nambé, Schuyler was plagued not only by the realization of his distraught mother's misery, but of Uncle Harry's hidden life.

Yet, Harry's life couldn't have been that hidden. Clementine must have known what he was. Why had Clementine never once brought up the subject? She would have supported her brother like a lioness. Defended him to the death. No doubt his father, Daniel Schuyler, knew Harry was gay. No doubt, also, Daniel had condemned and reviled what he'd categorize as a foul aberration. Uncle Harry's life had only been hidden from himself. Shock best described Schuyler's current mental and emotional state.

From here on out, however, he needed to put first things first.

Number one, he needed to figure out why anyone would choose to live in a state where the scenery was comprised of dirt, sand, and sagebrush, and why he'd been sent here rather than somewhere else. Next, he needed to record a satisfactory reply to Clementine's respiratory health tape. Having done that duty, what else could he say to his mother? Well, for starters, he'd let her know he'd taken a stab at getting the job. The designated job at Sam's Club. The sooner the better. Then he'd begin the task of mending fences with her.

$\backsim$

Schuyler let himself into the Nambé house through the carport door and dropped his flight bag on the kitchen floor, wincing at the sight of the bottle of Jack Daniels on the kitchen counter. After stripping down, he crashed on the twin bed mattress and collapsed into a dream world of nasal discharge, crowded flights with crying children, sagebrush, his own funeral rites, endless miles of dry desert, and Uncle Harry's ashes lying serene within a vault, their bed of infinite finality.

Vivid sunshine and a sky bluer than any hue he'd ever imagined awakened him much earlier than he had hoped. *Curtains.*

"Buy curtains, Schuyler," he mumbled to himself, stumbling naked into the kitchen. There, he faced only empty cupboards and the expectant bottle of Jack Daniels. Schuyler shook the bottle. Half empty.

"And another bottle of Jack." He could stock his pantry at the nearby Pojoaque Village Market but, first, he needed some breakfast.

Pulling on his brand-new jeans, the stiffest garment he'd ever worn, he headed for the bathroom. Brilliant light through the bathroom window illuminated what he least wanted to see in the mirror. Himself.

Peering into the glass, he scrutinized all the tiny lines around his eyes, and the many not-so-tiny facial lines. Despite his alcohol-burdened history he had none of the fine red veins or purple nose denoting a drunkard. Something to be thankful for. He also had a full head of hair, even if it was graying at a rapid rate. Despite his years he could still pass for a handsome man, thanks to Clementine's genes.

A sharp twinge of uneasiness prevailed, however, disturbing his self-contemplation. The image in the mirror wasn't a happy one. The man staring back at him wasn't at peace. When Schuyler frowned, the discontented countenance opposite him frowned back. All told, a harsh depiction.

"Take it in, old son," Schuyler muttered to his mirror image. "Take it all in. All the gory, gritty reality of guilt, age, too little sleep, more guilt and—exile in New Mexico."

He turned on the faucet, splashed cold water on his face, and dried off with yesterday's undershirt. *Towels.* He needed to buy towels.

Returning to the kitchen, he again picked up the Jack Daniels, fingered the now peeling, liquor-stained label, and placed the bottle back on the counter.

Hold off, old son. Wait till Happy Hour.

Grabbing his truck keys, he headed for the carport. The pickup soared down Road 503 heading toward I-25. It was a scenic drive and the New Mexico style houses Schuyler flew by on either side of the road claimed his attention. He was now expert at manipulating the clutch, but still unsure about when to use first or second gear. Choosing this battered and rattling truck, knowing her son had never driven anything but the Ford Fiesta, must be Clementine's not so subtle idea of a joke. Or, no doubt, another one of the many lessons in patience she felt he needed to learn. *Har-de-har.*

When he first became aware of the flashing lights behind him,was a question without a satisfactory answer. *Jesus.* What next? Pulling onto the shoulder, he quickly buckled on his seat belt and fumbled inside the glove box for the car registration.

"Good morning, sir." The officer touched the brim of his hat. "You're from Ohio? Just visiting?"

"Uh, no. I live here. Number 57. Up the road." Schuyler gestured over his shoulder.

"License and registration, please."

"Just a second. The license is in my back pocket."

"New York license." The officer scanned the documents. "But the truck has Ohio plates."

"Yeah. I just moved here from New York. My mother gave me this truck. She lives in Akron."

"Did you know you were exceeding the speed limit on this road? Twenty-five miles per hour."

"Geez—twenty-five! You're kidding—*right*? I mean—I—I didn't realize."

"There were signs posted two miles back, and one mile back. You were doing fifty."

"Gosh, I'm sorry."

The officer walked back to his vehicle and returned a few minutes later with a multilayered citation form. "Sign here. Then check a box. Indicate whether you accept the citation or choose to appear in court."

"I'll take the citation, I guess." What experience did he have with citations? "I didn't realize I was driving so fast. Twenty-five is the limit, you say?"

"This isn't the Big Apple, sir. And no honking." The officer removed his cap and ran his fingers through his hair. "Get your registration changed, get a New Mexico plate and driver's license. On Monday go to the DMV office in Española, up the road."

"Up yours," Schuyler muttered as the officer returned to his car, leaving his victim to contemplate the citation. "I haven't even been in your lousy state for a week." He watched the officer pull

onto the road and set off at a smart pace far in excess of twenty-
five miles per hour.

Motherfucker.

Somewhat shaken, wondering what the ticket was going
to cost him, he drove on down the road. He'd seen a café, the
Mockingbird, on the west side of the highway as he drove back
from Albuquerque last night. That would be his breakfast destination.

Since it was Saturday morning, not a work day, Schuyler was
surprised to be seated without waiting. He thought the place
would be crawling with patrons. *About time my luck turned.* He
could also eat here on Monday, before he made the drive into
Santa Fe to apply for the accursed but mandatory job at Sam's
Club. Clementine would be expecting a report on his success.
Funny—in his mind, his mother was always "Clementine." To
her face, she was "Mom."

He was escorted to a table near a window. Even better—he
could keep an eye on the truck. Supposing it got stolen from the
parking lot? Someone could hot-wire it, couldn't they?

He'd heard of these things happening. This was unknown
country and the truck was his lifeline. Surrounded as he was in
this godawful state of New Mexico, in Albuquerque and Santa Fe,
and in this funky restaurant by a sea of brown and red faces, he'd
best be cautious until he got the lay of the land. They all seemed
to be staring at him. Every person he laid eyes on looked shifty.
And why were so many people speaking Spanish? At least, he
thought it was Spanish.

"I'm Ellen. You ready?" A waitress with an order pad rattled
off the daily specials as he fingered a well-worn menu. Ellen was
dark-skinned like almost everyone else in the restaurant, the
gaunt fleshless type of woman he'd noticed working in so many
of the cafés he stopped at while driving west from Akron.

"I'd recommend you try the Ranch Special." She smiled, a
comfortable smile, as if she recognized his confusion. "That's two
eggs, your way, with two cheese enchiladas and chile."

"Sounds good." Schuyler felt sure his own smile was as winning as hers. "Scrambled."

"Red or green?"

"Uhh—what?"

"Red or green chile. I'd choose red."

"Fine. Make it red."

"Where'd you get your accent?"

"Me? I've got an accent?"

"Yeah. It's cute."

"Oh. I'm from New York."

Schuyler hoped he'd chosen a digestible meal. Many items on the Mockingbird Café menu were things he'd never heard of. Carne adovada? Chile con queso?

His stomach was delicate, fussy. He'd struggled with unpredictable bouts of IBS for most of his life. *What a curse.* As far as he could remember, the first bout happened when his father punished him by locking him in the closet. He'd messed his pants. Then, he was punished a second time for doing that.

He rubbed his hands on his thighs, convinced that jeans were the most uncomfortable garment ever invented and wondered what breakfast would be like. All he craved right now was a double cream cheese shmear on a sesame seed bagel.

"Excuse me, sir." Ellen was back again. "Would you mind if I seated someone at your table? We're swamped, and it would sure help me out."

Schuyler glanced up at the smiling waitress, then stared at the man standing behind her. A man whose face was red. Swarthy. A man whose coal-black hair was plaited in a long braid hanging down his back. Out of the corner of his eye he scanned the line of people hoping to get a table. *Wow.* The place had filled up fast. The line trailed beyond the restaurant door and onto the walkway outside. People were sitting on the hoods of their vehicles, smoking, chatting, laughing.

Brown kids swarmed the parking lot.

"Saturday morning. You know how it is." Ellen shrugged. "So?"

Schuyler nodded, then grimaced as his breakfast partner sat down across from him and proceeded to order two fried eggs over easy, hash browns with a side of posole, and coffee. *Posole?* The man wore a denim jacket and western-style hat. Looked like a movie cowboy's hat.

"Hey." The stranger's weathered face creased into a smile as he extended his hand. "I'm Thomas Jannssen. Two n's and two s's. J-A-N-N-S-S-E-N. Also known as Lone Goose."

"Glad to meet you." Schuyler hesitated before the piercing eye opposite him. Then he reached out to have his hand engulfed in a brief but crushing grip. "Aaron Schuyler." Maybe it was the custom in these parts to spell out your surname. "S-C-H-U—"

"I know who you are," interrupted Jannssen. "I asked Ellen to seat me with you."

"You did? Why?"

"You moved into number 57 on Road 503."

"How do you know that?"

"Word gets around. You're from New York," Jannssen offered further.

"Yeah. I am." Schuyler was concerned. He'd better be on his guard. He should have locked the back door when he left his house. But, why? There wasn't anything in it.

"Do you live around here, Mr. Jannssen?"

"Do now. Just rented a place a few miles west of the interstate. Call me Tom, or Lone Goose. What did you order?"

"For breakfast? The special. The Ranch Special."

"You getting red or green with that?"

"The waitress asked me the same question."

"And you said—?"

"I said, 'I'll take whatever you would have.' Was that a mistake? I wasn't sure what she meant."

"Chile. Red or green chile. Best to get red. It has a smoother flavor."

"I guess it will be okay." Schuyler felt no confidence in his answer.

"We'll see. You like your place? Why did you move here?"

The cadence of Lone Goose's speech, like that of the native staff he'd met at Pojoaque True Value Hardware, fascinated Schuyler. He'd gone in to buy a motion-detecting light for the back door of his house before he flew to New York. They tried to explain how he could wire and install the light by himself.

Fat chance that would happen.

What did he know about electrical wiring? He could get shocked. They laughed both at his questions and his accent when he said the closest he'd come to wiring in New York was handing a check to the electrician.

Maybe his landlord, this Hugh Leigh guy, would install the light.

"Yeah, I like the place. There's nothing in it right now. Nothing except a bed. I need to get some furniture." He sidestepped explaining why he had moved to Nambé.

"I can loan you a table. Kitchen table. Some chairs."

"Aw, that's okay. I'll buy something in Santa Fe."

"It's up to you," Jannssen answered.

"Where's the DMV office in Española?" Schuyler pronounced it Espa*NO*la.

"Turn right from your road and go north on I-25 a few miles. You getting New Mexico plates?"

"Yeah. License and registration, too. I just got ticketed. Can you believe the speed limit on 503 is only twenty-five? How much do you think the ticket will be?"

"Can't say. They always go after the out-of-state plates. Yours is Ohio. You better go to Española on Monday." Jannssen dug into his breakfast that had arrived at the table. "You'll like the red chile," he commented as he appraised Schuyler's plate.

Schuyler did like it.

"This is delicious." He had an adventurous palate and appreciated spicy cuisines. Except for Indian food. Curry was a no-no. "Mexican food in New York doesn't taste like this."

"Makes sense, doesn't it?" Jannssen agreed.

"Well"—Schuyler reverted to the topic most on his mind—"I can't go to Española on Monday. I'm going to Santa Fe to apply for a job at Sam's Club."

"Sam's Club, huh? Good luck with that."

The two men finished their meals and paid at the cash register. Schuyler noticed that the line of waiting patrons was even longer. The Mockingbird was a thriving business.

"Nice to meet you," he ventured, extending his hand to Tom Jannssen and, with surprise on his own part, realizing he'd enjoyed their conversation. Sort of. It was never a New Yorker's policy to encourage familiarity. Schuyler never had what you'd call "friends."

A foreign concept.

New Mexico was a foreign land. Jannssen was a foreign man. A very foreign man. You couldn't be too careful. Still, there was something about the guy. He was likable, although Schuyler couldn't bring himself to call his breakfast partner Lone Goose. That was a stretch.

"I'll be seeing you," said Jannssen, with a twitch of a smile as he read the uncertainty in his new acquaintance's eye.

Convinced everyone he encountered in New Mexico was laughing at him and that he would never fit in here, Schuyler climbed into the pickup and drove at a crawl across I-25 to the Pojoaque Village Market. He stocked up on what he thought he'd bother to cook for himself. *Let's be realistic.* With plenty of frozen dinners in his shopping cart he headed toward the aisles with wine and liquor.

He was about to snatch a bottle of Jack off the shelf when he noticed the alcohol aisle was roped off. No admittance on Sunday. Well, that was that. The half-empty bottle would have to suffice until Monday. He'd cash Clementine's check in Santa Fe and pick up more Jack on his return from Sam's Club.

What the hell was Sam's Club?

CHAPTER 7

Sam's Club

Schuyler glanced at the clock on the bedside table. Six a.m. Sunlight was pouring in through the window just as it would every day until he bought curtains, or a shade of some sort.

He was wide awake, and it was Monday morning. He'd spent his third night in the house and slept well, except when jarred awake by what he thought were coyotes baying, night birds trilling, and large rodents thumping across the roof.

Schuyler hoped they were only rodents. That was bad enough.

He lay in bed, staring up at the strange ceiling, again worried about what was living between the twigs and logs overhead. In response to his inquiry, Tom Jannssen had said the ceilings in these old adobe houses were made of *latillas* and *vigas*. It looked like a mass of dirty wood to Schuyler. The logs, *vigas*, still had bark on them and were covered with cobwebs. It gave him the creeps. He didn't like the house and once more wondered why Clementine had rented it.

Even worse, he still wondered why she had thrust him into this bizarre culture. She could have chosen upstate New York. Vermont, even. That was penance enough if she wanted to punish him, freeze his backside during the winters. There must be Sam's Clubs in those parts. He would have been with his own type of people. To close such a sweet deal, he would jump at the chance to sign a fourth notarized document and promise to do whatever dog tricks she wanted.

With a sigh, Schuyler rolled out of bed and stumbled into the bathroom. Shaved, showered, and dressed, he headed for the kitchen and opened the freezer compartment of the fridge, where he'd stored his frozen dinners. Chicken nuggets and these bizarre lumps of potato would suffice for breakfast. The only thing was, he couldn't figure out how to heat the oven.

He also had no cookware for heating his food on the range top. He stared at the label affixed to the appliance. "Amana Gas Range Superior."

Gas range. What the hell was that? Didn't New Mexico have enough electricity? His shabby Bronx motel–apartment had an electric range. *What the fuck?* This appliance had turn-on knobs for each of the four burners, and a dial for adjusting the degrees of heat in the oven, but he couldn't figure out how to get the range top or the oven started.

Returning to the bathroom, Schuyler brushed his teeth, checked his appearance in the mirror a second time, donned his sport coat, and picked up his truck keys. It would have to be the Mockingbird for breakfast. The third day in a row. Yesterday, Sunday, he'd wakened with the sun, explored the contents of the small shed behind the carport, and headed for the Mockingbird. After breakfast he spent some time at Ace Hardware in Pojoaque before heading back to the house. Today, however, there was no time for loitering. He needed to make time this morning, get to Santa Fe and find Sam's Club. He hoped Tom Jannssen wasn't at the cafe.

Once on I-25, heading south to Santa Fe, the tailgating he encountered was friggin' scary. No other way to describe it. By the time he reached the south end of Santa Fe he was thankful to be behind the wheel of a truck. It would be downright life-threatening to drive a sedan. He parked the Toyota in the Sam's Club parking lot, rechecked his appearance in the rear-view mirror, and headed for the store entrance.

"Can I see your membership card, sir?" asked an employee stationed just inside the door.

"Uh, I don't have a membership card," Schuyler responded. "I'm here to apply for a job."

"In that case, go up that set of stairs. Human Resources is on the second floor."

"Thanks." Schuyler again adjusted his tie, then climbed the stairs, wondering when he had last submitted to a job interview. He opened a door labeled HR.

"Good morning," said a young, dark-haired woman seated at a desk behind a windowed enclosure. "How may I help you?"

"I wondered if I could fill out a job application?" asked Schuyler, appalled by the plain appearance of the tiny office. His own office, back when he had one, was palatial.

That was then.

"Your name?" asked the woman. When he responded, "Aaron Schuyler," she surprised him by smiling, bouncing up from her chair, and opening the door into the enclosure behind her.

"Welcome, Mr. Schuyler!" Her tone was warm and welcoming. "I'm Janice Garcia. I'm the Human Resources receptionist. We've been expecting you." Her gesture indicated he should proceed.

We've been expecting you?

Puzzled, he smiled in return, then followed her down a hallway, surprised to see the Human Resources Department was larger than it first appeared to be. Ms. Garcia opened a door at the end of the hall and ushered him into an office not much bigger than the one she occupied.

"At last, here is Mr. Schuyler to see you, Ms. Chatterjee." Janice smiled at the woman seated behind a desk that filled most of her office. The desktop was stacked high with files.

Janice departed, closing the door behind her, and Schuyler found himself facing the most beautiful woman he'd ever encountered. She wasn't young—he guessed she might be in her mid-forties. But ignoring the fact that he must appear an idiot or a bumpkin by so doing, he couldn't stop staring, open-mouthed, as she rose to greet him. *Chatterjee.* Wasn't that an Indian surname? For some reason, it sounded familiar.

Ms. Chatterjee was neither blonde nor of fair complexion, and not at all the type to capture his fancy. Women of "foreign extraction" weren't his preference. Never had been. He seldom looked at them twice. But he was looking now.

"Mr. Schuyler, how nice to meet you, at last," said this smiling apparition with a voice like liquid music. She rose from her chair and extended her hand. "I'm Anita Chatterjee, director of Human Resources for Santa Fe Sam's Club."

Schuyler was a well-read man. Uncle Harry had seen to that. Had molded his literary tastes and encouraged his nephew to read widely. Although Ms. Chatterjee's beauty was of a type he had never admired—never, before today—he recognized at once that she was an image extracted live from a miniature Mughal painting. Perhaps the famed Mumtaz Mahal, adored by Shah Jahan, brought to life? Or, could she be Radha, the beloved consort of Krishna?

Her golden skin was smooth, flawless. Her coal-black hair, copious amounts of it, was pulled back from her forehead in what he assumed was a bun. Delicate brows sheltered the almond-shaped eyes so often lauded in classical literature. In books, in Uncle Harry's bookshop.

He was still staring. His mouth was hanging open. *Way to go, numbskull.*

He glanced toward her left hand, seeking evidence of her wedded status, hoping his observation went unnoticed. No ring.

Get a grip. Is this any way to land a job? Any way to make an impression? Schuyler struggled to find his tongue, abnormally dry, and remember how to use it.

"Please, make yourself comfortable." Ms. Chatterjee gestured toward the chairs on the opposite side of the desk. She dropped her eyes as if trying to suppress another smile.

"It's nice to meet you, too," Schuyler answered, clearing his throat, disgruntled by his banal reply. His formerly glib tongue having deserted him, he plopped down onto a chair.

"Thank you," Chatterjee responded. "Welcome to Sam's Club."

He knew she was laughing at him, just like Tom Jannssen and the waitresses at the Mockingbird laughed at him. Just like everyone he'd encountered in New Mexico. He swallowed hard. What was he—fifteen years old? Doing his best to imitate a pimple-faced adolescent? An awkward dweeb?

"So, you would like to come to work at Sam's Club, Mr. Schuyler?" Ms. Chatterjee's singsong lilt and British accent were proof she was not native-born to America.

"Yes, ma'am," he replied, nodding with vigor. "I need a job. It would be an honor to work here." He now wanted nothing more than to land a job at Sam's Club.

Yes! Clementine! Way to go, Mom!

He also wanted nothing more than to sit and listen to Ms. Chatterjee's clipped, flawless, perfect syllables. Her voice was the sweetest sound he'd ever heard. He imagined her honeyed voice dripping—drip-dropping—ambrosial nectar all over him.

You dunce.

"You think so?" she questioned, tilting her head to one side. "What type of work were you seeking, and what are your qualifications?"

"Well, I don't exactly know how my qualifications fit in here." Lame start. Be aggressive. "I have a college education. Master's degree in global finance," he offered. "What kind of jobs are available?"

"We have many jobs available, but my preference is to have new associates work their way up. Everyone starts out in the same way. At the bottom."

The last three words were stressed.

"In that way, the new associate experiences a variety of jobs and sees how the entire staff of associates functions as a team. You see, all the departments interact with each other."

Oh, yes, he saw.

"HR can then make a better decision as to where a person will not only be happy working long-term but will fulfill our needs and be an asset to Sam's Club."

"That seems sensible to me. A sound business practice," Schuyler agreed, his voice eager. "I, of course, would want to learn as much about operations as I possibly could."

"I'm glad to hear it." Ms. Chatterjee jotted some notes down on the paper in front of her. "And when do you think you would be able to start?"

"Well, I've only been in New Mexico a couple of days. I'm renting a place north of Santa Fe and just returned from my uncle's interment in New York—"

"Oh, please," interrupted Ms. Chatterjee. "How rude I've been. Allow me to offer my condolences."

"Thank you—too kind." Her sorrow, considering the fact he was a total stranger to her, seemed genuine enough, but puzzling. "So, as it is, I have no furniture—" His explanation ground to a halt. "I—uh, what I mean is I first arrived in New Mexico six days ago and then had to return to New York the day after that arrival—that *first* arrival. To attend the memorial. Is this making any sense?" he added in an ingratiating tone and with his most boyish grin.

"It makes perfect sense." Ms. Chatterjee tilted her head to the other side. "I understand the situation. You returned Saturday to Santa Fe after the funeral. A second beginning for you. Is that correct?"

"Yes, ma'am. I need some time to get settled. Get some pots and pans. Dishes. Table. Chairs." *Stop rambling.* "Cleaning supplies." *Zip it.*

Chatterjee was again doing her best to repress an amused expression.

"If you think you might hire me, a few days would be much appreciated."

"There is no question about me hiring you," she answered in melodic tones. "Consider it done, sir. Today is Monday. Would you be able to start next Monday?"

"Of course." Schuyler nodded, frowning. Confused. What was the catch here? This was like no kind of job interview he'd ever known. "I—uh—of course. Thank you."

"You don't seem entirely at your ease, Mr. Schuyler." It was Ms. Chatterjee's turn to frown. "Do you have some reservations? Are there any further questions I might answer about the Club? A job is yours if you want it."

"As a matter of fact—" Schuyler hesitated, mesmerized by the way her head swayed from side to side, but decided he had to speak up. "I do have some questions, if you don't mind me asking. First off, is this a real interview? I mean, you haven't asked to see my CV. You know nothing about my job history. Also, Ms. Garcia recognized my name as soon as I identified myself." He shifted his position in the chair. "How is that possible? I don't believe I've ever met her before."

Chatterjee was no longer smiling. The silence following his questions lengthened as she looked down, examining her hands clasping the pen.

"Ms. Garcia said, 'We've been expecting you,'" he continued. "Why was she expecting me? You seemed to know I'd walk through this door. You didn't ask for references or have me fill out a job application. I think—I don't know what to think. I'm not sure what's going on."

Schuyler watched her facial expression change several times, as if she couldn't decide what her response should be.

"Did you mistake me for someone else?" Schuyler prodded, now even more perplexed by her reaction.

"No, Mr. Schuyler. I did not." Chatterjee expelled a sigh, laid her pen down on the desk, and leaned forward. "You are entitled to an explanation and I have not been forbidden to give you one. I'm just not sure what to say. We hoped you would not enquire as to the, uh, the somewhat unusual details of your hire."

"What unusual details?" Schuyler leaned forward, elbows resting on his knees. "How could you know ahead of time that I'd come to Sam's Club and apply for a job?"

Again, Chatterjee struggled with herself. She emitted another sigh, as if resigned to an uncomfortable decision. "About three months ago our store manager, Alice Cordova, and myself, were contacted by your mother, Mrs. Clementine Atwater. Mrs. Atwater explained a few pertinent circumstances, the nature of which I am not at liberty to disclose. To put it bluntly, she asked us to employ you."

Schuyler blew out an exhale and slumped forward.

Betrayal. Major betrayal.

"There's no need to disclose anything," he mumbled, as he stood up and buttoned his sport coat. "I know those pertinent circumstances better than anyone." *Utter humiliation.* "I should probably leave now, Ms. Chatterjee."

"Not unless you are refusing the job I'm offering you."

Schuyler hesitated, then once more sat down in his chair.

"If you know what I think you know, then why would you want to hire me?" When Chatterjee made no reply, he continued. "Would you mind if I asked you one more question?"

"Please do, sir. I will answer if I can."

"I have an idea how she convinced you to take me on. If you confirm my suspicions I'm still going to leave, but at least I'll be able to get some sleep tonight. She bribed you, didn't she?"

Chatterjee bristled with a rush of syllables, raising her hands to ward off the very suggestion. "Please, Mr. Schuyler—do not mistake. I would not, could not, accept any sort of bribe and neither would Mrs. Cordova. Nor would any executive of Sam's Club."

"'Bribe' is not the term I would use."

"Then—what term would you use?" pursued Schuyler, in a hotter tone than he would have liked to employ.

"Your mother is a generous woman. She made a substantial donation to the Children's Miracle Network, a charity Sam's Club is proud to support," Chatterjee explained, swallowing hard. "It is my belief she intended only good with this gesture, that her only goal was to further your interests."

Schuyler wanted to throttle Clementine. She had gone too far. Way too far. Here was confirmation of what he'd long suspected. He was a mere puppet on a string. The puppy dog he'd likened himself to just a few days ago.

Arf. Arf.

Schuyler sat staring at the woman in front of him, certain his masculine sense of self had shrunk to nothing and was irrecoverable. Could never be restored, because it was mired in the depths of a swamp impossible to plumb. A mire of his own making. His gift for gab had deserted him and he, seldom at a loss for words, he who could sell anything to anyone, was speechless.

Yes, this time Clementine had outdone herself. Convinced he couldn't make his way in the world employing any degree of decency, she'd purchased him a job. *Unbelievable.* Schuyler could only wonder, then couldn't forgive himself for wondering, if Winston had anything to do with this scheme. Worst of all, in thinking such a possibility made sense and the long-deceased heroic PM had any power to influence Sam's Club, was he buying into his mother's madness?

"Mr. Schuyler?"

Chatterjee's concerned tone summoned him back to reality. A sinkhole of reality.

"Sir, I very much regret having traveled down this path of explanation with you." Her dismayed expression spoke louder than her words. "Please accept my apologies. My intention was sincere, but what I said was misguided. I see by your reaction, it was not my place to reveal such distasteful facts to you."

Schuyler glanced up from his hands clenched in frustration. This was a damned if you do, damned if you don't situation if ever there was one. Any further elaboration of circumstance, any excuse he might provide, would by necessity include the facts prompting his mother's interference and further muddy the waters. *Hell.* There was a 90 percent chance these sordid facts were already known to Chatterjee. Did humiliation or frustration top the lengthy list of negative feelings churning inside him right now?

"Is there anything I might say that would ease your mind?" Chatterjee added.

"No, I don't think so," he responded in a quiet, but steadier voice than he'd thought himself capable of. "What can I say, Ms. Chatterjee? To deny what my mother told you would be a lie. Untrue, not to mention useless."

"Will you still accept this job?" she urged. "We could use a man of your experience."

"And—my experience earns me a job at 'the bottom,' as you put it."

"Yes. Working on the dock, to begin with. Loading and unloading merchandise."

Aghast as he was at this dismal prospect, Schuyler made no answer. He desperately needed this job. If he failed to accept Chatterjee's terms, would Clementine pull the plug on his rent, his truck, his monthly allowance, and his inheritance? Leave him in the lurch, again a homeless bum?

"Let us leave it this way, Mr. Schuyler. The job is yours, if you want it," Ms. Chatterjee was saying. "If you arrive at 7:30 a.m. on Monday, I'll process a time card for you."

She rose from her chair and extended her hand.

Schuyler also rose, and accepted the hand. A warm and very delicate hand. Nodding, but saying nothing due to the lump in his throat and the frustration in his heart, he exited her office, walked down the hall, and offered another nod to Janice Garcia.

CHAPTER 8

Reflections

As he exited Sam's Club, Schuyler asked a man standing outside the store where he could find a decent bar.

"Try the lounge at the La Fonda Hotel," the man answered. "On the Plaza downtown. Very historical. Nice tourist place."

"Oh, I'm not a tourist," demurred Schuyler. "I live here."

With no idea where the Plaza was, or what a Plaza was, he headed north on Cerrillos Road until he found a sign indicating where to turn. He then drove at an annoying crawl through pedestrian traffic—why couldn't people stay on the sidewalk?—until he ended up several blocks away from the La Fonda. Finding a place to park was tougher than he expected but Santa Fe was, after all, a tourist magnet. Lots of people were looking for too few spaces. As he climbed out of the truck, he noticed his diary lying on the passenger seat. On a whim, he scooped it up. Laughing about his past escapades might offer some solace after his embarrassment in front of Ms. Chatterjee.

It was 10:00 a.m. when Schuyler ordered a double bourbon— no ice—at the lounge bar. He then settled into a comfortable booth and began paging through the diary, at first only half-interested in what he'd written there. Foremost in his mind was chagrin, as he reviewed what a fool he'd made of himself during the interview. Or, to be accurate, how Clementine had made a fool of him. The wheels wouldn't stop spinning as he seethed over the injustices he suffered. What must Ms. Chatterjee think of him?

He squirmed in his seat. His thoughts about the Human Resources director were even more unsettling than the interview debacle, not only because of her undoubted low regard for him, but because he didn't understand his attraction to her. She wasn't his type. She was Indian. Her unmistakable accent told him Anita Chatterjee was born either in England or on the subcontinent. He'd never cared for Indian people. *Point blank.* True, they were intelligent, like himself. But, unlike him, they worked hard for success. Hard work was never his ethic, even when he owned the investment firm. He preferred getting by with half-truths, outright lies when necessary, and skimping on vital paperwork. Whatever tactics worked for a given situation. Whatever made the most money with the least effort. In fact, he mused, "whatever" was almost his personal motto.

But—getting back to Indians. They stuck together and remained a tight-knit community when they settled in foreign countries. Could you trust such secretive people? Schuyler also had an aversion to Indian food. He detested curry. The odor alone made him desperate for a barf bag.

When his bourbon arrived at the table he toyed with the drink, taking long slow sips, then sucked on the ice cubes he'd specifically requested not be included. Did anyone ever get what they wanted? The lounge's soft light was comforting, unlike the harsh glare of an outside world hell-bent on pointing a finger at his peccadillos. The upholstered bench was comfortable. Why not enjoy this secluded ambience for a while longer? He could thumb through his diary, then head for home.

What a laugh. *Home?* How had he come to be stuck in this dry, dusty state with so few trees, people speaking a foreign language, and speed-mad drivers thirsting for his blood like an extraction from Hieronymus Bosch's *Last Judgment. If* they'd had cars in the Middle Ages. Or, whenever that was.

Paging through various dates in the diary, he came upon one he would rather have forgotten, given the shattering events of this morning. Events that were best forgotten, but never would be. How could he recover from his humiliation?

Buck up, Schuyler. Let's be honest here. Whose fault is this mess but your own?

Whoa. Where had that thought come from?

He considered closing the diary and not reading what he'd written in this entry. Better yet, why not rip out those pages? Never revisit them again. No one would be the wiser and he need not suffer further from his own folly. From having to read them again.

But what sort of solution was that? Not a satisfactory one. Wallowing in disgust and self-inflicted shame, Schuyler chose suffering. He soon regretted his rash decision to read the entry, but it was too late now for second thoughts. Humiliation morphed into dismay. A knife twisted inside his intestines. Now, he was even more grateful for the lounge's subtle lighting. His fellow pre-noon bar patrons couldn't see the crimson flush that seared his flesh.

Dear Diary,

I still can't believe what happened twice this morning, and all within less than three hours. Can't believe my luck. *Bad*, as per usual.

At the get-go it looked like the start to a pretty good day. I was in line at Goodwill by 9:00 a.m. and shuffled through the entrance when they opened, along with a bunch of low-class riffraff, on-unemployment types who'd never known what it was like to shop at a *really fine* store.

My goal was to find the racks with men's white shirts.

I almost didn't make it past the entrance. Almost couldn't take one more step due to the foul reek in the store. Didn't think I could stagger over to the shirts before puking. *No lie.* I'm no pansy but—gagging all the way. Body odor, moldy fabrics, and the unmistakable fragrance used to freshen up every thrift store I've ever been in stopped me in my tracks. The stink was more unforgettable than a skunk ever could be. You smell *one* thrift store, you smelled them all.

I tried holding my breath, but that didn't last long. There was nothing to do but suffer through it. Mustard gas couldn't be worse. If I found two nice white shirts by pawing through the rack, then it'd be worth it. I need to look decent, don't I?

Need to have a change of shirts?? Oh, how low I've stooped. Me—who patronized Dun & Bradstreet or bespoke my shirts in London. How have I *sunk so far*? It's not like my current financial state is my fault. Not all my fault. *The Feds* closed the firm on Wall Street. Not me. And I'd at least have a place to call home if Natalie hadn't kicked me out. Can't bunk with my kids. They won't speak to me.

So I did find two pretty good shirts, and I had this idea. What if I hid one shirt under the other? Could I get away with paying for only one? Worth a try. I had a client to call on at eleven and if luck was on my side, just this once, I could *maybe* talk the guy into buying into Stalwart Funds.

Diary, did I tell you about Stalwart Funds? That's the shitty company I work for. Commission only. One of their offerings is resort time-shares in *Antarctica*. Can you believe it? *Hah*. What a destination wedding that would make. People never cease to amaze me. If they fall for this scheme, they deserve what they get.

I handed the "shirt" to the clerk at the register. I needed to get the hell out of Goodwill and make this sales call. She shook the shirt before starting to fold it.

"Whoopsie!" she cries out. Then she says, "We have a second shirt stuck inside the first one. How could that have happened? Each shirt is $5.99, sir."

Smartass. With the emphasis on *sir*.

So I say, "Whoa—!" (Trying to save face.) "What do you know? I'll just take one." I flung some bills onto the counter and changed shirts in the store dressing room.

I needed to be on time for my appointment with this Mr. Amit Chatterjee. I thought I had a good chance at closing the deal. Getting a fat commission. Chatterjee had a Bronx address in a middle-class neighborhood. Just the demographic I was looking for. He owns a drapery factory, probably a sweatshop. *Child labor*. He uses fabrics imported from India. What a setup. If only I'd thought of that instead of going into financial management. You never know.

Chatterjee opened the door to his home at once when I knocked. And, guess what? The whole family was standing there. A man, Chatterjee, with a short woman wearing a sari to his right, and four little kids on his left.

And then—OMG—there was the stench. *Curry.* The aroma of curry slammed into me like a ton of bricks.

I staggered backward. Honest to God. Then, wave after wave of incense hit me. *Sickening.* I couldn't breathe. Incense is a heavy-duty *no-no.* And with curry? *No way.* No worse combination.

To top it off, it wasn't just curry and incense I smelled, but lamb. *Lamb.* The reek of roasted lamb flesh—

"Welcome, welcome, Mr. Schuyler," says Chatterjee with a thick accent. Plenty hard to understand. "Come in, come in. We have prepared a most excellent luncheon for you. Most delicious. My wife's best." And then he gestures toward his wife, who repeats. "Come in, come in! Eat your fill!"

I was ready to retch. Couldn't help it. The writing was on the wall. This would be a tough enough sell due to the language problem. Would Chatterjee even understand my sales pitch? And—there was no way I was going to *eat lamb.*

By this time, my temples were pounding and my head was swimming. (I blame it mostly on the curry.) I decided to handle it this way. I slapped my forehead *hard.*

"Good heavens!" I said. "I've forgotten the portfolio I prepared for you. I'll run to the office, pick it up, and be back here in an hour. Or two. Or—tomorrow. Even better."

So Chatterjee says, "Oh no, Mr. Schuyler! Come in and eat. The meal is most delicious. Then you can go home and fetch your portfolio. Let us not waste this food."

I wasn't going to be one-upped by a drapery salesman. I said, "Absolutely not! Kind of you, Mr. Chatterjee, but I wouldn't think of imposing. I'll get the portfolio and be back before you know it."

The guy grabs my sleeve. I jerked it away from him, but he seemed alarmed. Confused. So did his wife and kids. I almost felt sorry for them. Chatterjee gestured toward the interior of his home. "Our meal—!" *Very* dramatic.

Well, I wasn't doing so hot. Coughing up a storm. Needed to make tracks.

"Later, dear sir." I gagged again. "So thoughtful. Too kind! Appreciate the thought. Really do. Lovely family. Lovely home." I said whatever came into my head, then took off.

I tripped going backward down the front step, twisted my ankle, and limped off, breathing into my handkerchief. Got to thinking—buying the shirt was a waste of cash. A rip-off. I was taken in again.

It was a close call. I swear the incense odor chased me down the block all the way to the subway entrance. *Indian food.* Not my cup of tea. Never will be.

July 19, 2011

Chatterjee. Amit Chatterjee. Anita Chatterjee. The same surname.

Could these two be even tangentially related? If so, Schuyler knew his cause was lost. He chugged his drink, shook his head in despair, and with eyes downcast, peered through the dim lounge light at the floor beneath his table. *Holy hell.* What was happening? Horrified, he watched the aged oaken planks start to smolder. The odor of wood burning and then charring rose upward and enveloped not only the bench he sat on but his person as well. The mellow boards turned to cinders and revealed a gaping hole through which he spied seductive crimson flames beckoning to him. He hadn't the strength to resist their allure. They would suck him into their fiery depths. *Shades of Bosch!* He'd suffer a punishment the likes of which he could not imagine.

A punishment he well deserved.

He'd already toppled off the ladder to success. Now, the ladder of salvation was being jerked out from under his feet. There would be no forgiveness. Not for him. He was damned.

Schuyler recalled researching Amit Chatterjee before that ill-fated sales call. He learned Chatterjee was a common Bengali name. Considering the vast number of Chatterjees in the vast Bengali population, and how many had emigrated to the United States, there was, at best, only a marginal chance he was related to the Human Resources director at Sam's Club.

The opening in the floor beneath his feet resutured itself and the wrathful blaze subsided, but his throat was parched and he couldn't swallow. Closing the diary, he motioned for the bartender to bring another double.

The entry he'd written in his diary was disturbing. Beyond disturbing. He was not happy with himself. *Who would be?* How had he churned up the gall necessary to inscribe his foul interpretation of that incident with Amit Chatterjee onto paper? His life path seemed to progress like a ping-pong ball, bouncing from embarrassment to humiliation and then back again. What kind of progress was that? Schuyler retrieved a pen from his jacket pocket and thumbed through his diary until he found a blank page. If he put some of his scattered thoughts down on paper, maybe he'd have a better chance of making sense out of them.

Dear Diary,

I just reread what I wrote after making a sales call on the Amit Chatterjee family a few years ago. Looking at that entry now makes me sick to my stomach. I make myself sick to my stomach. It's a two-part sickness. My rudeness to them was disgusting. Writing about it in the diary like it was an amusing escapade, was worse.

What kind of asshole does that?

If now I am still overindulging in liquor, still driving too fast, and still mooching off Clementine and—all the facts point to it—unable to get a job without her paying some business to hire me, am I as vile as the version of myself who wrote that disgraceful entry in the diary. Am I that same person?

Despite indisputable evidence to the contrary, I don't feel I am.

Don't *feel* I am. What the hell do *my feelings* matter? Have I ever paid a mite of attention to the feelings of other people?

Those of Natalie, my ex-wife. Those of my three kids. Bert, my former business partner, when I cheated with his wife. Or, maybe worst of all, Clementine. What about *her* feelings?

I just saw the gates of hell open up beneath my feet. I don't want to end up *Down There*. I'll scourge myself bloody to prevent it. I don't have to search for words to describe my *unforgivable* behavior toward the Chatterjee family. It was vile. Wait. I already wrote vile. *Churlish.* That's a good one. *Disrespectful. Rude. Boorish.* Boorish is too much like churlish, but a lot of other adjectives will fit.

Uncivil. Crude. Inconsiderate. Selfish. Selfish. Selfish. How about that?

I haven't acted like a man. Like a gentleman. Even if I despise Stan Atwater—who will be forever in my face—the man has class. I have to hand it to him. A tough kind of class. He loves my mother. She deserves to be loved, and I don't know if she ever was loved *until now*. Am I capable of offering that kind of love? That kind of devotion? To anyone?

I've broken all the rules of common courtesy that were Uncle Harry's pillars of civility and decorum. Considering how much I looked up to Harry and benefited from his mentorship, why didn't those same standards become *my own*?

Am I so ego-driven and self-absorbed I'm beyond redemption? I don't want to be,but that's what it looks like. Why else would my mother force me to live in New Mexico? What other conclusion can I draw if whatever pitiful inner strength I have, isn't enough to put the brakes on my descent into the flames of hell?

April 17, 2017

Schuyler left the second drink unfinished and eased himself out of the booth. As much as he wanted to dump his finger-pointing diary into a trash can, he didn't. He placed a tip on the table and staggered out of the lounge. With the diary.

He had towels to buy. He had dishes and pots and pans to buy. Next time he saw Tom Jannssen he'd take him up on the loan of chairs and a table. He'd probably turn up at Sam's Club next Monday and accept the job offer.

He also needed to get home. His new landlord, Hugh Leigh, was scheduled to arrive at the rental home at two o'clock that afternoon.

CHAPTER 9

Hugh Leigh

Schuyler purchased more groceries, an alarm clock, and other household goods at Walmart, then headed north on I-25 after refueling the truck. The cost of gas for the gallons the truck consumed was both a wake-up call and a blow to his pocketbook. With daily treks to Santa Fe, driving back and forth was going to cost an arm and a leg. He'd need to be thrifty for a few weeks, and sound financial management was never his strong suit. That precarious line of thought led him to wonder if he'd ever had a strong suit, and just what it might be.

At 2:10 p.m. he pulled into the driveway of his Nambé rental home where a battered and ancient vehicle was parked in the carport. The rear-end logo read "GMC Jimmy." This piece of junk, no doubt belonging to Hugh Leigh, looked old enough to be an original model. That would make it what—1970? The courtyard gate Schuyler had not yet had time to explore beyond stood open. Since the front door was located on that side of the house, Leigh was probably there. Schuyler hadn't given any thought to whether or not his landlord might have keys to the home. *Shit.* He hoped not.

As he hauled the Walmart bags out of the truck, he spied his diary lying on the passenger seat. The diary was beginning to function like a personal albatross, hung about his neck, dogging him with the tenacity of a second shadow or, God forbid, an auxiliary conscience. He stuffed the diary into a shopping bag.

"Hello there!" he called out as he ducked his full height under the gateway arch, crossed the courtyard and rounded the corner of the house, heading for the front door.

Several yards away a man of slender build, but taller than average height—a physique, in fact, much like that of Stan

Atwater—stood facing away from Schuyler toward a grove of oak trees near the west wall of the property. Standing with his hands clasped behind his back, the man's stillness appeared almost meditative, as if he were lost in thought.

"Hello!" repeated Schuyler, walking toward the unresponsive figure.

After another moment of what could be interpreted as indecision, or disinterest, with a resigned shrug of his shoulders and an audible sigh the man turned around. He didn't reply to Schuyler's greeting but stared with discomfiting intensity, appraising the one who had spoken.

Even from a distance that stare was so penetrating Schuyler felt he was being examined from the inside out. Turned inside out. *What was happening to him?* A churning of energy in his stomach was followed by a wave of heat that engulfed his entire frame. Was it the alcohol? This sensation diminished by degrees, leaving behind the perception of a pleasant glow. Was this guy some kind of Marvel Comics superhero? Keeping his eyes glued to those of the person he assumed was Hugh Leigh, he leaned over and placed his Walmart bags on the flagstones.

He'd never met Leigh, but he'd seen Leigh's photo and what a shock to his system that had been. *Oh, yeah.* It would be hard to mistake the coal-black skin, willowy build, and gray locks braided tight to the scalp of the person who stood before him. Only days before while visiting Uncle Harry's bookshop, Schuyler had perused a travel memoir entitled *The Ultimate Journey*. This volume was authored by Harold Neuville—his Uncle Harry—and another man, but the second author of the volume wasn't listed as Hugh Leigh.

One photo in that volume was a stunner. It revealed two men, his Uncle Harry and another, kissing each other. A much older version of the man locked in a passionate embrace with Harry then stood before Schuyler now, and stared back at him with a peculiar combination of disinterest and curiosity. The memoir's black-and-white photos hadn't hidden the second man's black skin, but it did fail to reveal his startling blue eyes. Right now, those eyes were grilling Schuyler like a human X-ray machine.

His new landlord was Harry's partner in the pilgrimage to Mount Kailash. Harry's partner in more than one way. Harry's lover. *Huey Lee.*

Sonofabitch—was there no end to the unwelcome coincidences he encountered at every turn? Is this why they called New Mexico the Land of Enchantment? It mesmerizes you until you give up trying to figure it out and think it's a normal place?

"I'm Aaron Schuyler. Your tenant, I guess." Schuyler shrugged, suppressing a smirk as he recalled that flaming photograph. "You are Hugh Leigh?"

With a snapping head motion, as if to clear his mind or break a spell, Leigh's stony expression softened. His whole being relaxed and changed. He smiled as if he were not the same man who had almost, like a basilisk, stared Schuyler out of existence. Or, into hell.

"I am." Leigh's voice was deep, his smile engaging as he bowed and extended his hand. "Welcome to your new home."

"Thanks." Schuyler was relieved to see the forbidding scowl disappear yet surprised by Leigh's formality. He reached for Leigh's outstretched hand. This muddle of linked relationships and overlapping connections he seemed doomed to encounter was brewing up a migraine.

Please don't let this bring on a bout of IBS.

That often happened with stress, but what was one more comeuppance after the string of humiliating events he'd endured today? With a rapidity beyond belief, he was becoming accustomed to having his world turned upside down. Or—was he only now beginning to understand his world was upside down to begin with?

"I hope the house didn't look too messy when you went in." Schuyler bared a lot of teeth, displaying his most ingratiating smile. Might as well get on this guy's good side. "I haven't had time to get organized. I've covered many miles in the past few days."

"I didn't go inside the house," responded Leigh. He spoke in quiet, even tones, but his smile dissolved into his former harsh, piercing glint of appraisal. "It's your home now, Schuyler. I only came by to meet you and to show you around, if you would like."

"Uh, well, sure. I guess." Schuyler again shrugged in an offhand way. "Nice of you to offer. I'll put these bags in the kitchen. My key works on the back door. Will it fit the front lock?"

"I don't see why not." Hugh Leigh's smile returned.

Swallowing hard, hands shaking, wondering if it was wise to turn his back on this man, Schuyler unlocked the door. Leigh followed, and they entered a living room with a large fireplace. Schuyler was familiar with this room since the hallway from the carport entrance passed the bedroom he slept in, a bathroom, another bedroom, and then ended here. On the other side of this living room was the kitchen. Beyond that lay another entire wing he hadn't yet explored.

Leigh at once strode through the kitchen, but paused on the threshold of this second wing with its smaller den, built-in bookshelves, and a second fireplace.

"This is the sitting room," he announced without preamble. He then circled the room at a slower pace, taking time to linger before each bare wall and each empty corner, as if remembering what had happened here.

Schuyler also glanced around this room that was new to him. His attention was caught by the fireplace, the oddest one he'd ever seen. As rotund as a Santa Claus, its rounded chimney was stuccoed, just like the walls on either side of it.

"That's a kiva fireplace," stated Leigh, as Schuyler paused to examine it.

"Huh. I suppose I'll need to hire some peon to chop wood," Schuyler quipped.

"A kiva fireplace is quite a common feature in southwest architecture, and you can chop your own wood." Leigh walked on, down a broad hallway with a bank of windows on its south side. "We called this our gallery. We hung paintings and photos here."

Who, exactly, was "we"? Schuyler had a pretty good idea what the answer to that question was. He followed Leigh down the gallery to where his host opened another door. This space was not much bigger than a large closet, its windows covered in heavy layers of foil.

"This is the darkroom." Leigh's expression tightened into a grimace. Suddenly turning away, in an uncomfortable attempt to disguise emotion, he became quite still, just like when Schuyler first approached him. As if searching for something to do while Leigh recovered a measure of poise, Leigh opened the doors of the cabinets hanging on the wall. These were empty. "We were both into photography." Leigh cleared his throat. "We studied with a friend who was a photographer. For a while—"

With an abrupt turn, he passed by Schuyler and exited the small room.

Schuyler waited a minute or two, then followed Leigh back down the gallery and into the sitting room with the oddball fireplace.

"Here is the third bedroom." Leigh opened yet another door. "And this door leads outside into another courtyard."

The two men exited into a smaller cozy, flagstone-paved courtyard behind the house. Two cheap, plastic lawn chairs, placed side by side with a small folding table between them, seemed a forlorn reminder of long-forgotten intimate conversations. For a brief moment Schuyler could have sworn he saw his Uncle Harry comfortably sprawled in one of those chairs, a cigarette dangling from his lips and a vodka tonic close at hand on the small table. With a broad smile on his face, Harry looked happier than Schuyler had ever seen him in life.

He nodded, more to himself than in acknowledgment of Leigh's words. What Leigh had not said, as well as his struggle to contain a deep and heartfelt sorrow, revealed far more to Schuyler than the scanty verbiage and this brief guided tour ever could. Was it Leigh's unstated intention to impart information about his life with Harry Neville without appearing to do so? That's how Schuyler chose to read it.

The plain fact was, this house contained two well-designed and separate apartments connected by the kitchen, a shared space. Two people living here, one in each wing, could be as private or as intimate as they wanted to be. Two gay guys. Hugh Leigh and Uncle Harry.

Schuyler had a lot to think about.

"Well, thanks," was his laconic reply, given with another noncommittal shrug of the shoulders. "I appreciate your time. If you could show me the fuse box, and give me your cell number, that might be a help. In case I need to get hold of you. Otherwise, I think I can figure it all out for myself."

For the time being, during this tour, he would feign ignorance of the plot masterminded by his mother. But Clementine and Winston had been quite busy, hadn't they? *Friggin' right.* His meddling mother had maneuvered him into a house previously owned by his Uncle Harry.

Clementine's interference, he further guessed, extended far beyond today's events at Sam's Club and the arrangements made for renting this house. Far beyond making Uncle Harry's summer hideaway her son's permanent abode, and meeting his uncle's secret life partner.

Oh, there was going to be hell to pay.

But—would he be the one repaying a debt to hell, or would she? Earlier today he'd seen what hell had in store for him. Just for once, maybe it would be best to bide his time. See how events unfolded during the next few months. He wouldn't hesitate to drag the miserable truth out of her if he had to, and he wanted the whole story—Clementine's every motive and machination revealed. She owed him that much, didn't she, if she expected him to make a life for himself in this desert hellhole?

Although seething with a sense of injury and victimization, Schuyler also felt something akin to sympathy for Hugh Leigh. Here was an unusual man by any standard, a wounded and grieving man who had loved Harry. Some barrier separated Leigh from himself. Was it Leigh's perceived air of aloofness or his possible higher perspective on the ways of the world and the pitfalls of life? *Maybe.* But that barrier might well be Aaron Schuyler's own smelly and unsavory reputation. Who could blame the man for being wary of such a lifelong jerk?

He itched to bombard Leigh with questions, but the ones forming in his mind weren't appropriate between strangers. Now was not the time for questions. Or answers. But the time would come. Schuyler was sure of that.

"This is a nice cherry tree." Leigh was chuckling now, his black face crinkling into a smile as the two men passed through a narrow gateway into the backyard. "Old, but dependable, if you pick the fruit before the birds make a mess of it. We used to make some good pies. Really good pies."

We. Again. *Baking.* That about clinched it. Two grown men baking.

Leigh walked farther up a gentle incline beyond the backyard, with Schuyler in his wake. Stopping in front of a large metal square fitted over a concrete base, he strained to lift what Schuyler now realized was a lid.

"This enclosure houses the well pump," said Leigh. "If your water stops running, let me know at once. It could be the pump's gone out."

As Schuyler leaned over to better explore the dark interior of the space below, Leigh restrained his outstretched hand. "Wait— don't go sticking your hand down there. Be careful of those black widows. Let the experts take care of things."

Schuyler recoiled. Black widows. He'd never seen one before, but there it was. The spider's size and glossy sheen were at once startling and fascinating. *Shit.* If they had those things in New York City, he, at least, had never seen one.

Leigh continued his progress, explaining about the irrigation system for the apple orchard as he walked along. "When it's time to harvest the fruit, give me a call. I'll come by to help you." He showed Schuyler the turn-on valves with hoses connected to them for watering each tree. Then he headed back down the slope and into the carport.

"Well, that's about it. These are the numbers for the gas company and the city utilities. You have to haul your garbage to the dump." He opened the Jimmy's door, reached inside the glove box, and retrieved a piece of paper which he handed to Schuyler. "This is your dump permit. I paid your fees for one year. The dump is up the high road a few miles. You can't miss it." Again, he extended his hand. "Nice to have met you."

"Where do you live?" Schuyler blurted out. He couldn't help asking.

"Up near Los Alamos," was Leigh's curt answer. "I need to be getting back."

"I—I owe you a lot," Schuyler began. Why was it so hard to say goodbye to this strange man? Why did it seem like they hadn't said enough, and why did he feel this aching sense of loss? Of loneliness. Of times lost forever, precious times that could not be retrieved. "I feel like I know you, although we've never met. As far as I know—"

Leigh made no response.

Schuyler thirsted for more information about his uncle. There was no end to the questions on the tip of his tongue, and only Leigh had the answers. Or, maybe, Clementine. Those two knew a side of Harry never shared with him. Maybe the story of Hugh and Harry was common knowledge to others, as well, but it was unknown territory for Schuyler. He felt a closeness to Leigh. A tie. A link. They had both loved the same man, although in different ways.

"Maybe a cup of coffee? Sometime? If you wanted to stop by—"

"It's unlikely." Leigh opened his car door and slid onto the seat. "Out of my way. Goodbye to you, Schuyler."

He coaxed the Jimmy to life and backed down the driveway, seemingly oblivious to the vehicle's noxious exhaust and rattling vibrations. Pausing on the dirt road, Leigh glanced toward the carport and raised his hand. A kind of salute, thought Schuyler, who waved back eagerly as Leigh then turned west onto Road 503.

He stood in the carport for a long time, pondering the multiple encounters of his day, ignoring the overpowering fumes that lingered like a ghost behind his departed guest. He was beginning to get the gist of how he fit into this panoply of events, of what his role was in this contrived but superbly stage-managed play.

He was meant to go along with everything, wasn't he? Like those three Chinese monkeys—blind, deaf, and dumb. And if all his spoken lines and actions were predetermined, then all he need do, as far as he could see from his perspective, was respond on cue. He would continue to play Clementine's game and see what was in it for himself. After all, he'd met Ms. Chatterjee, hadn't he? That was a five-star plus, a worthy bonus for what he was being forced to endure. But his mother's machinations didn't deceive him for a moment. From the get-go, she and Winston had always been one step ahead of him.

What the hell. Why had he never seen this before?

Tomorrow was Tuesday. He'd phone Anita Chatterjee and accept the job with Sam's Club. The job Clementine intended him to have. The why was what he couldn't figure out. For the time being he'd cede control over his life and future to her, and maybe to Hugh Leigh, as well. Always a gambler, he was willing to take his chances. What did he have to lose?

A good measure of trepidation accompanied these ruminations. Since he couldn't help speculating what he might next discover about himself, his mother, or his uncle, he wondered what his own next step should be? And if he didn't make the correct next step, what reprisals of Clementine and Winston's contriving were in store for him? Maybe it was best not to speculate.

Having entered the house, he closed the door behind him, exhaled with relief, and wiped away the sweat on his forehead. Only then did he realize he'd left his grocery bags sitting on the front porch.

CHAPTER 10

Walmart

A slew of impressions converged in Schuyler's sleep-drugged brain as he struggled to waken. And—why was it necessary to wake up? What day was it, anyway? With one eye open, he squinted at the bedside clock. *Six a.m.?* Again? The same thing it said yesterday. To his way of thinking, 6:00 a.m. was almost the middle of the night, yet the sunshine streaming through the bedroom window was as bright as high noon.

Bemused and groggy, he lay there reviewing what he could remember of his to-do list. Today was Tuesday. Today he must buy some curtains. Today he must phone Anita Chatterjee.

True to his vow, he placed that call at 9:00 a.m. On the dot. Ms. Chatterjee seemed pleased to learn of his acceptance.

"I'll be sure all details are attended to, Mr. Schuyler." On Monday, his time card would be waiting for him in her office, along with his *Sam's Club Associates' Handbook.* "We will be ready for you, and we are all pleased you have accepted the position."

He could picture her head listing from side to side as she spoke, so clearly did her voice relay satisfaction. Could he say—smug satisfaction?

No.

There was no taint of triumph in Chatterjee's tone. Yet, he had no doubt she would phone Clementine in Akron to say her son's employment was a sure thing, as soon as he hung up. Chalk another one up for his mother and Winston. The Dynamic Duo.

Determined to make the most of the day and get his house in order, he made a mental list of necessary purchases. Yesterday's encounter with Hugh Leigh was unsettling, and he'd forgotten to ask his new landlord how to operate the range. His only breakfast option was the Mockingbird. Then he'd drive into Santa Fe and finish his shopping. A change of clothing was needed so he didn't stick out like a sore thumb in his flannel slacks and a sport coat. He couldn't show up for work on the loading dock wearing that garb, or his funereal black suit. Except for the stiff pair of jeans, these few items were about the extent of his current wardrobe.

"Could you do me a favor?" he asked Ellen, the waitress, as he sat down in his now familiar booth at the Mockingbird. "If I leave a message for Tom Jannssen, would you give it to him the next time you see him?"

"Sure thing. No problem. But hurry up." On a napkin he explained his dilemma with the range and scribbled his phone number. Ellen snatched the note and stuffed it into her bra. "I'm slammed right now."

On her recommendation, Schuyler chose huevos rancheros with extra bacon and a tortilla. Not bad. The chile was still too spicy for his non-New Mexican palate, but this time he at least knew what to expect. He left a bigger tip, having asked her to do him a favor, and headed south to commence his errands.

Yesterday, Monday, he'd bought sauce pans, a cast iron frying pan, a boxed set of dishes for eight, and Joy liquid. He also purchased bath towels, toothpaste, a toothbrush, and soap, but he needed sheets for his twin bed. *And curtains.* For the time being he'd make do with the lumpy spring-ridden mattress, but a new pillow would help. Most of all, he needed clothes. Even if he didn't want to be here, he should at least look like he belonged in New Mexico.

As he drove south, however, Schuyler wondered if, perhaps, he really did want to be here. *Perish the thought.* Where had that come from?

Looking as closely as he dared with the hectic pace of driving, he became more aware of the desert's scenic intricacies. He revised his first judgment that it was the ugliest place he'd ever seen, worthy only as the backdrop for a cheesy sci-fi movie. It was weird, yes, but now he focused on its delicate distinctions. The variations in the red and rusty hues of the sandstone bluffs. The elegant contortions of this irregular landscape, contortions so refined no human art could have devised the prospect. The array of squat bushes in subtle shades of grayish-green that graced hills and depressions at uneven intervals, resembled a polka dot fabric draped at random over the land by the hand of an ancient divinity. The effect was profound. Alluring. Odd, yet somehow satisfying.

He couldn't say he liked it, but, he grudgingly admitted, he admired it.

Schuyler was responding to his desert surroundings in a way unthinkable, impossible to achieve with the concrete sidewalks lining mile after mile of blacktopped streets in New York. Only a paucity of sky was visible between the high-rise buildings of his native city. He couldn't help speculating whether New York skies had ever been this blue. For sure, they couldn't compare with the intense, almost purple stain of the New Mexico sky overhead.

Huh. Here he was, waxing poetic in a place where he didn't even want to be.

What the hell had happened to him?

The Walmart parking lot was jammed with cars so he settled for a spot quite a distance from the entrance. It was exercise, wasn't it? Grabbing a cart, he reviewed his mental list to see if he could afford flatware and drinking glasses. His cash had to stretch a long way, and there was a substantial difference in price between glass or plastic glasses. The plastics were a garish shade of green and came shrink-wrapped in a set of six. A sign above read "Add a splash of color to your table."

Yuck.

Jack Daniels wouldn't taste the same in plastic, splash or no splash, but plastic fit his budget. And it was better than chugging from the bottle. It struck Schuyler how he'd left the bottle of bourbon untouched last night—although he hungered for its sustenance—despite the embarrassing, if not shattering revelations he had endured. A staggering weight of revelations.

Was he sunk beneath reproach, he questioned, recalling yesterday's embarrassments. He might as well have been bare-assed. He still felt like he'd had a good tanning.

Sunk beneath reproach. *Huh.* The sonorous phrase kept playing in his mind, but he had no idea what it meant. Could it mean someone was buried beneath an abundance of reproaches? Or, had someone sunk so low they were not worth reproaching?

Back to the shopping list.

As he placed the green plastic glasses in his cart a melodious voice sounded behind him.

"Mr. Schuyler! Good morning!"

There stood Anita Chatterjee, looking up at him, displaying her brilliant smile, her arm draped around the shoulders of an older woman. Ms. Chatterjee was wearing jeans and a T-shirt, but the older woman wore an ensemble Schuyler recognized as uniquely Indian. Her turquoise-blue tunic fell to the knees, over a pair of loose-fitting trousers in the same color.

He stood speechless for a moment, stunned once more by Chatterjee's striking features, before he found his tongue.

"Uh, Ms. Chatterjee, hello! What a surprise." He answered her smile with his own. "I'm picking up a few necessities before I start work on Monday."

"And how nice it is, Mr. Schuyler, that you are patronizing our sister establishment."

"Your what?" Had he missed something?

"Yes, indeed! Sam's and Walmart are owned by the same corporation." Chatterjee nodded. "Oh, you will learn much in your orientation session. But enough shoptalk. I'm off duty now. I work a split shift on Tuesdays. Please, Mr. Schuyler, allow me to introduce my mother, Yuthi Chatterjee."

"It's a pleasure to meet you, ma'am." With a slight bow Schuyler extended his hand but, instead of accepting it, the older woman placed her palms together at chest level. She nodded her head forward as she smiled. Schuyler wondered if she spoke any English.

"You are no doubt wondering if Mother speaks English, but, yes, she does," Ms. Chatterjee offered. "She is often just a bit shy, Mr. Schuyler."

"Well, my own English is somewhat rough around the edges." *That should smooth things over.* He hoped he was presenting the appropriate combination of affable personality—attractive to a woman like the Human Resources director—with the gratitude a respectful employee should display when the boss acknowledges him in public.

"I have no doubt your English is flawless." Chatterjee laughed.

Here, again, was that sound like the tinkling of a bell, the perfect complement to the lilt in her voice when she spoke and, well—*enough of that line of thought.*

"I shall see you at 7:30 a.m. this coming Monday," she finished. "Enjoy your week!"

"The same to you, Ms. Chatterjee," Schuyler returned, almost unable to control his compulsive grin. "I'll be there. And it was very nice to make your acquaintance, ma'am."

He again made a slight bow toward Mrs. Chatterjee, knowing he couldn't manage a satisfactory imitation of her clasped hands posture. For a moment, he thought he caught a knowing look, a faint hint of laughter, of understanding, in Mrs. Chatterjee's eye. She looked slightly familiar to him, but why? He couldn't possibly have met her before today. Could he?

He assigned his uncertainty to the fact that New Mexicans considered him some kind of joke. A joke he didn't get, yet they all seemed to find his confusion hilarious. Mrs. Chatterjee was politely laughing at him. There was more to "Mother" than met the eye, no matter how self-effacing Mrs. Chatterjee chose to appear.

As the two ladies retreated down the housewares aisle, his attention again settled on the younger of the two. He was not only uplifted by this brief encounter, but unable to tear his eyes away from Chatterjee's posterior. He watched her disappear into the crowd, her mother's bright ensemble flitting among the more somber colors worn by other shoppers.

Hands down, his new boss looked better in a T-shirt and jeans than in a business suit.

And, was there any way at all to explain his attraction to her? Whatever this "something" was, it wasn't merely physical like the flirts he had heretofore pursued. It wasn't plain old lust. No way. His attraction to Ms. Chatterjee was more like a yearning for completion. He felt she had crawled inside his body and was a part of him. Already a much-cherished part of him. He didn't even know the woman, yet he felt he couldn't live without her.

Whatever.

Don't go waxing poetic again, Schuyler. Shaking his head in self-disgust, he tossed two bed pillows and a set of sheets with pillowcases into the cart. He couldn't take another night of unrest on the sour-smelling sheets he had thus far endured. Unsure what work clothes were suitable for a loading dock, he chose the safe bet. Another pair of jeans. Stiff as a board. *Stiff as a stiff.* These were followed by a denim jacket and a blue plaid cotton shirt.

He noticed the sign above an end display of men's lace-up work boots: "Leather Uppers. Soles Manmade. $39.95."

Was that a reasonable price? Boots might be the best choice for his new occupation, so Schuyler hunted for his correct size, then tried them on. He walked up and down the aisle, surprised at the weight of the boots on his feet. A far cry from Ferragamo loafers. For a moment he struggled against the force of the inevitable, then resigned himself to the fact that, for him, the era of high-ticket suits and even more expensive footwear was as dead as a dinosaur. Even more surprising, he realized he didn't much care. *Good riddance.*

No matter how well-shod he'd been, it had never stopped him from acting like a louse.

Standing in the checkout line, Schuyler again recalled his fumbling attempt to cheat the clerk at a Goodwill store in New York before his appointment with the Amit Chatterjee family. He shifted his stance, aware of the abdominal gurgling so often a precursor to an IBS episode. *Uh-oh.* He needed to get the hell out of Walmart. Before locking his car and heading into the store he'd glanced at his gas gauge and decided to top off the tank in Santa Fe before driving back to Nambé. His next stop would be the Chevron station farther north on Cerrillos Avenue. He could use the restroom there.

A niggling possibility troubled Schuyler. He couldn't quite see the connection, not yet. It was dim at best. But could the increased frequency of these intestinal attacks be linked to memories of his past regrettable behavior? Could recalling those shameful incidents trigger a colonic impulse to rid himself of a load of shit?

No way.

More likely, the temptation of this "new age style" line of thought was only a nonproductive pile of pseudo-psychological crap.

CHAPTER 11

The Dog

Bang. Bang.

Holy hell. There it was again. The loud thumps put an end to Schuyler's dream. Why was someone pounding on the back door? He forced his eyelids open and glanced at the clock. Six a.m. Just like yesterday. And the day before. His best sleep was always between 5:00 and 7:00 a.m. and the clamor had jarred him out of the joyous vision of an intimate moment with Ms. Anita Chatterjee.

Hauling his stiff body out of bed, he struggled into the jeans he'd dropped on the floor at midnight and pulled on a T-shirt. He padded barefoot out of his new bedroom—he had moved into the second wing of the house—through the sitting room and kitchen, through the living room, and down the hall to the back door, hand-combing his hair as he hurried along.

Through the door window he recognized his visitor. It was Tom Jannssen, the man he'd had breakfast with last Saturday, a week ago today. Schuyler opened the door a few inches.

"Hey, man." Jannssen's bulk blocked the morning light.

"Good morning," responded Schuyler, clearing his throat and frowning. His visitor was holding a rope tied to the collar of a scruffy looking animal. "It's six a.m."

"I brought you your dog," Lone Goose said as he offered the rope to Schuyler.

"No." Schuyler shook his head vigorously. "It's not mine. I don't own a dog. I don't want a dog."

"Yes, you do."

"Why?"

The dog sat down, mouth open, tongue out, panting in time with the rhythm of its thumping tail, looking for all the world like it was smiling. *Did dogs smile?*

"A dog discourages snakes, coyotes. A dog will keep cats from using your garden as a litter box."

"I don't have a garden."

"You might change your mind. You never know."

"What kind of dog is this?" The smiling animal was black-and-white, its shaggy coat matted with dirt and bits of twig.

"We're not sure. Some kind of shepherd mix."

"Who's 'we'?"

"My mother and me. The dog showed up at my mom's place. She has three dogs of her own. Maybe four."

"So you're sticking me with this mutt?" growled Schuyler. "Instead of taking it to a shelter?"

"You'll thank me. Just wait."

"Is it male or female?" The rope was now in Schuyler's hand.

"Female. Do I smell coffee?" Jannssen asked with a straight face.

"No. Uh, not yet. I just woke up."

"You should ask me in."

"Yeah. Right." Clementine's protocol of politeness took command. "I should." With a sigh of resignation, Schuyler stepped back and opened the door wider. "Is she fixed?"

"You'll find out," answered Jannssen as he stepped into the house. Schuyler glanced down at the rope in his hand. What the hell was he going to do with a dog? Another expense. Shrugging his shoulders, he led his new companion back down the hallway and into the kitchen.

There was nothing to attach the rope to, so he dropped it onto the floor.

"Keep your eye on her. I'll be right back." After peeing and scrubbing his face, Schuyler headed back to the kitchen. "Does the dog have a name?"

"Mom called her Tinkerbell," Jannssen answered.

"*Tinkerbell*?" Schuyler's laugh was harsh. "This mangy mutt? Have you ever seen anything that looked less like a Tinkerbell?"

"I see your point. Call her Bella."

"That's still a stretch." Schuyler caught the twitch of amusement hovering at the corner of Jannssen's mouth just before it disappeared. "Look, man. I'm sorry I made such a big deal out of this. Thanks for the dog."

"No worries."

"And I'd offer you the cup of coffee, but I don't know how the range works."

"Got any matches?"

"Yeah. So what?" Schuyler withdrew a book of matches from his jeans pocket.

"It's a gas range. You turn the knob like this. See? Then you light the burner with your match." With a whoosh, and like a miracle, flames emerged beneath a stove-top burner.

"What about the oven?"

"Same thing. See this hole? Turn the oven dial a bit. Then hold your match over the hole." Jannssen lit the oven. "Turn the dial again to whatever temperature you want."

"I'll be damned. I've never used a gas range before. Hold on and I'll get the coffee going." He opened a can of Folger's and started measuring. "Sorry I can't offer you a seat. I want to take you up on your offer of a table and chairs."

"That's what I figured." Jannssen nodded. "Ellen gave me your message. The furniture is in my pickup. Let's unload the stuff while the coffee's perking."

Schuyler wondered why Jannssen kept chuckling as the two of them situated the table and three chairs in the empty space meant for that purpose.

"What's so funny?" Schuyler frowned although he was, by now, used to everyone enjoying an obscure joke at his expense. *Once a butt, always a butt.*

"Not much. The table and chairs sat in this same spot for years."

"You're saying this set belonged to Hugh Leigh." Would he ever connect all the dots?

"Hugh Leigh and Harry Neville."

"You knew my uncle?" Schuyler was flabbergasted. "What the hell's going on here?"

"I was a little shaver when I met the two of them. Maybe about eight years old. They used to come to all the dances at Santa Clara Pueblo, where I lived. Harry saw a drawing I did with chalk on a paper grocery sack. He told me to keep drawing. I did. Entered local art shows. He and Hugh paid my tuition for the Pratt Institute."

"*The* Pratt Institute?" Schuyler was stunned. "*You*?"

"Greenpoint. You know—in Brooklyn?" Jannssen clarified.

Schuyler was speechless. Of course, he knew Greenpoint. Once again his brain's ability to function was ensnared by the tangled web of connections mysterious to him, but which every other human being he encountered in New Mexico seemed familiar with.

"Look over here." Jannssen strolled toward a wall in the living room and gestured toward a large rectangular space a shade or two darker in color than the rest of the wall. "For years one of my paintings hung here. Look around the house. Wherever there's a rectangle? Well, most of those are where one of my paintings hung. Hugh took them with him when he decided to move out and rent the house to you."

"You're an artist," Schuyler stated the obvious.

"I got a couple of paintings hanging at MOMA. The Museum of Modern Art."

"I know what MOMA is. Hey—wait a minute." Schuyler shook his head. "I saw a painting of horses at a creek in my uncle's bookstore in New York. It's signed 'L.G.' That was yours?"

"L.G. Lone Goose. I already told you that."

"What the flip. I just saw your painting a few days ago."

"Yep. The bookstore staff is shipping it back to us. Hugh wants it for his Los Alamos house. Always one of his favorites."

"And how did you end up with the table and three chairs if they belonged in this house to begin with? Why are there only three chairs?"

"Answer number one. Harry's cancer spread faster than anyone expected. He needed to be back East near the best docs. When Harry left, Hugh moved the best antiques to Los Alamos. He's an analytical chemist, you know."

"I didn't know."

"Hugh sold some of the furniture, and I'm storing the rest for him in my studio. Answer number two. Hugh and Harry bought the table and four chairs at a yard sale in Santa Fe and strapped everything on top of the old Jimmy to bring it up to Nambé. They always figured as they drove home one of the chairs fell off the roof of the car, because when they got back to this house they only had three. They never bothered to go back and look for it. Three is a better number than four, you know."

"Why didn't Hugh return to New York with Harry?" asked Schuyler, ignoring the ubiquitous "you know." "It seems sacrilegious, to me, to abandon your partner."

"If that's what you think, you don't understand Buddhist principles." Jannssen shook his head. "Those two had a long and wonderful life together. A loving life, a journey together as life partners. That journey ended sooner than either of them expected." Jannssen paused, and Schuyler felt the weight of his emotion.

"Harry didn't want Hugh to witness his day-by-day deterioration," Jannssen continued. "They both knew it was time to part and say goodbye. Time for each of them to let go. Start the next adventure. Don't you find there's a bittersweet taste to aging?" He glanced over at Schuyler who was startled, knowing he was unable to answer that question. "Both Hugh and Harry were good at accepting, at yielding, at laughing at what comes next in life. End of story."

Schuyler's head was swimming. Oh yeah, he got the bittersweet part. More bitter than sweet, to his way of thinking. The rest of Jannssen's explanation was more like a pile of doo-doo. New age doo-doo with a nice spin on it, but doo-doo nevertheless.

"I just don't get it. My uncle was the most important man in my life and I never knew any of the things I'm finding out about him now. I knew none of this shit I've heard since moving to New Mexico."

A surge of fecal matter gurgled through his intestines.

"Yeah." Jannssen pulled a chair away from the table and sat down. For several minutes the two men shared a heavy silence.

"Maybe that's why you're here, Schuyler. To learn a few things," Jannssen suggested. "I know all of this is news to you. I never understood why that crazy lot, the two guys and your mother, kept you in the dark. As for me, I wanted to meet you, but you had your own life and had drifted away from your family. You probably never knew Clementine invited me to spend weekends at her condo while I was at Pratt." Jannssen's expression as he gazed at the stupefied Schuyler was kind, empathetic, concerned. "I think your coffee's ready, man."

"Pour me a cup." Schuyler swallowed hard. "I need to use the bathroom," he called over his shoulder as he raced out of the room.

CHAPTER 12

Flashback

After the two men drank their coffee and polished off plates of scrambled eggs, Jannssen drove away leaving Bella behind. Schuyler frowned at the sorry-looking dog as she stared out the kitchen window at the back end of Jannssen's departing truck. She looked like she'd lost her best friend. He poured himself another cup. What a sucker he was, allowing himself to get stuck with this dog. *Jesus.* Tom Jannssen saw him as an easy mark, as much a patsy as some of the clients Schuyler, himself, had fleeced back in the day.

Although unimpressed by his tail-thumping acquisition, he did realize she might need to pee or poop. Better outside than in. Putting on his new denim jacket, he picked up the dog's rope leash and led her out through the bedroom door and into the smaller courtyard. When he unhooked her leash, Bella made the most of the opportunity. She leaped over the courtyard wall, squatted on the buffalo grass lawn, and did her business.

Schuyler settled down in one of the weather-stained plastic chairs, a bit wobbly under his weight, and propped his feet up on the other. His bum was soon frozen to the rigid plastic, but he felt more ill at ease with the worshipful gaze Bella fixed upon him. There was more to this woebegone mutt than met the eye. He squirmed in his chair, knowing how unworthy he was of any form of adulation. But just why did he feel uneasy? Because he had done a good deed by adopting her, or because he had in his lifetime very few other good deeds to brag about?

Bella commenced scratching her ribs with her hind foot. Was it fleas? He hoped not. Observing the mangy dog's misery, not of its own doing, made him think about his past, so riddled with willful errors. Would she prove to be an unwelcome key inserted into the rusty padlock guarding his withered conscience? On the rare occasions that seldom-used capacity escaped its dungeon, his thoughts made a beeline for the squalid zone of shame and regret.

That pitfall must be avoided at all cost or he would be obliged, again, to reevaluate his life path and all the crap he'd dealt out to other people. Other people meaning not only complete strangers or business associates, but his nearest and dearest. His wife. His children. His mother.

Harry.

Schuyler had met his future business partner, Robert "Bert" Bradford in 1985. He and Bert were both twenty years old and frat brothers at Yale. When they graduated in 1987 Schuyler stayed in school and got his master's degree in global finance. Bert volunteered for army service so his master's studies would be paid for, and never failed to remind Schuyler how he'd come up the hard way. Together, they founded Bradford-Schuyler Investments LLC in 1991.

Prior to that, Schuyler was donning his undergraduate cap and gown in preparation for the graduation ceremony in 1987 when a jolt of clarity leveled him. There was no telling why this unpleasant realization hadn't struck him before, but it did now. *Reality check.*

One week after receiving his bachelor's degree, he would be marrying his sweetheart, Natalie Weston. Natalie was four months pregnant.

His relationships with women had been, and he was convinced always would be, akin to labyrinthine nightmares. Weren't his constant attempts to outwit and deceive Clementine worthy of that description? Labyrinthine? Her relentless determination to reshape his life, and his unending resistance and petty provocations of her should have been warning enough.

Bloody hell.

Yeah. Bloody hell. Nothing better described the marriage coil than his British-born mother's go-to phrase when faced with inescapable consequences. He'd been forced into marriage, and what had he done to deserve such a fate, just as his foot was poised on the lowest rung of the ladder to success?

"It's a good thing I've never had a big appetite, Aaron," Natalie had chortled as she cut the first slice of their wedding cake. "I won't gain much weight during the next five months!"

From Schuyler's perspective, her belly already looked swollen. Unable to swallow his sinking feeling of desperation, akin to that of a POW, he choked on a mouthful of chocolate ganache. He was trapped. Soon he'd be a father and Clementine was ready to throttle him. He felt her fingers squeezing his throat. *Squeezing.* Her frustration and fury were directed at him not because he'd gotten Natalie pregnant, but because he point-blank refused to stop seeing Janelle Pearson, his study partner since their freshman year at Yale.

From then on, his bouts of IBS became wholly unpredictable.

Soon after the June wedding, Schuyler began to demonstrate his renowned ability to disengage from any confrontation or unpleasantness he didn't wish to face. That ability became a life-long habit. It was Clementine, five months later, who rushed Natalie to the hospital when her water broke. Schuyler was out of town for a "job interview." He'd felt it expedient to take Janelle with him, since her advice on structuring impressive interview responses was invaluable.

"Honey, forgive me! I'm so sorry!" His apologies to Natalie upon arriving, too late, at the hospital were profuse. "I got my timing all wrong. Rushed back as soon as I got Mom's message. I thought you weren't due for two weeks." He clutched his fore-head. "What was I thinking?"

Clementine snatched the massive bouquet of roses out of his grasp and thrust them toward the attending nurse. "Please put these in a vase. Don't come back. We need privacy!"

While Clementine ripped her son up one side and down the other, berating his callous behavior, Natalie maintained a stony silence. As Schuyler hightailed it out the front door of the hospital, feeling as raw as if the hide had been scraped off his rear end, escaping the wails of an abandoned wife and a hungry infant, and charged with the task of picking up their baby crib and changing table at Sears Roebuck, he realized he'd forgotten the sex of his offspring. Already.

Natalie had told him, hadn't she?

He'd also forgotten to take a peek at the newborn. Had forgotten to hold his—*son? Daughter?* As if he wasn't already in deep shit, that day he tumbled into a hole he never climbed out of during his marriage.

Three years and another child later, with Bradford-Schuyler Investments thriving, Schuyler was unsure just who snitched to his mother. How did she find out BSI had hired Janelle Pearson as their waiting room receptionist? The day Clementine, like some reincarnated vengeance-seeking Medea, stormed their offices, pulled Ms. Pearson's chair out from her, and kicked her out the front door remained the most odious yet awe-inspiring of all his Clementine-related memories.

"What the hell do you think you're doing?" he raged, as his mother threw Janelle's handbag out the door after her. "I told you never to come here without first calling!"

"Bollocks!" Clementine shouted back in fury. "I'll come whenever I bloody well feel like it! And what the hell do you think you're playing at? Get rid of that woman! We have a respected name. Beyond that—you're *married*."

"I never wanted to get married!"

"Then you should have kept your pants zipped!"

On hearing a door squeak open, Schuyler swerved around to see the two clients who had sought his advice on hedge funds slink out of the conference room and edge past him and Clementine, making for the exit.

"Tight schedule, Mr. Schuyler." Lacey Taylor's smile was grim, her voice small. "We'd best move on. We'll be in touch."

"Hello, Mrs.—uh—Mrs.—" Tim Taylor tipped his hat but left his sentence unfinished. The Taylors were Clementine's social equals, belonged to the same country club, but the astonished Tim couldn't recall the last name of Clementine's current husband. "So sorry. Ta!"

Now, sitting in the quiet courtyard, surrounded by a forest of barren cottonwood trees and the evening scent of sage, his rear end numbed with cold, Schuyler felt the oppressive weight of his past sins. It was more than he could bear. *Really.* Regret caused stress, didn't it? Couldn't stress bring on a heart attack? The revelations of hindsight, acknowledging his follies, had never proved to be of any help. And he needed help if he was to change his ways once and for all.

If he were a Catholic, he could confess to a priest. Get rid of the whole rotten burden. Shove it onto someone else. He should have thought of that earlier. Too late now. Hindsight, again. He shivered.

Assuming Bella knew he was her meal ticket and would stay in the yard, he retreated into the house and grabbed the half-empty bottle of Jack from the kitchen counter. He snatched one of the lime-green plastic cups from the cupboard and carried bottle and cup outside.

The dog was waiting for him, nose to the screen door, worried that her new best friend might have ditched her. *Why not?* All the others had. This time, when Schuyler plopped his bottom onto the stiff plastic seat, Bella curled up as close to his feet as she could manage. Her chin and paws were resting on his shoes. When he leaned over and scratched her matted ears, he could have sworn the dog started purring.

Having now opened the floodgates of his long-repressed and shameful memories, he was so fascinated by his own lurid history that he couldn't lock the past back into the dungeon where it belonged. He poured half the bottle's remaining contents into the garish green cup.

"Let's see," he muttered. "How long did I keep seeing Janelle? Freshman year in college, that would be 1982, at least until 1993." Their affair continued even after Clementine booted Janelle out of the investment office.

"Yeah, 1993." He nodded. "Then, she ditched me. Women are so damn fickle."

In 1993, Janelle finally finished her degree in social work at NYU, graduated, and married one of the psych professors. Last he'd heard, they were living in Rochester. He couldn't imagine why. Her husband must be teaching at one of the colleges there. Thinking back on the messy break-up with Janelle, Schuyler speculated how he might still have made a go of his marriage to Natalie if he hadn't met Rose Rafferty.

Natalie, having wept with relief when she learned from Clementine that Janelle was out of the picture, broke down again when she found out about Rose.

"Why, Aaron? Why can't I be enough for you?" She poured her desperate sobs into the comforter on their king-size bed, wretched and unhappy, scarcely able to breathe. Was there no end to the humiliation her husband heaped upon her?

Schuyler was unmoved. Or, rather, he was moved, but only in the sense that her red, scrunched-up face, her swollen eyes, smeared makeup, and runny nose, repelled him.

"I want you to stop seeing this other woman!" she cried.

"Who gives a shit what you want!" The words flew out of his mouth. To his credit he wanted to take them back as soon as he'd said them—after all, she was his wife—but it was too late. Also, it was too true.

He didn't give a shit.

Natalie turned as white as a shroud. The color drained not only from her face, but from her entire being. He had savaged her soul. Ripped the heart right out of her. She said nothing, but her expression, now devoid of all hope, spoke volumes. In that moment, Schuyler realized he had lost her love forever.

No. That wasn't true.

He had discarded her love as being worthless long ago. Tossed it aside as something of no value to himself. A very long time ago. Now, with just seven words he stripped them both naked, down to their most essential and vulnerable selves. *Ugly.* The sight of them that way was ugly. But nothing was as hideous as what his words had just done to Natalie. All he wanted was to shield himself from the sight of his wife's betrayed and obliterated self.

All he wanted to do was leave.

Infuriated by his loss of self-control—she had egged him on to it. She had started it, hadn't she? Angry at being cornered, nauseatingly guilt-ridden, he'd stormed out from the bedroom, stalked past his three frightened children, and charged out of the flat. *Way to go, guy.*

And—what was the name of the gorgeous black girl who came after Rose Rafferty? The one with the incredibly long legs.

Who gives a shit what you want.

Schuyler choked on the Jack Daniels. Had he really spoken those words to Natalie? The crudity of it so struck him now that if he'd been standing up, he would have fallen to his knees, shattered by the enormity of his own baseness. He was wilting beneath the weight of these flashbacks, this barrage of offal. His self-disgust was more than any man could bear. Sweat streamed down his forehead. Was there any way to turn off the faucet of sewage pouring out of him? Out from his mind. Out from his heart.

If he didn't stem the flow of his own waste he would drown in it. Suffocate. *Whoops.* It was coming up again, he was vomiting up his own crap.

Who gives a shit what you want?

Had he really said that to his wedded wife? He poured the remaining Jack into the lime-green cup and chugged it, hoping the liquor would burn through the lining of his throat. Make him suffer. Absolve him of the filth he had generated and enjoyed. Purify him.

His affairs had not only destroyed Natalie but devastated his children and harmed all the women he had ever seduced.

～

An unfamiliar noise roused Schuyler from his nightmare. Bella was softly whining. She shifted her position on the flagstones and pawed at his shoe. He reached down again to scratch her ears. Had his self-torment disturbed the mutt? Had his foul, putrid emotions spilled over onto her? *Another victim.* He forced himself to shift his attention away from what he could not undo and into the present where he could do something useful.

Maybe the dog was hungry. That was as good a guess as any. Feeding her would take his mind off his own shit.

Schuyler hauled himself off the chair, pounded his frozen backside with his fist, and held the screen door open. Maybe he could coax Bella back into the house. "Come on, sister."

Hoping to improve his diet and overall health, he'd purchased whole grain wheat bread instead of the white he'd craved since childhood. He twisted the tie loose on the loaf and extracted five slices from the plastic wrapper, then slathered each one with mayonnaise just the way he liked it. Since he had no dog food he dropped these onto the floor, one at a time, fascinated by how Bella swallowed each in a single gulp.

Guess she was hungry.

Later in the evening Schuyler stripped the twin bed of its musty sheets and tossed them in the trash. After his guilt-ridden rehash of that episode with Natalie, he was ready for an early night. While unwrapping the new sheets with their welcome store-fresh fragrance, he realized he had no dog bed. One more thing for the shopping list.

The lack of a bed didn't seem to bother Bella, who climbed up and lay down next to him. *What the hell.* He had no better company. He reached over and started rubbing the dog's ears. At such close quarters he couldn't miss her rank odor. Pondering how he'd go about giving the dog a bath, he drifted into an uneasy slumber punctuated by wakeful starts and nightmares worse than the memories assaulting him while he was awake.

His pillow was damp with sweat as he rolled away from the snoring dog. A clear image of Grace Bradford, Bert's wife, sprang to his mind.

Oh no—not that one again.

Schuyler couldn't remember the exact year, but he knew his two oldest kids were in high school when this mishap came to pass. He, Natalie, Bert, and Grace must have been somewhere in their forties. On that Friday night of infamy, he'd been stuffing documents into his briefcase and was ready to close the office for the weekend, when Grace Bradford bounded through the door and into the reception area.

"Hi, Aaron," she gasped, out of breath. "I just missed the elevator, so I walked the whole three flights. Where's Bert?"

Schuyler gulped. He had a very good idea where Bert was, but it would do no good to share that information with Grace. "He caught a train to Elizabeth. He has a wheelchair-bound client over there who never comes into the city." His facility with a quick but believable lie often amazed himself.

"Oh." Grace frowned, looking downcast and sounding disappointed. "How strange. He asked me to come downtown and have dinner with him tonight. Maybe catch a movie like we sometimes do on Friday nights."

"Did he now? *Huh.*" Schuyler's laugh was too jovial. "Sometimes I think he's losing it, Gracie. I can't tell you how often I've asked him to jot down his commitments. It makes things so much easier in the long run."

"No kidding. I gave him a datebook for his birthday, and he's supposed to carry it in his briefcase."

Well, he does have a datebook, mused Schuyler, but I hope he doesn't keep it in his briefcase. He was thinking fast. Grace wasn't really his type, not that he had a type. Or, at least there were very few exceptions to his type. She always reminded him of Doris Day or Debbie Reynolds. He'd seen their old films late at night on Turner and was puzzled as to why men had found them attractive. All bubbly. With bubbly hairdos. Still, Grace was cute. She had a totally different figure from Natalie. Not at all a bad figure. A bird in the hand . . . as they say.

"I can't do anything about Bert's forgetfulness." He laughed again. "But I'll remind him about keeping the diary. And I can't do anything about your movie, but I can buy you dinner."

"Dinner? Us?" Grace's surprise was genuine. "You need to get on home. That's a bit of a hike, heading out to the island."

"I'm staying in town tonight. Yesterday, Natalie took the kids to Miami to visit her mother." *That had turned out to be convenient.* Schuyler snapped his briefcase closed, then locked his private office. He also locked Bert's. "Long weekend. Since there's no school on Monday they can all hang out on the beach. With them away, it's easier for me to stay midtown. I can work in my hotel room after dinner and get back to the office at the crack of dawn."

"You work on Saturdays?"

"Nose to the grindstone. So, what do you think?"

"Oh, Aaron. I don't know." She shrugged. "I should probably have you call me a taxi and get on home."

"Bert will probably eat in Newark. What's your hurry? You'll be back home long before he rolls in." Schuyler shrugged himself into his suit jacket and gave Grace a hug. Like she was a pal, or something.

"Come on, Gracie. I know you've got photos of the kids in your handbag. Photos I haven't seen yet. Bert never brings photos to the office. You can show me while we have a nice cocktail," he urged, following this with his patented innocent schoolboy grin. "Maybe two cocktails."

"I'm not sure." Grace looked uncertain. "Anyway, I need to use your ladies room."

"Be my guest."

⌣

Once inside the restroom Grace exhaled. She'd been holding her breath almost since Aaron issued his unexpected invitation. She hadn't needed to use the toilet, but she did need time to think. Where could Bert be? She was confused by his absence, more than a little peeved at being stood up, and very hungry. How polite it was for Aaron, always the gentleman, to offer dinner and at least try to assuage her disappointment.

But—was this a dinner invitation, or a proposition? "I'd like to think I still know the difference!" she muttered to herself. "It's been a long time since any guy—for sure, not that loser, Bert—expressed any interest in my company."

Grace had always liked Aaron. What difference did it make? Really. It would be just a dinner, after all. Aaron, so affable, so easy to talk to, was a likable guy. She had never understood why he and Natalie had such problems. Grace stared at her image in the mirror. *If I was honest with myself, I'd admit I've lusted after Aaron more than once.*

Aaron Schuyler was handsome, and he understood social niceties. He knew how to treat a lady. Bert would never acquire such graces in a million years. *You can't teach an old dog . . .*

Grace searched her handbag for a lipstick. *Darn.* Nothing. She wished she'd taken time to apply some makeup before leaving home, time she would never have taken for Bert. She felt an unfamiliar thrill. The daring of anticipation. Excitement—like something long forgotten, but not quite dead. She exited the ladies room with a bright smile.

⌒

"I'll take you up on that dinner invitation, Aaron," Grace smiled. "Why not? I'm starved. Where were you planning to eat?"

"I'm staying at the Marriott Marquis, so I thought I'd try one of their restaurants. That sound good enough?"

"Better than good."

"Let's go." Once out of the building and at the curb Schuyler hailed a cab. He ushered Grace into the back seat and didn't fail to notice how she scrutinized him. Sizing him up. "Hey," he said, "This is a first for us, isn't it? We've never had dinner together, just the two of us. It's always been a foursome."

"No extra baggage tonight," she giggled.

Pick up your cue, dude. Schuyler draped his arm over the seat behind Grace.

"I always thought Bert was a lucky guy, Grace, but with him being my best friend, I felt I couldn't say it. Obviously."

"I'm not sorry to hear that, Aaron," she whispered. "Thanks for the compliment. It's nice to be appreciated."

Once they were seated in the restaurant, Schuyler made a show of turning off his cell phone. "No unwanted interruptions," he said with a meaningful look as their waiter approached the table. "Not tonight. What would you like to drink?"

"A grapefruit vodka martini."

"Hey, that sounds good. I've never had one. Make that two," he said to the waiter. "Now, what photos of the kids do you have in your handbag?"

They consumed three martinis apiece before dinner and their wine arrived. Grace was having a hard time putting a sentence together, although she laughed constantly at Schuyler's jokes. He was slurring his words. Everything was going according to plan even if her laugh was a bit shrill. Irritating. A little went a long way.

It was about 11:00 p.m. when the hotel house phone next to the bed woke Schuyler. He had dozed off and Grace, lying next to him in the nude, was sound asleep.

"What the hell, Schuyler!" roared Bert. "I couldn't reach you on your cell. Did you turn it off? We agreed not to do that! Good thing I remembered you were staying at the Marriott."

"What's up?" muttered Schuyler through a yawn.

"I don't know where Grace is," hissed Bert. "We were supposed to have dinner tonight. I just now got back to town. I forgot about her. Shit. Did she come to the office?"

"She did, and she was pissed you weren't there. She said you two were going to a movie," Schuyler said in a low tone, concerned that Grace might waken. "What happened?"

"You know what happened. I got tied up with Mrs. Samuelson. Literally. Grace isn't here. Why didn't she come home?"

"I can't tell you. She really wanted to see a movie. Would she have gone by herself?"

"Even if, she shoulda been home by now."

"She should have. Would she have stayed the night with her sister? Don't know what to tell you. It's your problem. I need to sleep, so don't call again. My cell is off until tomorrow morning." Schuyler replaced the receiver, turned off the bedside light, and, wrapping his arm around Grace, lying back down on his pillow.

We've all got problems, Bert. At least you're not married to the "Hyper Nutcase."

Natalie.

⌒

Was it worth it? Schuyler agonized as he tossed on the soaking wet mattress next to a smelly Bella. A lot of good it had done to put clean sheets on the bed. Clean sheets did nothing to stave off the barrage of memories that kept on coming.

⌒

Just a bit guilt-ridden, Schuyler arrived at Bradford-Schuyler Investments early the following Monday morning. He considered locking the door to his office until he remembered he and Bert had keys to each other's offices. No protection there. Waste of time to lock the door. He knew he'd have to face the music sooner or later. There was no way Grace would keep her mouth shut when Bert started grilling her. Schuyler was no scrapper like his business partner, who was built like a bulldog. Even so, he wasn't prepared for the pain when Bert charged into his office at noon, leaped over the desk, knocked him flying out of his swivel chair, and planted a well-aimed fist square on the jawbone. Bert had a brutal left. He had boxed in the Army.

Schuyler, sprawled on the Berber carpet, prepared himself for the next blow, sure he'd receive a vicious kick in the ribs. But, no. Bert picked up the chair and brought it down on his back. Schuyler, gasping and wheezing, sprawled on the floor, dared not move lest his opponent heave the chair at him again. Was this guy a Hulk wannabe? All he heard was heavy breathing as Bert decided what to do next.

The expected sharp kick to Schuyler's ribs came next. Bradford stood over his prone victim, appreciating the effects of his handiwork, then walked with a measured step to the door and closed it quietly behind him.

That was *so* Bert.

⌐

Was it worth it? He hadn't given a thought to Grace's predicament when Bert saw right through her flimsy excuse and learned she'd slept with Schuyler. How had he underestimated Bert's fury when Grace told him she wasn't sorry, and said she'd do it again in a heartbeat? Was that one-night stand worth Natalie's meltdown when Bert took a mean, lowdown revenge? He phoned Natalie and squealed about her husband's fling with Grace.

Natalie, mad with grief and jealousy, squealed on him in turn. She phoned Grace and said she'd kept her mouth shut for far too long. For fourteen years, in fact. All along, she'd known Bert was a philandering louse and making a fool of his wife. That would show squatty little Grace how it felt to be cheated on.

⌐

Was it worth it? Schuyler hauled himself to a sitting position on the edge of the bed, careful not to disturb the sleeping dog. He lumbered into the kitchen where the clock above the sink said 4:00 a.m. No point trying to go back to sleep.

I can't live this way any longer.

The words, "Please help me, Winston!" hovered on the tip of his tongue but he wasn't that desperate. Or that insane.

I don't want to be a louse anymore.

I won't live this way any longer.

CHAPTER 13

On the Dock

Sunday was uneventful, and Schuyler couldn't have been more grateful. If his luck held out, no one would stop by either to visit or to give him advice, or another dog, and his memory might be once more occluded. He couldn't remember ever being more depressed.

After heating a frozen dinner for breakfast, he sat down at the kitchen table only to have his attention diverted by Bella who, as she inched closer to his chair, never took her eyes off his plate. *Holy shit.* He still had no dog food.

Schuyler laid his plate on the floor, opened the freezer compartment of the fridge, and placed another frozen dinner in the oven. He turned around seconds later to see Bella's plate licked clean, her eyes once again focused on his movements.

"You're out of luck, sister. I'll get your food at the market today." He picked up the dog's leash, then eased her out the front door and into the large courtyard.

Sitting down again, eager to forget the horrors of last night's self-incriminating and scathing review of past misdeeds, he assessed the household purchases he'd made so far and started making a list. *Bookcase?* The sitting room had built-in shelves on one wall. Getting up, he arranged the books he'd selected from Novel Ideas on those shelves. No need to buy a bookcase. Almost as an afterthought he dug out his copy of the *I Ching* from his luggage and placed it on the shelf. He hadn't consulted the oracle for several years, but now felt a pressing need to do so. He needed all the help he could get.

He wasn't sure how efficient his furnace was and wondered if he should buy wood for the two fireplaces. Where would he purchase some wood? No doubt Tom Jannssen could answer that question.

Despite his defects of character and personality, and his previous shoddy lifestyle, Schuyler couldn't tolerate grime or untidiness. He must have clean surroundings. That meant buying a broom and a dust pan. Oh, and more matches. Jannssen had advised him to get a couple of oil lamps, and lamp oil, so he added those to his list.

Oil lamps. What a backwater he was stuck in. Still, he remembered the inconvenience of East Coast blackouts. Oil lamps were a good investment. And curtains. Would he ever remember to buy curtains?

It was time to visit True Value Hardware in Pojoaque. He could buy some of these items there. It wouldn't hurt to pick up a quart of milk at the market. And dog food. Speaking of quarts, he glanced toward the kitchen counter where the empty Jack Daniels bottle stood.

How funny. Ever since his debauch in the Plaza Lounge, then running into Chatterjee at Walmart, he'd had no taste for liquor. Until last night he'd forgotten all about the bottle of Jack abandoned on the kitchen counter.

When he walked out the back door, ready to drive into Pojoaque, he almost stumbled over Bella lying on the doormat, tail wagging.

"Come on, sister." Bella jumped onto the front seat as soon as he opened the truck door. She must be used to vehicles, but where did she think she was going?

In the late afternoon, on returning from Pojoaque, he lay down on his bed for a nap. Assuming she had a right to half that square footage, Bella jumped up beside him. Schuyler guessed this would be their customary routine, at least until he bought a dog bed. And that better happen soon. She was one stinky dog. Bella smelled worse than the discarded sheets, and her idea of half the bed left him with twelve inches of mattress.

After dinner, Schuyler set his alarm for a six o'clock wake-up the next morning, and that magic Monday morning hour arrived all too soon. He struggled out of bed, anxious to arrive on time for his first day of work at Sam's Club. A hot shower restored him, and he dressed in jeans and his flannel shirt. He was about to pull on his new boots when he remembered Tom Jannssen's caution. Jannssen had seen the box containing the boots sitting on the kitchen counter.

"You might want to use Bag Balm on those once in a while. Keeps the leather from cracking and drying out. Also, you might want to turn your boots upside down and shake them before you put them on."

"Bag Balm? Where do I get it? And, why shake the boots?" asked Schuyler.

"You can get Bag Balm at Walmart. You shake out your boots because something could have crawled inside during the night. You never know."

"What kind of something?"

"We have a lot of black widows around here. Centipedes. Scorpions."

"Holy shit." Schuyler recalled the sizable spider inside the pump housing. "Is there anything nonlethal around here?"

"That little tree out back, behind the small courtyard, gives great pie cherries. That is, if the birds don't get them first."

Schuyler shook out his boots, although he doubted a spider or scorpion had crawled inside the boot box. *You never know.* He boiled water and poured it over his instant oatmeal, made a cup of coffee, and turned off the range burners. As he poured dog food onto a paper towel, he wondered how long the bag of kibble would last. Bella seemed to have a hollow leg. And she needed a dog food dish.

The drive south into Santa Fe took far longer than he'd anticipated due to the stream of cars and trucks. Who knew there'd be so much commuter traffic out here in the Wild West? Maybe he should set the alarm for five thirty instead of six. Disgusting thought.

Having parked his truck, he hurried into the Club through the employee entrance. Janice Garcia had left him a message on how to find this. He climbed the stairs to the second floor and on entering the Human Resources Office was greeted by Ms. Chatterjee herself, now attired in her business suit. No jeans. What a shame.

"Welcome, Mr. Schuyler," she beamed. "It's not yet eight o'clock, and we are off to a good start."

"I'm happy to be here," he grinned, wondering if she would monitor his arrival each and every morning. "And it was a pleasure to meet your mother last Tuesday."

"Oh, Mr. Schuyler, I can assure you she felt exactly the same as you. Just exactly."

Schuyler doubted the truth of that statement. More likely, Chatterjee had told her mother all the sordid details related to his forced employment at Sam's Club.

"Please, take a seat," she continued. "I have some papers for you to fill out. Then why don't you glance over the associates' handbook to see if you have any questions. You may do a more thorough reading tonight."

As if—Schuyler sat down to read the handbook. *I can hardly wait.*

"You may have noticed I did not require a drug test before hiring you. I am positive we have no such issue to contend with, but tomorrow morning before coming to work will you please report to this clinic for your test."

Chatterjee's pleasant expression never changed as she placed a card with the clinic address in front of Schuyler. Absorbed in perusing the employees' handbook, he failed to notice how she studied him with a more appraising eye than an indifferent employer might bestow on a new hire.

"So, if you have no questions, let's go to the dock and I will introduce you to the people you will work with." She handed him a pullover cotton vest that read "Sam's Club. Happy To Help" on the back.

Schuyler donned the vest. He followed Ms. Chatterjee the length of the store to the back wall. They went through swinging doors with an overhead sign reading "Associates Only."

"Mike!" Chatterjee hailed a younger man who raised a hand in greeting. "This is Aaron Schuyler, our new associate who is joining your staff. Mr. Schuyler, Mike Three Rivers. Mike is our dock manager, and he will assign you your duties. They're on a first-name basis out here. Now, when it is time for your break please visit the service desk staff. They will take your photo and make an ID tag for you. "He's all yours, Mike," Chatterjee called out as she headed back toward the swinging doors. "Good luck, Mr. Schuyler!"

"Welcome." Mike extended his hand. "Nice to meet you."

"Likewise," hissed Schuyler, trying not to wince at the crushing grip. He checked out Mike's full head of hair. More hair than he'd ever had, even in his teens. Mike's coloring was about the same shade as Jannssen's, and he had a similar round face.

"Are you from Santa Clara Pueblo?" he asked.

"Hell no!" Mike laughed. It was a good-natured spontaneous laugh. The kind that comes easy to some people. "I'm from San Ildefonso. You know about the Pueblos?"

"Not really." Schuyler shrugged. It didn't hurt to admit he knew nothing. "Just learning."

"You've got your work cut out for you," Mike chortled. "Let's see how much weight you can lift, Aaron. I need to see what shape you're in."

Schuyler frowned. When had he last worked out at a gym? Or played tennis? Rowed? Gone hiking with Harry?

"Can you manage fifty pounds? That's a pretty typical average for incoming goods," said Mike. "Here, try lifting this box." He handed Schuyler a pair of leather work gloves.

Schuyler pulled on the gloves and leaned over the box.

"Wait. Not yet!" cried Mike. "You always need to wear a back brace. See? Like what I'm wearing. Hold on a sec."

Schuyler stared at the strange contraption strapped around Mike's waist. Mike opened a cupboard and pulled out a similar brace for Schuyler.

"I'll put this on for you." Mike gestured with the brace. "Then you'll know how to do it. Don't ever let me see you working without your brace."

With the brace adjusted and cinched in, Schuyler leaned over again to hoist the box.

"Wait. You gotta bend your knees before picking up anything. Bend your knees first."

With his back braced and his knees bent, Schuyler made a third attempt to retrieve the box. It was unbelievably heavy. Once he managed to get his gloved hands underneath the box he was able to lift it, then staggered back a few steps and almost lost his balance.

"Whoa!" Mike steadied Schuyler's shoulders and stopped the backward motion.

"Wow," gasped Schuyler. "Fifty pounds is quite a load."

"That was thirty-five. I wasn't gonna start you out with fifty." Mike turned to greet two men now emerging onto the dock from the swinging doors.

"Good! Ernie and Jesús are back from lunch. Now we're back to full staff and we can get some work done." Mike beckoned to the two men. "This is Aaron, the new hire."

"I'm Ernie. Ernie Daniels." The taller of the two men reached for Schuyler's hand. Again, the brief but punishing grip.

"Good to meet you." Ernie had the same facial coloring as Mike Three Rivers. "Are you also from San Il—San Il—?

"San Ildefonso? No, man. I'm Pojoaque Pueblo."

"I live up near there. Road 503." Schuyler was anxious to find common ground with these hefty guys. He extended his hand to the second man. "I'm Aaron Schuyler."

"Jesús C. deBaca. Con gusto! Welcome to the dock."

"Are you from Pojoaque Pueblo?" asked Schuyler, freeing his hand from a third crush.

"No way! I'm not like them." Jesus poked Ernie in the ribs. "I'm New Mexican."

When Schuyler looked puzzled, Jesús added, "A Hispanic native. My family has been in New Mexico for five hundred years."

"No kidding." Schuyler whistled. His own lineage, the Dutch in America on his father's side, was equally impressive.

"Enough bullshit, you slackers," Mike growled. "Time to get to work."

"Come on, old guy." Jesús chuckled. "Let me show you the ropes. You gotta pull your weight around here. Before you know it, we'll have you driving the leveler/stacker. And remember, what happens on the dock stays on the dock." He slapped Schuyler on the shoulder. "Five o'clock, man, we hit the Cheerful Tortoise for brewskies!"

Old guy?

Unsure of what a leveler/stacker or a brewski was, skeptical of his ability to lift fifty pounds, wondering how many Pueblos there were altogether, and what the difference was between them, Schuyler followed Jesús toward a massive truck loaded with boxes. Each box looked like it weighed far more than fifty pounds.

Yeah. *Old guy.* If the shoe fits, wear it.

At 5:00 p.m. Schuyler declined accompanying his workmates to the Cheerful Tortoise. When had he last felt so tired? This bone-weary exhaustion where every muscle in his body begged for relief, and his arms felt too weak to control the steering wheel, was different from the wrung-out feeling of headache, dizziness, and stomach-aching-from-too-much-vomiting that followed an over-the-top bout of drinking.

And—that had been his idea of fun? *Yowzer.* What age will do to you.

The drive north to Nambé was tedious and stressful, with the same congestion and erratic driving he'd encountered on his commute into town. Was he the only one minding the speed limit? And what about this New Mexican custom of tailgating, where cars would rush up to within an inch of his rear bumper, hang there for a few seconds, then pass him up like a dirty shirt. Where was that asshole cop when you needed him?

Thankful to be alive, he turned right on Road 503, soothed by a previously unthinkable thought. Twenty-five miles an hour was a sane speed. That seemed as fast as any decent person should drive.

What to do with Bella had been a question when Schuyler left for work in the morning. He had put her outside, thinking if she was still there when he returned home that would be fine. If not, that also was fine. As it turned out, Bella was sitting in the carport as he drove in, thumping her tail like crazy. She knew where her meal ticket was.

Schuyler poured some kibble onto her paper towel, placed a frozen dinner in the oven, then stripped down, tossing his shirt, belt, and Sam's Club vest onto the floor as he headed for the bathroom. He lingered in the shower until the hot water started cooling down, then toweled off, pulled on clean shorts, ate dinner, brushed his teeth, and fell into bed. His clock stated it was 8:00 p.m. Ludicrous. He also set the alarm for five thirty hoping an earlier start might mean a less hair-raising drive into town.

"Come here, sister," he beckoned to Bella, who didn't hesitate. She accepted his invitation and jumped onto the bed.

CHAPTER 14

Days at Sam's Club

Schuyler never thought about how long he'd worked at Sam's Club until he arrived one Friday morning to find the store decorated for the Fourth of July. Wow. He hadn't even noticed the ramped-up deliveries of barbecue supplies that should have been a clue. And, during early morning staff meetings, how had he failed to miss any mention of this important-for-business holiday?

The answer to his question wasn't hard to find. As if he didn't already know.

No-brainer.

At the early morning staff meetings, he hunkered down at the table farthest away from where the store executives sat. Thus positioned behind other associates, he was hidden from the view of the Human Resources director, Ms. Chatterjee. She'd never guess he spent the entire meeting staring at her, while remaining oblivious to whatever business was conducted.

Things had gotten out of hand. Even from his lopsided perspective, he realized that. This coming Monday, June 26th, he'd have been working on the dock at Sam's Club for two whole months and the frequency of his treks up the stairs to the Human Resources department, after conjuring up some lame excuse, or a lamer question, was beyond embarrassing. Most often, Janice Garcia answered the question after she asked him what his business was and he, frustrated, hurried back down the stairs and returned to the dock.

Give up, Schuyler. You're making an even bigger ass of yourself.

There were enough times, however, when Janice was not on duty and, on hearing the buzzer ring at the front desk, Chatterjee would emerge in all her glory to attend to the needy associate. Having figured out this repeated pattern, and more or less aware of when Janice was away from her desk, Schuyler timed his work breaks and treks up the steps to coincide with her absence. Then he was able to question Chatterjee about crucial or confusing points in the associates' handbook, about necessary safety regulations on the dock, and what he might do to improve his employee performance pending his upcoming six-month review that was only four months away. It was vital he serve the Club to the best of his ability.

"I was just wondering, Ms. Chatterjee, whether the breaks I'm taking are too long?"

"That would be a matter for your supervisor, Mike, to decide, Mr. Schuyler."

If Chatterjee suspected these frequent visits were ploys to spend a few minutes with her, and he often felt she saw right through him, she never let on. Each time, she folded her hands on the desk and focused her lovely smile and sparkling eyes upon him, as if his concerns affected the welfare of the entire worldwide corporation.

By this point, Schuyler felt like such a fool he didn't care if she already knew he was a goner. Hopelessly in love with her. As far as he could recall, he'd never felt like this about any woman. Certainly not Natalie. Not even Janelle. This was the real thing. He was running out of excuses for trudging up to HR and, worse yet, he was a laughingstock for the guys on the dock. They heckled him without mercy.

"Still SOL, *Viéjo*?"

"Hey, you're huffing and puffing up those stairs! Get some Viagra!"

"Buy a bottle of dye first, old man. No one as hot as Chatterjee will fall for gray hair."

No letup. The assholes. He was miserable, not only because he was the constant butt of their jokes—nothing else amused them from 8:00 a.m. until quitting time—but because he was beginning to see the light. He'd never get to first base with the object of his adoration.

"Ms. Chatterjee," he began during their most recent interview, desiring nothing more than to sit on the other side of the desk and listen to her musical voice, "I was rereading page eleven of our handbook, the guidelines for washing hands after using the lavatory. Please understand, I'm not complaining, but often there isn't any soap in the dispensers. I don't want to get anyone in trouble, but it seemed best for both staff and customers if I mentioned this to you."

You sick suck-up. He detested the agony of his fruitless penitential routine.

Chatterjee's smile was ever gracious. She was adept at maintaining both eye contact and an even voice. "You can rest assured, Mr. Schuyler. I will take this up with the custodians, and do so in a manner which in no way can be construed as censure, but as a recommendation only." She was good at her job.

At this point, feeling he was unable to endure the torture of one more such smile, Schuyler lost all sense of reality.

Was there a suggestion of coyness in that smile? In the tilt of her head? In the brighter light of her eye? In the warmth of her voice? Was she, despite rank and title, signaling her interest? Hinting that some deeper connection between the two of them might become manifest? A deeper connection than his devotion to mastering the thirty-five pages of the associates' handbook, and her expertise in explaining its intricacies.

This was a now-or-never situation.

"Ms. Chatterjee." Schuyler cleared his throat and leaned forward on his chair, speaking in an earnest tone. "Um, I hope I'm not crossing a line here, but I wondered if you might—sometime—be interested in doing something on a Saturday afternoon. With me? Maybe a trip to the zoo, or the botanical gardens. In Albuquerque." He felt he had a better chance suggesting afternoon than evening. A better chance with the zoo, than a movie where they would naturally sit right next to each other. In the dark.

He fell headlong into the pit he'd been digging for himself.

"Mr. Schuyler—" Chatterjee hesitated. She frowned. She unfolded her hands and picked up a pen from the desk. Her unsmiling gaze was focused on the plate of glass covering the desktop, rather than on Schuyler. "I am honored that you asked. Such an invitation is always flattering and, believe me, I have no wish to hurt your feelings. But, however, there are some unwritten rules pertaining to Sam's Club associates, a code of ethics, so to speak, that precludes socializing with fellow employees of the opposite sex."

If her turndown was spoken in too much of a rush, almost as if she had once, or maybe more than once, considered the likelihood of him asking her for a date, wasn't sure herself of how she wished to answer, and had, therefore, preplanned her response, Schuyler failed to notice. He also missed the brief flush that tinted her cheeks, then vanished.

He was stunned. Speechless. Once, again, the dunce. He had failed to play the right card. But—how could he play the right card when he had so few in his hand? She held all the aces.

"Mr. Schuyler?" Chatterjee stood up from her chair, seeking to regain his attention, this time looking him straight in the eye. "I am so very sorry." Her sincerity could not be mistaken.

"Oh, no problem," he mumbled, as he also rose. Interview over. Strategy unsuccessful. "I am the one who is sorry. I was out of line. Inappropriate. I—uh—guess I should get back to work. Thank you for your time."

In his hurry to leave her office, he stumbled over the threshold. Pitiful.

"Sorry," he called back over his shoulder. Pathetic.

His hopes were shattered. Dashed. His world had crumbled to dust. All he now had left of the world Anita Chatterjee inhabited was his work on the dock. All he had to look forward to was hiding behind his fellow associates at the staff meeting each morning and staring at her.

There would be nothing more. He beat a scrambling retreat down the stairs.

Since the onset of his infatuation, he'd warned himself she might have no interest in anything beyond a professional relationship. That she might, in fact, turn him down. True to his self-acknowledged egotistical perspective and his lengthy history of positive results in dating, he had dismissed this possibility as remote, if not nonexistent.

"In all probability, she'd jump at the chance," he had mused.

After all, he was a good-looking man. Well spoken. Not like some of the bozos working at the Club. But as the pain of her refusal cut deeper, he was forced to admit just how strong the feelings were. *On his part.* All hope was now lost, and the agony of unrequited love welled up within him until it squeezed the very blood from his heart.

Schuyler had suffered no such pangs when Janelle broke up with him, nor when Natalie divorced him. Their divorce was nothing compared with this. He never glimpsed the potential for intimacy with his ex-wife, nor in any of his romantic liaisons, that he knew existed on so many levels with Anita Chatterjee. *Goddammit.*

He made an instant vow. No matter how long he worked at Sam's Club, he would never again, ever climb those stairs. It was better to hide out on the dock. Better to eat lunch in his truck than sit in the Club café and risk having *her* walk by and offer him an indifferent greeting.

His intestines gurgled. Catastrophe loomed. He dashed to the men's room, realizing he hadn't a moment to lose. IBS had struck again.

When Schuyler returned to the dock, Jesús, noticing his morose aspect and suspecting what outcome lay behind it, suggested he join the dock crew after work at the Cheerful Tortoise. Schuyler did not refuse and, at closing time, he followed the other guys to the bar.

As it turned out, the Cheerful Tortoise was a happening place. The music mix was pleasant, the turkey sandwiches were bountiful, and the bartender's pour was generous. Even better, tonight Schuyler's dock buddies were out of character in their sensitivity.

None of the three inquired too closely into the details of what had happened in Human Resources. They made only general references to the quirks and fickleness of women who, in their collective opinion, couldn't recognize a good thing when it was right in front of their eyes.

Schuyler was having a fun time. As fun a time as possible, given the painful circumstances. The usual two doubles hit him harder than usual. His stomach was churning and his bowels were unhappy, but maybe a chaser would settle him down. He ordered the third drink. When the group agreed to call it a night at 8:00 p.m., Schuyler eased himself out of his chair, grabbed the edge of the table, then slumped back onto the seat.

"You okay, man?" Mike Three Rivers was concerned. What had happened to Schuyler with Chatterjee wasn't something a man could blow off. "Can you make the drive to Nambé?"

"A little light-headed. I'll be okay."

"I'm also heading north. Española. I'll follow you," Mike added. "Just take it real easy."

The drive north on Cerrillos Road took forever. Schuyler hit every red light. Each time he checked in his rear-view mirror, however, Mike was behind him. That was reassuring. There was no logical reason why the liquor had hit him so hard tonight. Could it be old age? Like the guys kept kidding him? In the past, his younger days, three doubles had never been a problem. If he wanted to admit the truth, which he didn't, his liquor-soaked binges were beyond the counting.

When he reached the 503 cutoff north of Pojoaque, he honked to let Mike know he was okay, then turned right.

Schuyler wasn't sure how it happened, how it came about that he took the curve too wide when he made that turn, but the unmistakable crunch of metal meeting metal confirmed a serious lapse in judgment. What the fuck! He'd collided with the driver-side front bumper of a pickup coming toward him!

Despite the fog in his head, Schuyler managed to pull off the road as far as he could and turn off the ignition. The other driver did the same, on the opposite side of the road. *Screwed.* Schuyler reached into the glove box, pulled out his registration and proof of insurance, then fished his license out of his rear pocket. Glancing across the road, he saw the driver of the truck he'd hit making a call on his cell phone. *Totally screwed.*

To Schuyler in his hazy euphoria, a state patrol car arrived in what seemed like no time at all. How fast did these guys drive? The officer pulled off the road behind the victimized truck, leaving his headlights on bright. Schuyler squinted into the glare as he watched the officer listen to what the other driver had to say. When the patrolman started to cross the road toward his pickup, Schuyler recognized him as the same man who ticketed him in April, when he first arrived in New Mexico. *Dang.*

"License and registration, please."

"Right here, Officer." Schuyler passed the documents out through the window.

"Can you tell me what happened, sir?"

"Well, it's dark. Obviously. Dark. I took the turn a little too wide and didn't see the lights coming toward me."

"How could you not see the lights coming toward you?" The officer frowned.

"I don't know, Officer. I guess I didn't time my turn right."

"I guess you didn't." The officer leaned a little closer toward Schuyler. "Don't I know you?"

"I don't think so."

"Yeah. I do. You're the dude from the Big Apple. I ticketed you a while back. You just can't get it right, can you? We have laws in New Mexico. What's your name again?"

"Schuyler. I'm sorry, Officer. I made a big mistake. We have laws in New York, too."

Shut your trap, you moron.

"O-kay." The officer breathed in the fumes emanating from Schuyler's mouth, and heaved an exhale. "I think we have a problem here. Sir, please step out of the truck."

"Why?" At this point, Schuyler saw headlights in his rear-view mirror. Mike's truck had just pulled up behind him. Mike must have heard the resounding metal on metal clash.

"Mr. Schuyler, step out of the truck."

"I know him, Officer. I'll vouch for him!" Mike cried as he jumped out of his truck and strode toward the officer.

"Back in your vehicle, sir. Now."

There would be no argument with this command. The officer patted his side holster and Mike did as he was told. As he retreated toward his truck, the officer called for backup.

"Sir," he said to Schuyler as he moved away several paces, "you are going to walk toward me, heel to toe, in a straight line. Start now and walk toward me."

Schuyler's head felt heavy, his temples pounded, and his bowels gurgled. He took one step, a second step, then stumbled, listing to port as sure as a sinking ship. He righted himself, taking one step, two steps. *This was going well.* On the third step his legs wobbled, his left foot tripped over his right, and he fell to his knees. Another patrol car pulled up. A second officer emerged and took up a position near Mike's truck.

"Okay. I've seen enough. Breathe into my phone, Mr. Schuyler." The officer checked the readout, then called out to the second officer who had just arrived. "Andy, can you drive him into Española? I've got patrol all the way north to Las Trampas."

"No! Wait!" Schuyler objected. "If you'll let me go home, I'll sleep this off. I'll be fine in the morning."

"And will his vehicle be fine in the morning?" the officer growled, jerking his head toward the crushed front fender on the opposite side of the road. "Will yours? You've got some major body work coming up, Mr. Schuyler."

"What's your name? I demand—" Schuyler cried out to the first officer as the second one gripped his elbow and steered him toward the patrol car.

"Gomez. Archie Gomez. Have a nice evening, sir." He handed his paperwork to the second officer, hopped into his car, made a swift U-turn and headed north up the High Road.

"Hey, I'm sorry, man." Mike's expression was pained. "Really sorry. Wish I could help."

"Thanks anyway," mumbled Schuyler as he slumped onto the back seat of the patrol car. "Wait—Mike!" he called out through the open window. "Can you drive to my place, number 57? Feed my dog? There's a key under the pot with the dead cactus."

CHAPTER 15

In Jail

Schuyler lay on his bunk in a holding cell in the Rio Arriba County Jail in Española, not wondering what he did to deserve being here—his guilt was obvious—but reviewing the steps in his faulty reasoning process that landed him in the clinker. What led him to conclude last night that getting drunk was an adequate solution to any given problem? How many more times would he choose to soak himself in liquor because Chatterjee had turned him down for a date? Once more? Twice? Where was the logic in such a remedy? And hadn't he, just two months ago, sworn to mend his ways?

Forever.

Despite his taste for bourbon, he was never once cited for drunk driving in New York.

"You loser, that's nothing to crow about!" Schuyler chided himself. For many years he had the services of a chauffeur. When he didn't, he usually had the wherewithal to take a taxi. Only later, after his bankruptcy, was he forced to get a license and drive the dilapidated Ford Fiesta. A discarded relic that had previously belonged to Clementine's cleaning woman.

There was one time during his New York years when he'd ended up in jail, but it wasn't due to drink. Although Schuyler and his business partner, Bert Bradford, were indicted for investment fraud, they'd ducked a prison term. The vast amount paid to their team of lawyers did the trick. That was the downside to the dismissal of their case, the extortionate fees those shysters extracted. Repayment to investors—at least some of them—following upon those attorney fees, bankrupted the Bradford-Schuyler firm. Both partners ended up penniless and wifeless. But, not in prison.

The reason why Schuyler spent a night in jail a few years back stemmed from a very different cause. Since then he'd often revisited the incident and made a dogged effort to understand why he so often chose the path of sleaze when it would have been just as easy to make a different, wiser, better choice. Committed as he now was to mending his ways and becoming a reputable member of society, it was important to dissect whatever baser motivations revealed themselves.

Schuyler had described the incident in his diary after being bailed out by Clementine, who also paid his court costs and fines. The entry, written soon after his release, revealed neither regret nor guilt concerning his misdeed. It was, instead, a blatant defense of shameful choices. Excuses. He was always good at making excuses. Nothing was ever his fault.

A well intentioned hint from Uncle Harry on the value of changing his course in life had fallen on deaf ears. Give up women and greed? *Hah.* Easier said than done. Only much later had he begun to reflect on the wisdom of Harry's advice. After Harry's funeral. After moving to New Mexico.

In trying to determine the rationale behind his disgraceful life choices, Schuyler reread that entry so often he'd now memorized it. Lying in his cell, nursing a rotten headache, he recalled its entirety.

Dear Diary,

My mother bailed me out of jail last night, expected me to thank her, and went so far as to say, "Winston wasn't pleased." Will she ever give me a break? Are any breaks at all, *even one*, coming my way any time soon?

What I did wasn't that bad. I didn't deserve jail, that's for sure. I was just doing my civic duty. Word had gotten out, hush-hush, that a potential GOP nominee was paying people to picket his Demo rival's speech and rally in Central Park. *Paying.* That's the key word. I contacted some of my fellow event crashers and we hightailed it over to the park. Action like this was just up our alley. That pinko leftie Demo scum candidate would put everyone in the country on welfare if she got her way.

Bankrupt the army. All the crashers were going to do was liven things up a bit and shut down the rally. Have some fun. Earn our forty dollars. *Yeah.*

Well, things got a little out of hand what with jostling a few of those bleeding hearts. Busting a newsman's camera. Routine stuff. As for me? I went above and beyond the call of duty and belly-bumped some duffer wearing a hat with a *blue* donkey on it. Some tree hugger. How was I to know he had emphysema? Sure, I saw the oxygen tank but I thought it belonged to *someone else*. Who knew the guy was such a basket case he'd have a coughing fit and fall and hit his head on the sidewalk?

No one would let me explain. I ended up thrown in jail on an assault charge. Where was the justice in that?

"Are you listening to me? I don't belong here!" I kept yelling but the jerk pig at the front desk could have cared less. He totally ignored me. I got so angry I slammed my forehead against the bars of the holding cell number four, Precinct 47. *Big mistake.*

"Call my lawyer!" I told them I had rights. Did they care? What kind of country is this, what kind of *system* when decent citizens get jailed for supporting their political party? That lump above my left eyebrow was plenty tender. Hurt like hell. I tried to get the cop's attention again.

"This is an election year, man, in case you hadn't heard," I yelled. Then someone in another cell started giving me grief.

"Hey!" This jerk farther down the row, in number six, bangs on his bars. "You with the mouth!" he snarls. And what a voice! Harsh, hoarse. A *nasty* kind of drunk.

"You in number four—" he yells. "Some of us wanna sleep. Shut your trap!"

Who was he to tell me what to do? Wasn't this just what I was protesting in the park? I dealt with this crap the whole time I lay in that smelly cell. *Three hours.* Low company. No respect. Threats from a *nobody* sounding like a mafia wannabe. All because I tried to earn a few extra bucks.

Diary, you can't believe how my head hurt with that bruise bulging above my left eye. Friggin' cell bars. Here I end up in jail and hadn't gotten paid for putting on the show in the park. Life really *sucks*. Same as usual. Tell me, is anything fair? Not for me.

Not for a good long while. Not since before the crash of '08, back when Bradford-Schuyler was thriving.

I needed the forty dollars so *bad*. My suit and tux were long overdue for a trip to the dry cleaners. You know those clothes are my livelihood. Put the *food* on my plate. Still, there's a chance I might get paid. The big shot might end up being the candidate. You never know, and we were tight once. Sat on the board of Winthrop Worldwide back in the day. He might remember me though he never had a good rep for keeping his word.

You think this was bad? Things at the jail got even worse. I heard someone yelling up front at the admitting desk. On hearing *that* voice, and I think you know *who* I mean, my intestines started gurgling!

"Hey—you tore my shirt!" Came this unmistakable Brooklyn accent. "Pig—get your hands off me!"

Are you getting the idea? That voice was way too familiar. In a very bad way. The cop marches this guy who's struggling down the row of cells and they stop outside *my cell*. Number four. There was no escape, I turned my back. I heard the cop's keys jangle. Then I heard the door open. Go figure. It had to be my cell.

"Pig! H-hamhock!" The prisoner is so angry, he's stuttering as the cop shoves him into my cell.

"Sober up!" growls the officer as he bangs the door shut.

I crept as far into a corner as I could, but it only postponed the inevitable.

"Did you see how he manhandled me?" says the voice I know all too well. "You saw! You're a witness. Police brutality!"

He stands still for a moment, expecting me to support him. *As if.* When I don't say anything, he jams a fist into my left side ribs. "Hey! I'm talkin' to you—"

What could I do?

"And I heard you, Bert," I answer, but I have to squeeze the words out between my teeth. My ribs hurt like hell and I ask you—could this day get any worse? You know by now my cell-mate is Bert Bradford.

"You—what—? Ohmygod—!" Bradford's eyes bulged wide. You should have seen it. He stares at me, speechless for a moment. Then, like the fool he is he throws himself against the cell door frame. A steel frame.

"Hey!" he shouts. "Lemme out of here—you locked me up with a pervert! I'm tellin' you! A philanderer! A lowdown cheat!"

"Show a little class, Bert," I answer back, thinking of all we'd been through together, what a rotten business partner he was. Now I was pissed. "You're calling me a pervert? You—who made up lewd nursery rhymes for your granddaughter!"

He wasn't gonna go punching me in the ribs! I jostled my former business partner up against the bars. *Good riddance.*

"You—who ate sauerkraut at your desk in front of our clients, Bert, are calling me a pervert? That's rich. Let me remind you we were in it together. Up to our necks in it. Took the fall together. Your hands are as dirty as mine, you dumb shmuck!"

By this time, Bert was shaking with fury. Ready with a come-back. His comb-over flopping into his eyes as he vaults away from the bars.

"Not quite, you friggin' cheat—!" he cries as he swings at me. Missed! He pushes back his hair and lunges. Punches me below the belt. "I lost everything because your big ideas went south!"

I'm hauling myself off the floor, hoping the cop knows what's going down here.

"And I mean *everything*!" Bert continues. "I'm living over in Jersey. My boys had to drop out of college and join the Peace Corps!" He lands me another stomach punch and I'm on the floor again. Diary, you can't believe the pain. I'd forgotten what a left Bert had. I'm going to need the toilet fast. IBS.

"They coulda got part-time jobs. Studied at night—right?" I gasped, hunched over and trying to protect my ribs. "That's what my girls ended up doing."

"Wrong! You fucking liar!" yells Bert. "I know Clementine paid through the nose so all your kids could graduate college!"

"You think I'm better off than you?" I tried stretching out my arm, waving it back and forth like a flag of truce, or surrender. Whatever it took. "I live in a lousy motel room, and I do mean lousy. We both made bad calls, Bert." I was panting by now, hoping I had a prayer of reasoning with this maniac. "Some very bad calls. Who knew we'd be the ones to get hurt when it all crashed down?"

"You bastard," he yells back. "You think this is about losing millions? You screwed my wife! Ex-wife, I should say! What kinda partner does that? You think that's forgivable?"

"A crucial point—not forgivable. I'll not deny it." I tried to calm him down. Bert was breathing hard and clutching his chest. "Still, we managed to keep working together, didn't we?" I tried to sound earnest, engaged. "I admit we have some things to discuss."

Diary, there was no reasoning with the guy. He was livid. Irate.

"There was only the one night with Grace. Only a couple of times. And, as for forgivable? Well, we have some talking points, don't we? We share a concern. Her welfare? You can grant me that much, can't you?"

I took a third punch to the gut and hugged the floor. A floor that stunk of piss. To make matters worse, the lamebrain in cell number six starts sounding off again, wanting peace and quiet. Don't we all?

At last, the duty officer opened the cell and yanked Bert out. He was locked up down the row and I never even found out what he was in for. What a lousy night, and not made better by my mother coming to bail me out. Not that I wasn't grateful.

But—*my mother*. Whose mother comes and bails them out? June 10, 2016

Recalling this diary entry did nothing but exacerbate Schuyler's headache and roil his intestines. He tossed on a bunk even less comfortable than his mattress at home. He tossed and turned, yet when he wakened in the morning his punishing headache was only a minor throb. He sat up and rubbed his temples, trying to recall the order of events in the past thirty-six hours of his life. Thank heavens, it was Saturday. If he got released from jail today he could go home and sleep for the rest of the weekend.

If he got released.

This depressing thought was followed by the sound of the officer striding down the row again, accompanied by the jangle of his keys. He stopped in front of Schuyler's cell and inserted a key in the lock.

"Your bail's been posted."

"Who posted bail?" Schuyler was astonished.

The officer indicated by a jerk of his head that the question wasn't worth answering.

"Move it. You can claim your personal effects at the duty desk."

"I need to use the restroom."

"Take a left before you reach the desk."

When Schuyler arrived at the duty officer's window, a clear plastic gab with his watch, keys, wallet, registration, and insurance cards was handed to him. "Sign here, please."

With a click, the automatic door opened. He was a free man, maybe, but who had posted bail? There was no way Clementine could have found out about his citation, even with Winston's intercession. And where the hell was his truck?

Schuyler exited the station to find Hugh Leigh standing on the steps outside, facing toward the Cowboy's Emporium on the opposite side of the street.

"*You?*" Schuyler croaked, swallowing hard. "I mean—*thank* you. That's what I meant to say. You posted my bail?"

Leigh turned around and nodded, giving Schuyler an appraising up-and-down look before he spoke. "You need a shower, boy."

"I'm not a boy."

"Then don't act like one."

"Look, I'm grateful to you, Mr. Leigh." Schuyler shoved his hands in his pockets. "But if you don't mind, let's skip the lecture. I've been beating myself up for the past twelve hours."

"Good for you." Leigh didn't crack a smile.

"How did you know I was in jail?"

"Lone Goose called me."

"Jannssen? But, how did he know where I was?"

"Mike Three Rivers told him."

"You've lost me." Schuyler shook his head and wondered how bad his breath smelled.

"Jannssen's sister married into San Ildefonso Pueblo. He is Mike's uncle. They spend a lot of time together. Jannssen had told Mike he knew you, asked Mike to keep an eye on you, so Mike didn't waste any time contacting him. Jannssen phoned me. For some reason he figured I'd want to know." Pausing, Hugh Leigh shrugged. "I didn't, but I'd promised Harry a long time ago I'd look after you if the need arose. He was sure it would."

Schuyler put a lid on his arrogance and stifled a wise ass reply. Was he still a boy? It sure looked like it.

"Well, sir, I'm very grateful to you. Does my mother know about this?"

"There's no reason why she should." Leigh gestured with his head. "Let's go get your truck. It's in impound. Do you have money to pay the release fee?"

"I'm not sure. I've never paid an impound fee. If I need to borrow the money from you, I'll pay you back for both the impound costs and my bail fees."

"Good enough," said Leigh with an appraising look at Schuyler. "I figured you would. Between us we should be able to cover the fees. Let's go."

Schuyler released a deep sigh as he climbed into the ancient Jimmy. For some reason he felt buoyant, but couldn't figure out why. The loss of a chance to date Anita Chatterjee had torn a hole in his heart that might never mend. Even worse, he was beginning to see what people meant when they said, "What goes around, comes around."

That wasn't the corny platitude he'd always thought it was. That was how life worked. When had he ever played fair? When had he treated anyone, even his wife and children—especially his wife and children—with the respect and consideration they deserved? And what about love? In that department he was always a taker, never a giver. Payback time.

Right now, he hurt like hell, and not just from a headache. In fact, he needed to be hit over the head a few more times. Then, maybe, he'd have it down pat. *Life.* How to live one's life. As for Chatterjee, he suspected his heart wouldn't heal for a very long time. If ever. What was wrong with those poets who extolled the agonies of love? He could empathize with their pained perspective, but that didn't seem like any reason to put pen to paper and write about it.

Hugh Leigh wasn't such a bad sort. Maybe a little stiff in the rump. For sure a bit skeptical about getting involved with his deceased partner's nephew. Who could blame him? Whatever the root of Leigh's brusque behavior, Schuyler owed him a debt of gratitude.

With the impound fees paid and the pickup now released, the two men shook hands.

"Just saying thanks doesn't seem like enough, Mr. Leigh." Schuyler's tone was grave. "I am indebted to you for helping me."

Leigh said nothing but stared into Schuyler's eyes. Although tempted to look away, squirming with discomfort, Schuyler held steady before that visual evaluation. Leigh seemed lost in thought until, at length, he nodded in response.

"I'll stop by for that cup of coffee."

◞

Bella was sitting near the back door when Schuyler drove into the carport, her tail swatting the door mat at a furious pace.

"Hello, Sister Bella." As he reached down to scratch the dog's ears before unlocking the back door, he realized he was glad to be back home. *Home.* In the kitchen he filled Bella's water pan with fresh water, then dumped a generous portion of kibble into her dish. Bella looked different, somehow, and he puzzled over what could have changed in the past twenty or thirty hours. Was her belly even bigger?

Opening the fridge, he stared at the eggs he'd bought, not at all sure what to do with them. He'd never learned how to fix eggs. Might as well pop another frozen dinner into the oven, then he wouldn't have to wait for a table at the Mockingbird. He filled the tea kettle with water and lit the flame under a burner.

"Instant coffee coming up. And, boy, do I need the fix." Relieved to be home again, Schuyler found himself enjoying the rhythm of his simple kitchen routine. Of sitting at his own kitchen table. Drinking the coffee he made, even if it was a store brand and not barista quality. In New York, every meal he ate was at a deli, of which there was an abundance near his motel. Cooking, if you could call it that, was a novel experience.

The water was taking a long time to boil, and as Schuyler drummed his fingers on the kitchen counter the ever-present bottle of Jack Daniels, standing in its assigned station next to the sink, caught his eye. Like so many of its predecessors, this one was half-empty. *Half-full?* Just like life, wasn't it? All in one's chosen perspective. He removed the cap, tilted the bottle, and watched the contents trickle down the drain.

While he was waiting for the water to boil, he might as well walk across the road to his Route 503 post box. Inside were two envelopes from the New Mexico Department of Motor Vehicles. One envelope held his voter registration card. The other one was marked "Second Notice" in bold red letters. This was a statement demanding immediate payment for infraction of Motor Vehicle Code. The date of offense was listed as April 15, 2017. *No argument there.* Schuyler had thrown the first request in the garbage, thinking they weren't serious. To his way of thinking then, New Mexico wasn't a real state. It was just an afterthought.

If you feel this fee is in error, or issuance was improper, contact Rio Arriba County Courthouse in Tierra Amarilla. If the fee is in order, please at once remit the amount of $65.00 plus $15.00 interest applied for late payment either in person or by check to Department of Motor Vehicles, etc. A Santa Fe address was given.

Ouch. Eighty bucks.

The mailbox also contained a manila envelope with protective padding sent from his mother's Akron, Ohio, address. Schuyler had received many envelopes of similar size. This one, he knew, contained more tapes concerning the degraded condition of Clementine's sinuses. He couldn't help wondering if she ever complained of this ailment to Stan Atwater?

Never. She wouldn't dare. Too big a risk. That revelation, on top of Atwater's knowledge of her devotion to Winston Churchill, might be sufficient grounds for divorce. Her son would always be the only one privileged to witness the near-insane level of her hypochondria.

CHAPTER 16

Flashback

Having finished his frozen dinner breakfast and put Bella outside to do her business, Schuyler brushed his teeth and retrieved his diary from the bedside table. God, he didn't want to do this. But, sitting down at the kitchen, he poised his pen above a blank page. Each word he squeezed out onto paper, gritting his teeth with the effort, felt like something between a heart attack and a cerebral hemorrhage.

Dear Diary,

Here's what it looks like. I am at last forced to choose between thinking myself the most abused, misunderstood human being who ever lived or *facing the fact* that for my whole life I've been a cowardly egotistical self-fucked-up *shmuck*. Hah-hah. Better late than never. Having realized that for the first time in my life I am truly in love, and that the woman is *out of reach* and will never return said love or, even if wishing to do, so *cannot* return it due to corporate regulations, how am I supposed to cope with this frigging flood of emotion? The dam is *blown up*. I'm at the mercy of the flow.

Yeah, I get it. My plight is just punishment for the wrongs I've committed, but if I consider it that way then I must do something about it. Change the course of my life. Hard, *if not impossible* when you're not quite sure where you first went wrong. How can I make amends to just about every human being who crossed my path in my adult years?

There's no point in blaming my parents. There's no point blaming my father's instability. *Sadism*, if truth be told. No point blaming my mother for being so off her rocker and unable to stand up to him. This is my life and I am responsible for *How It Goes*. Did I just write that? I am responsible. Me.

After landing in jail last night and this morning's debt owed to Hugh Leigh, almost a total stranger, I realize a lot of truths that have been out there all the time but have evaded my notice. Or, *I avoided noticing* those truths. On purpose.

Beyond all the sorrow I caused my mother, I also dumped on my uncle and caused Harry as much grief as I caused Clementine. Despite my current surfeit of pain and humiliation due to Anita Chatterjee's rejection (and, let's be honest, any attraction I thought she felt toward me was totally MY IMAGINATION), this truth about Clementine and Harry can no longer be denied. BY *ME*. And *why* have I arrived at this moment of truth so late in life? Here I am, almost in the home stretch. Galloping toward sixty. Is it because of Anita? Or because life in New Mexico turns everything upside down?

The *best* question of all—am I the *boy* I am constantly being labeled as? Have I sinned further by casting blame for my fuck-ups onto anyone who was in my way, so as to excuse my rotten behavior and lousy choices. Here's me talking—so listen up. "For the first time in your life, Schuyler, you realize you're an *overgrown version* of the child who cringed at your father's sarcasm, hid in the closet when he got drunk, saw your mother flogged with a cane. All done by a man so crippled from mental illness there was no way he could help himself, even if he wanted to. *Big* if."

You are no longer defenseless, BOY!!! Will you keep making excuses or face the music? Could this *humiliating* downfall of my *own* making—aren't they all—be a beginning and not an end? Think about that one for a while.

June 24, 2017

Yeah, you shithead, think about that one for a while.

Schuyler almost wanted to laugh. Talk about humiliating downfalls. Could anyone else's descent from power and privilege match the swiftness of his own? How was it that from the get-go he and Bert felt it was okay to deceive their clients? To cheat. That wasn't a business practice taught at the Yale School of Management. That wasn't an ethic learned from Harry, nor a family value promoted by Clementine. He alone was responsible for the deserts he'd earned due to greed, his conviction of personal entitlement, and his callous disregard for any human being on the face of this earth besides himself.

How had this happened? Schuyler laid his pen down on the table, sat back in his chair, and pondered that question. He could only answer it by delving into his lurid past.

Bert Bradford's brilliance at putting together a presentation portfolio, Schuyler recalled, was unmatched. His facility with written composition was slick even if his Brooklyn accent was low-class. The Bradford-Schuyler Investments engraved glossy folder, the result of Bert's artistry, was a tangible something a client could hold in his hand. It was solid, like the firm's offerings. Investors could read, then reread, how Bradford-Schuyler would ensure their future stability.

The package provided an easy-to-understand explanation of how the stock market functioned. Its simple terms demystified tax shelters and hedge funds. It described how the firm's strategy of investment in the real estate boom worked. The huge profits to be made from real estate properties guaranteed retirement security. If the big banks weren't concerned by the proliferation of subprime mortgages, why should clients worry? Potential investors could expect a reliable rate of return, thanks to the Bradford-Schuyler management team's expertise.

And if the paper portfolio wasn't evidence enough of a diligent and conservative firm, their scheduled appointment with the affable Aaron Schuyler clinched the deal. He answered all questions and addressed all concerns. Until, that is, December 10, 2008 . . .

"Bert! Haul your ass over here!" Schuyler shrieked, his eyes glued to one of the three computer screens on his desk. "Have you seen this? They arrested Madoff!"

"Calm down, you shithead philanderer!" From his own office Bradford shouted the epithet he'd assigned to Schuyler after learning his business partner had seduced Grace. "You're not the only human with internet, Schuyler. What the fuck! Bernie's kids ratted him out."

In the interests of financial solvency, more important than marital commitment, the two men had continued as business partners. On the light side, their shady interaction with clients, their fumbling hustle to keep the firm afloat, as well as their personal friction, provided an ongoing source of amusement for the two secretaries and the receptionist.

"Bert! What are we going to do?"

After a hurried conference, the partners let the receptionist go with two weeks' pay. Bert directed the secretaries to cancel the day's remaining appointments, as well as the Thursday and Friday appointments. He phoned the firm's attorney, Merriweather Layton of Layton, Schirmer, Jones, and Kurkowski, and pretty much told him to hotfoot it over. ASAP.

As for Schuyler, he dashed out of the building to lay in a supply of bagels and cream cheese, extra-large pizzas, hot dogs, and beer. On returning, he unplugged the office phones. The constant ringing was more than annoying. It was intrusive. He needed time to think.

Merriweather Layton, J.D., was not pleased with this summary command. He had long wished to dissociate himself from the questionable practices of the partners, but what could he do? He was one of Bradford-Schuyler's original investors. The firm had made him a lot of money with a less-than-crystal-clear paper trail. He was in deep. In stark contrast with the firm's later investors, he wouldn't suffer at all if these two sleaze-mongers went belly-up.

"Look—I can't tell you two anything I haven't tried to drum into your thick heads a dozen times," Layton growled. "It's a rotten shame, but the Ponzi as a vehicle for making money is dead. At least, for now. You think I don't watch the market? I told you to get out of mortgages."

"Enough with the hindsight, Merriweather," hissed Schuyler, slamming his fists down on the burled maple surface of the conference table. "Are we going to lose everything?"

"If you'd followed the previous advice of your attorney— myself—that wouldn't even be an issue. You wouldn't be in this position with your shorts in a knot." Layton sipped his scotch in its elegant Venetian cut-glass tumbler. No beer for him. He knew where Schuyler hid the Laphroaig.

"We *are* in this position. It's damned uncomfortable and you better get us out of it." Bradford's Brooklyn accent thickened as his anxiety mounted. He pushed back his comb-over. "You're no innocent, Merry!"

"Don't threaten me, Bert. I'll remain your principal, but I'm assigning Giovanni Jones as defense counsel, if it comes to that."

"This wrangling is getting us nowhere." Schuyler shook his head. "We get it. You're saying we need to pay off investors. We'll do that, but we're nowhere near having the cash flow to repay everyone. It'll bankrupt us and even bankruptcy won't satisfy all the investor demands."

"Then go bankrupt. That shows good intention. It's better than prison."

"Can the courts come after our homes? Personal possessions?" Schuyler's chauffeured Bentley was almost his reason for living.

"What about my condo in Cabo? The one in the Keys? Can they take those?" asked Bert.

"Expect the worst. But if you think bankruptcy is intolerable, let me ask you this—do you have any idea how severe Madoff's sentence is likely to be?" Merriweather Layton's grim expression hardened further on observing his two clients' dumbfounded silence and blank expressions. "I didn't think so. Take the bank-ruptcy."

〰

For seventeen, nearly eighteen years, Bert Bradford and Aaron Schuyler fulfilled every consumer want of their respective clans, yet never gave a rat's ass about basic family values. Being worthy fathers or faithful, loving husbands wasn't on their radar.

"Get out!" Natalie cried when she finally understood the full impact of their financial debacle. "I can't take it any longer! We're done, Aaron. I'm through with you!"

Bradford-Schuyler Investments had taken bankruptcy. The attorneys were paid. Schuyler was penniless. Clementine assumed mortgage payments and condo association fees for Natalie, so she and the girls still had a roof over their heads. She also paid college tuition and expenses for Nate, who was a freshman at Penn State. She did the same for both girls after they finished high school.

Natalie gratefully accepted Clementine's help and started job hunting. For the first time in nineteen years, she felt free, joyful. Her relief when the longtime burden of her husband's marital infidelity was lifted from her shoulders made life, once again, worth living. There was no way she'd miss the friggin' idiot. The only good thing her ex-husband Aaron had done for her was to father their three children.

When Schuyler stalked out of the flat with a suitcase in each hand, his departure didn't even faze his two daughters. *Whatever.* Nora Clementine was watching Oprah and texting her boyfriend, Michael, whom Schuyler had never bothered to meet. The kid attended Phillips Exeter Academy and that met with his approval. That's all that mattered. Really.

"Nora? Will you put down your phone and listen to me?" He frowned as Nora clapped her free hand over her mouth, tears welling up. *Teenagers.* So moody. "You owe your father that much. I paid for that phone. Your mother wants a divorce and I'm leaving."

"Don't talk to me!" Nora sprang up from the couch. "My heart is breaking!" she cried, and texted Michael the same message as she fled to her bedroom and slammed the door.

Sandy was already locked inside her bedroom. She refused to come out.

"I hope you're gone for good!" was her muffled comment from behind the door. Who could have missed the latest row between her mother and father? "You've said you were leaving so many times, what does it matter? Why don't you really do it? Don't ever come back!"

To herself Sandy admitted it did matter. Very much. But there wasn't anything she could do about the situation. Hopeless.

"Parents are irrelevant, Dad!" she screamed. "Especially *mine*!"

Later that evening Schuyler texted Sandy and Nora, asking them to reply. They never did. Over the years he continued sending birthday cards to both girls and honored all appropriate occasions with gifts. These, and his occasional texts, were never acknowledged.

Nathan Daniel, Schuyler's son and oldest child, the one whose birth he hadn't been present for due to a tryst with Janelle, had already escaped to Harrisburg. It was early August and he was settling in for his first year at Penn. Eager to begin premed studies, happy to be out of his nightmare family, the few words Nathan exchanged with his father during their brief phone conversation left the young man sad and exhausted.

"So that's pretty much the long and the short of it, Nate. This time we really are getting a divorce," Schuyler concluded. "Your mother and I are through."

"Yeah, Dad."

"So, maybe I can make it to Harrisburg for the homecoming game."

"Okay."

"If not, I'll see you at Christmas break."

"Okay."

"Well, good luck in school."

"Thanks, Dad. See you."

When Nate's phone went dead Schuyler wondered why he had a lump in his throat. This was something new. Unpleasant. He wrote it off as the stress of the whole damn divorce debacle. How was he supposed to deal with his kids' indifference, on top of now being a bankrupt has-been? The settlement with Natalie would swallow what little money remained after Bradford-Schuyler's court-ordered dissolution. *Damn lawyers.* He swallowed hard to rid himself of the lump. It wouldn't go away.

∽

The sound of Bella whining at the back door, seeking re-admittance, roused Schuyler. Once again, he'd lost himself in the maze of dead ends that comprised his disgusting past. This well-traveled road map wasn't just unpleasant. It was shameful. A nightmare. He poured more dog food into Bella's dish, noting how her tummy nearly dragged upon the floor. Schuyler was by now resigned to his canine partner's pregnancy, but apprehensive about how he was going to deal with puppies. *Oh, well.* Last week he'd bought a king-size dog bed.

Putting pen to paper and writing the diary entry lying on the table in front of him had meant reliving every horror he'd hoped was laid to rest forever. These written words, his very own, dredged up all the dirt he'd tried so hard to bury. Yet, he'd had to do it. He had no choice.

Rethinking his previous judgment, he realized the day when Ms. Chatterjee said "no thank you" wasn't the worst day of his life. Not by a long shot. That prize belonged to the day when he'd last spoken with his only son, the day when his two daughters turned their backs on him and never acknowledged him again. Schuyler realized the lump in his throat had never gone away. It was still there.

He forced himself to reread what he'd written, then deemed it satisfactory. It included most of what he wanted to get out of his gut. He could add to it later, couldn't he, in another entry? His heart and mind were in turmoil, contesting each other in a tug-of-war as if there could be only one winner in that confrontation. But, why couldn't they both win? Heart and mind could pull together, instead of struggling at opposite ends of the rope. Or, in this case, his heart strings.

Hallelujah. The light dawns.

The whole point, as Schuyler saw it, was that he'd written down his feelings. When, before today, had he ever admitted to having feelings? His callous tough guy persona had taken shape so long ago, it might have hardened as early as when he exited his cradle.

His father. When had he not had to deal with his moody father's frame of mind? When Daniel Schuyler was at home, there was a constant need to gauge "the Atmosphere." Would rage be the order of the day? His boyhood safety depended on being wary and alert, yet safety sometimes meant taking the punishment meted out to him, because things could get worse.

"Taking the patriarchal temperature" was young Schuyler's only defense against the barrage of verbal abuse aimed at himself or Clementine. He must always be prepared for "worse," and ready to find a place to hide.

In his very early years Schuyler's father shut him in a closet as punishment. This was a frequent occurrence since Daniel felt so many offenses deserved punishment. There came a time when young Aaron sought refuge in the closet because its darkness was no longer frightening. It was safe. Dependable. As the years passed, however, he discovered the best hiding place was deep inside himself. This was what he once, in youthful confidence to Uncle Harry, termed his "Shield of Steel."

"You are, indeed, a warrior, my boy." Harry gave Aaron a copy of *Shambala: The Sacred Way of the Warrior.* "This book," said Harry, "is a trustworthy path to warriorhood."

Harry's lips had smiled, but his nephew had a difficult time interpreting the mix of emotions he read in his uncle's eyes.

Yes, today's diary entry was satisfying. Well done. Written in his own hand was an admission of love and loss. He owned to have broken many hearts, those of his entire family. He owned to his own broken heart. The misery and frustration he'd be living with due to his unrequited love for Ms. Chatterjee was a cruel sentence of undetermined length, yet the loss of his children was forever.

The more meditative aspect of his nature, as nurtured by Harry Neville, acknowledged how the river of life flows onward, and that its course over rocky shoals might change. That was a rational statement, wasn't it? Things might get better.

In an effort to be rational, Schuyler labeled himself "a late bloomer." He was just now understanding some of the facts of life that most people knew by the time they were twelve. Given that premise, then, wasn't it also rational to accept that some lessons, at least for him, were meant to be learned later in life? Eventually his heart would mend. At some elusive future point in time, he might even fall in love again.

That statement seemed the very antithesis of rationality.

CHAPTER 17

Hugh and Harry

After parting ways with Schuyler, Hugh Leigh left the Santa Fe County impound park, prey to many thoughts and emotions. Foremost among these was the heartache of loss and sorrow. Foremost among these would always be the heartache of loss and sorrow. But, lagging not far behind was his admitted surprise that Aaron Schuyler's expression of gratitude was sincere. Although unexpected, this apparent change in Schuyler's demeanor was most welcome. Leigh saw none of the surly, blasé I-know-all-the-tricks-in-the-book attitude he'd found so distasteful at his initial meeting with Harry's nephew.

In accordance with his and Harry's agreement, he had not attended his partner's interment and funeral wake. Their very private last goodbye was shared two days prior to Harry's passing, in Harry's ninth-floor hospital room in New York. Hugh had made no attempt to disguise his distress.

Harry, his own eyes brimming with tears, understood Hugh's sobbing breakdown. His grief at this final parting was monumental, not because he was leaving this earthly realm—there were unknown realms to explore—but because cancer was wrenching him away from the man who was, in every sense of the word, his soul mate. His other half in a loving partnership that spanned the decades. Forty-six years. Now, Hugh would be alone.

"You've moved out of the Nambé house?" groaned Harry, his pain-wracked body laden with plastic tubes and lines.

"Yes," Hugh replied in a low voice, "I moved what I wanted to keep to Los Alamos, gave quite a bit of furniture to Lone Goose, and left a few things in the Nambé house."

"If you have any difficulties with Aaron, but I don't imagine you will, just contact Clementine—" Harry's laugh ended with a choking cough. "She'll take care of everything. I have no doubt she and Winston will straighten him out. Claim victory, in the end. Even as we speak, Aaron is driving my old Toyota pickup back to New Mexico. Clementine wanted to keep the truck in the family. Hah! Right about now he should be crossing into Kansas."

"You're more optimistic than me. I don't know if I can deal with Aaron." Hugh gripped his temples. In sympathy with Harry, his whole body ached. "He's caused you and Clementine nothing but trouble."

"True enough," Harry gasped, trying to grin. "Dealing with Aaron was always a daunting prospect.

"He's over fifty—" Harry wheezed with the effort.

"Stop. You don't have to talk." To Hugh, Harry's whisper was noticeably weaker.

"Please—I must. Aaron—in many ways he's worse than a self-centered child. Grasping and selfish. Yet, there's an innocence about him, Hugh—if you can get past his tough guy act. When he clearly sees the right thing to do, he—does it. Sad to say, those times are rare. His vision is clouded by—always putting his own interests first."

As Harry paused, Hugh's thoughts drifted back to the strong and virile man he had met in their youth. That seemed so very long ago. Another lifetime, really, for it couldn't have been the two of them, now aged and frail, who had loved each other with such nonstop exuberant passion.

Harry Neville and Hugh Leigh first met at Yale in 1971, when Harry was twenty-nine years old and Hugh was twenty-six. Harry was completing a doctorate in comparative religions, and he was well-housed in a spacious apartment. Hugh had recently submitted his doctoral thesis in analytical chemistry to his review committee. He lived in university-underwritten accommodations and worked on-call shifts at McDonald's to make ends meet.

While he was waiting to defend his thesis, Hugh spent his free time pursuing his avocation, Buddhist studies. That was how, one night, he encountered Harry Neville in the Philosophy

Department's library. Their attraction was immediate. Hugh was fascinated by Harry's precise British accent, and Harry poked fun at Hugh's broad Alabaman vowels.

They first slept together two days later, after several hours at the library spent delving into the origins of Jain festival customs. "Slept together" didn't exactly describe a night that provided no sleep for either of them, but did include the stimulus of sex and endless rounds of discussion concerning the future of Buddhism in Tibet under Chinese occupation.

Now, in the hospital room that contained the last earthly objects he would ever contemplate, Harry reached toward Hugh. Hugh gently caressed his beloved partner's hand.

"Clementine has high hopes for the New Mexico experiment." A wave of pain, all too evident in his contorted expression, assaulted Harry. "Do—do what you can, my dear, if you feel you can stomach his company. That's all I ask. You can do no more."

"I haven't seen Aaron since 1974. His tenth birthday party," Hugh mused, as he removed the oxygen tubes from Harry's nostrils, wiped his nose, and helped him sip water through a straw. He then refitted the tubing. "He won't remember me, so it'll be a fresh start. I give you my solemn promise to do my best by him, although I have no idea what that might be."

"Neither do I," whispered Harry. "Aaron's history is—unfortunate. His father was mentally ill, never cognizant of how abusive he was. To this day Aaron has no idea how much my sister, Clementine, endured for his sake. Daniel's death—was no loss—to anyone."

"Families," mumbled Hugh, recalling the trials of his own boyhood. No picnic, that, with the untimely deaths of so many relatives. "They can be a real tragedy."

"I couldn't provide the home life he needed, but I tried to give him stability and example, even through his college days." Harry shook his head. "It just—wasn't enough."

"You did wonders, Harry." Hugh smoothed out the wrinkles on the back of his partner's gnarled hand. "Don't ever doubt it. I remember how much time you spent with Aaron. Camping trips. Foreign travel. If I'm skeptical about Clementine's current scheme to reform him, that only concerns my part in the plan. How much support I can actually give her. You know what a loner I am. Happiest with you, in my lab, or reading a book. I don't enjoy being with many people."

"One breath at a time." Harry pressed Hugh's hand. "That is— enough. *Always*. And only one step at a time."

With the greatest reluctance and heaviest of hearts, Hugh choked out a goodbye. His beloved partner was so fragile he was afraid any embrace at all might be painful. He kissed Harry on the forehead, kissed his hand, and took an elevator down to the main entrance. With his tear-filled eyes nearly swollen shut, his shoulders slumped, and his head bowed, he failed to see Clementine enter another elevator and press a button for the ninth floor.

Preoccupied as she was with disguising her own sorrow from strangers and presenting a cheery face to Harry, she in turn failed to see Hugh depart the building.

CHAPTER 18

Performance Review

The following day, Sunday, Schuyler's sleep was shattered by someone banging on the back door. He shuffled barefoot down the hallway in the gloom of early morning, wondering what time it was. Tom Jannssen was standing outside.

"Let me in, man. Did you forget?" Jannssen had suggested they drive to Taos for a weekend festival today, July the 1st.

"I did forget. Sorry. Tell me again why we're leaving so early?" groused Schuyler. He had promised to be ready to leave at 5:30 a.m.

"We're taking the High Road. It's a longer route but much less traffic. Awesome scenery. We want to drive while it's cool. Don't be a wuss. Where's your spirit of adventure?"

"It's still in bed and I haven't had breakfast."

"We'll get some food up at the Pueblo. I've got a thermos of coffee." Jannssen leaned down to rub Bella's swollen belly. "She's gonna drop these pups any day now."

"Yeah, and what am I going to do with puppies?" Schuyler yelled from the bedroom as he pulled on jeans and a T-shirt. "It's your fault. You knew she was pregnant when you brought her over here."

"Don't worry about the pups. Just put up a sign at the Mockingbird, or at Sam's Club. You'll have plenty of takers."

"But how do I deliver pups? What am I supposed to do?"

"Bella will take care of everything. Make her a nice nest with blankets. Keep her warm. She'll pretty much clean up the pups but you can wash them, and her, with some warm wash cloths. Feed her real good after she delivers. Be sure she has plenty of water."

To Schuyler's astonishment—he wasn't present for the births of his son and daughters—Bella had delivered a litter of three males and one female by the time he and Jannssen returned from the Taos jaunt. Without his help.

He'd never seen anything like the soft-skinned puppies, who were most often piled in a heap of legs, ears, and tails. Their ravenous lust to nurse was fascinating, as was Bella's long-suffering patience. He sat on the floor next to her, hand-fed her, and wrapped the pups in a fleece blanket whenever she went outside to pee. Honest to God, he couldn't remember the last time he'd had so much fun. He wished Clementine was here to see Bella and her brood.

The third week of August brought a hint of sharpness to the air, foretelling the arrival of Autumn in the high desert. On Jannssen's advice, Schuyler warmed up the old truck daily before driving down to Santa Fe. Sometimes after work he sat in the gathering dusk, repeating the same process of warming up the truck. On many an evening as he waited in the associates' section of the parking lot, he watched Anita Chatterjee walk to her bespoke parking spot, unlock her Prius, then head for home. She never knew he was watching, and he never considered this stalking. It fell into the same category as his confirmed habit of sitting at the table farthest from the executives' table during morning staff meetings, so he could stare at her from that vantage point.

Schuyler lived those fleeting days in something like a daze. The four pups were now more than six weeks old, weaned, and busy peeing on a kitchen floor littered with newspapers. They were getting better about letting him know when they needed to go outside, however, and all five dogs spent the day in the apple orchard while he was at work. Schuyler wasn't in any rush to put up a "Free Puppies" notice at the Mockingbird.

"You need to advertise," urged Jannssen, who came by to see Bella's brood. "It's easier to get rid of them while they're this cute. They're weaned, so they're ready to go."

"It seems wrong to separate them from Bella," muttered Schuyler.

"What are you going to do? Feed five dogs?" Jannssen smoothed the plaits of his long braid. "If you can't unload them, I'll take one of the males off your hands."

"I'll think about it," was Schuyler's noncommittal reply.

He had more urgent matters on his mind. Yesterday, Friday, August 25th, he found a note from Janice Garcia in his associate's mailbox. Written on an official-looking "Sam's Club" memo the note advised him:

> *Your Associate's review will take place on September 7th. This change in scheduling was necessary since the director of Human Resources will attend a conference during the week when your review was originally scheduled. Human Resources apologizes for any inconvenience this may have caused you. Please report to Ms. Chatterjee's office at 9:30 a.m. on the date indicated.*

Oh, no. His interview was only two weeks away. Schuyler broke into a cold sweat. A million thoughts coursed through his brain, not least of which was whether his ill-timed invitation to Anita Chatterjee might affect the review.

Chatterjee was pleasant enough when they encountered each other at work, and he greeted her in a respectful but impersonal manner, doing his best to avoid eye contact. She always smiled and responded in kind with a brisk businesslike comment. At times Schuyler thought she lingered, for a mere second at best, before walking on. You could read just about anything into that. You could pretend she wanted to say more than hello. He was tempted to encourage her with a bit of shop talk. Say something about the loading dock or the leveler/stacker.

Forget it, man. How many times do you plan to make an ass of yourself?

But—if I could hold her interest for a moment. Let her get to know me—

Don't stumble down that path again. Don't repeat your subpar performance.

Smarten up. Be thankful if you get a good review. Then, you can keep staring at her at staff meetings.

September 7th arrived all too soon, and Schuyler dressed with more than his usual meticulous care. He read a section from *Shambhala: The Sacred Path of the Warrior*, while he breakfasted. His reverence for Choegyam Trungpa's Tibetan Buddhist teachings was one of his most gratifying legacies from Harry Neville.

"Authentic presence is the result of a gradual, developmental process of letting go of ego fixation." It was time to go to work and take one more step toward letting go of his friggin' ego fixation. Make that plural. *Fixations.* Time to take one more step toward enlightenment. Toward Jesus. Winston. *Whoever.* Was enlightenment always this painful?

After dishing up a vast amount of puppy chow and patting Bella on the head, he drove into Santa Fe, manipulating the hectic traffic on Cerrillos Road with what he hoped would pass for tolerance and not road rage. He spent the lengthy minutes on the dock prior to his review in something more resembling a daze than a state of meditation. His three workmates gave him his space and said very little until it was time for him to report to HR.

"Good luck, senior citizen." Mike spoke for the group. "You can fill us in at lunch."

Schuyler's walk through the Club sales floor and up the stairs to Human Resources seemed endless. He was sure every associate wearing a Sam's Club vest like his own knew it was his review date and was betting on his chances of permanent hire. Or, not.

"Welcome, Mr. Schuyler." Janice Garcia's bright smile greeted him. "You can go on in now. Ms. Chatterjee is ready for you."

I'll bet she is.

Schuyler had a hard time swallowing. As he opened the door to Chatterjee's office, it dawned on him, as it never had before, how much he enjoyed his shitty job at Sam's Club. It would be hard to say goodbye.

"Hello, Mr. Schuyler. Please have a seat and make yourself comfortable. This won't take long." Again, to his ear, Chatterjee's melodious singsong tones more resembled the delicate sound of doves cooing than a human voice.

"Good morning, Ms. Chatterjee." Schuyler's throat felt dry, his knees weak. This interview would be agony. He was lost. *Save me, Winston. Save me, if you're up there watching.*

Chatterjee's smile remained bright as her victim lowered himself into a chair on the other side of her desk. "Here is your copy of the points we will discuss today. This is the standard review administered annually to employees of Sam's Club. As you can see, I have rated your performance as either 'very good' or 'excellent' in all categories, but two."

Very good or excellent.

His expression vacant, Schuyler watched her head list gently from side to side.

"Administration is very firm in its policy that all associates, with no exceptions, park in associate-designated parking spots. You have violated this policy several times and parked in guest parking. Thus, I have been forced to mark 'fails to meet expectations' for the section entitled 'Comprehension of Company Policies' and I will need your initials here." With a pencil, she indicated the appropriate line.

"Thank you." She smiled brightly, as Schuyler affixed his initials to the appropriate box with his own pen.

"I am sure we'll see an improvement in that category. The second area where I hope to see a change is in your understanding of 'Break Time Parameters' in chapter three of the associates' handbook. Mike Three Rivers sets high standards for his crew, and I applaud his enthusiasm. However, it is mandatory that *all* associates take breaks in accordance with State of New Mexico regulations for the workplace. Mike is negligent in this area. I have discussed with him the necessity of enforcing break times."

Ms. Chatterjee paused, searching Schuyler's face, which was, in truth, a total blank.

"Is this clear, Mr. Schuyler? Do you understand that you must take two breaks each work day, besides your lunch hour?"

"Yes, ma'am."

"Loading and unloading the trucks is very important, but this duty is second to ensuring that the dock crew takes their required breaks. No exceptions. We honor break time."

Schuyler's tension drained away. His habit of cynicism surged to the fore, but was ruthlessly subdued. *Was she kidding?* He was parking in the wrong section of the lot and he wasn't taking enough work breaks. Were these the only issues?

"Please affix your initials here. Well done. Now, also sign and date on this line. Mrs. Garcia will place a copy of this signed original in your associate's mailbox."

After Schuyler signed, Chatterjee again paused. Her mouth opened as if she had something further to say.

"Is—is that all?" interrupted Schuyler, hesitating, unsure if he should leave her office.

"Well, I suppose—" she hesitated. "Do you have any questions about your work status, Mr. Schuyler?"

"Uh—do I have a work status? Am I a permanent employee?"

"Ah, most definitely." Her smile was angelic. Heavenly. "Mike Three Rivers is happy with your performance. You fit in well with his crew, although I am led to believe you put up with an excess of hazing."

"Uh, no." Schuyler's head shake was vigorous. Firm. "I don't think so. Not really." What had she heard? Did Chatterjee know they tormented him all day long about being a lovesick sap?

"It's just guy stuff."

"Well, the Club is happy to have you as an associate." Another lengthy pause suggested Ms. Chatterjee might have more to say.

"I guess—I should get back to the dock." Schuyler gestured toward the door and started to rise from his chair, but Ms. Chatterjee raised a hand to forestall him.

"Oh, please! One moment, Mr. Schuyler—" Chatterjee began in a rush. "Please, one more thing." She cleared her throat. "If you are free on Sunday, my mother has invited you to dinner at our home. She would very much like to have you join us."

"Your mother?" Schuyler fell back into his chair. "Dinner? Would I be rude if—um. I, uh, don't understand."

"Mother at once took a liking to you when we met you in Walmart a few months ago. She has ever since been wanting to prepare some curries for you."

"Oh. I am so sorry." Schuyler had never uttered a more truthful statement. There he was, elevated for a brief second into nirvana, then at once dropped headfirst, back to earth. *Kerplunk.* "I don't tolerate curry well. In fact, I don't like curries and wouldn't want to offend your mother." He blanched at the prospect of puking all over Mrs. Chatterjee's carpet with his first whiff of turmeric. Cardamom. *Whatever.* "I don't see how—"

"Do not worry, Mr. Schuyler," Ms. Chatterjee soothed. "I understand. Many people feel as you do, but I assure you there are many ways to remedy the difficulty. Mother and I will put our heads together and work out a menu. The two of us will prepare an Indian meal in a satisfactory way to suit your tastes!"

Her smile, not to mention her enthusiasm, was so contagious Schuyler could do nothing but nod his acceptance, hope for the best, and write down the family's street address. The Chatterjees lived in south Santa Fe, not far from Sam's Club.

He bowed himself out the door, wondering if he'd even said goodbye. Had he shaken Ms. Chatterjee's hand? Had he thanked her?

Although highly doubtful the dinner would be palatable, Schuyler was euphoric. Bowled over, in fact. He needed time to think. He needed to take his lunch break *now*—9:45 a.m. There wasn't even time to ask Mike's permission. The dock could wait. How had his fortunes changed from the depths of despair to the heights of euphoria within the span of fifteen minutes?

Holy shit. Was this Winston's doing?

⌒

Leaving Sam's Club, Schuyler drove to McDonald's.

"Let's see—I'll have one large fries, two Big Macs, and a chocolate shake. *Yes*—large. Also, two chocolate chip cookies."

He sat in the truck devouring his order while he pondered the unexpected outcome of the past quarter hour in Chatterjee's office.

"Who the hell cares if, on occasion, an associate might park his truck in guest parking?" he muttered to himself. By any standard of evaluation, his demerits were ridiculous. "The only time that lot has been full was during the Fourth of July shopping rush." And to chide someone in writing for failing to take work breaks? Unheard of.

"What corporation is going to censure an employee for being a gung-ho eager beaver?"

What a pile of crap.

"She must have been looking for points to pick on. Minor points, at that." To Chatterjee's way of thinking, he concluded, it mustn't look like she was playing favorites or being too lenient with him. That must mean, therefore, his work performance was close to perfect. Thank you, Mike Three-Rivers!

What would happen next? Was she required, according to the pact with Clementine, to report the evaluation to his mother? *Probable, if not mandatory.*

Did Clementine already know he'd been invited to dine with the Chatterjees? *Maybe—maybe not.* As Schuyler became more familiar with the intricacies of his mother's far-reaching plot—indeed, a spider's web of intrigue—he began to view himself as a hapless beetle trapped beyond hope of escape in those sticky filaments. Just how far did Clementine's reach extend?

"Who cares? Wise up, you cretin," he self-admonished. "You're on a steep learning curve. Be honest, just this once. Have you really suffered from Clementine's machinations?"

Not much.

"Think about it. The only negatives you've endured since moving to New Mexico are those of your own making. They're nothing, compared to all the positives."

The Santa Fe Opera season, just ended, had given him a good culture fix. He was now crazy about the soulful desert scenery he'd first dismissed as a sandy replication of Dante's *Inferno*. He only missed New York when he craved a pumpernickel bagel or a dog with the works.

"And not even that much. Carne adovada is better. Really."

His perspective had traveled more than mere miles. He'd come to appreciate the quiet of his Nambé home, and the spacious quality of his lifestyle compared with its previous hectic East Coast pace. He had a dog and four puppies, although that was a somewhat dubious benefit. He'd made new friends. Tom Jannssen, Mike, Ernie, and Jesús weren't in the same class as his previous cronies, but that difference was all to the good as he saw it. Wherever his victim stance had gone, he wished it good riddance.

"I'm a really lucky guy." His perspective had traveled far, but the change in his circumstances was, perhaps, not so radical as what he had, at first, raged against.

In New Mexico, like New York, he never knew what was coming at him next. *True.* The difference between life in New York City and life in New Mexico couldn't have been more extreme. *Also true.* Conversely, though, the two were very much alike. In both places, there was no such thing as black and white. It was all shades of gray. *Yeah.*

His baptism as a New Mexican had been a rough one. He could almost say the dunking had threatened to drown him and left him gasping for air, if it wasn't for the fact that there was hardly enough water in this friggin' state to drown a rat.

In New Mexico you held on for dear life and you didn't let go because you wanted to be here. If you needed a safety net, it would have to be one of your own making. Reaching out to new friends, for instance. Conjuring up changes in yourself. *Deep changes.* Being willing to adapt to and be assimilated by an almost foreign culture. Say—preferring a taco to a pastrami sandwich.

And then there was the awesomeness of the landscape itself, ensnaring you with its freaky beauty. Grabbing you. Sucking you in. Owning you. And nothing, no matter how bad it got, was going to make you give up.

It had taken a while but, yeah, now Schuyler understood his trial by fire.

You either "get" New Mexico, or you get out.

As incredible as it seemed, he was going to dine with Anita Chatterjee and her family. She had turned his world upside down once before, and now she was doing it again. He could stare at her across the less unbridgeable gap of a dining room table. Who would have thought? He almost wanted to thank Winston again, but Clementine's weird and wacky world was not for him.

Get a grip, man.

He burped. Twice. This was followed by a hint of intestinal gurgling. God almighty, would his massive fast food lunch bring on a bout of IBS? It was time to get back to work.

CHAPTER 19

Ms. Chatterjee's Dilemma

Anita Chatterjee's own odyssey of self-discovery was no less fraught with chance and mishap than Schuyler's. Her life in Kolkata, India, where she was born, had more than its share of wrinkles. At the age of sixteen, Anita was married to Raju Mukherjee, her senior by fifteen years. This was a not an uncommon arrangement.

Raju was a kind man, an engineer with the Indian army, and often away from home working on projects throughout the country. Just where, or when, he contracted dysentery was unknown. Pressed for time in a stressful job, he managed what he termed "an annoyance" as best he could but delayed in consulting a doctor. His dehydration soon became debilitating. The symptoms, too long neglected, were at last so severe Raju could not recover.

Anita had been living with her husband's mother and father for three years. Now widowed at the age of nineteen she returned to her family home and resumed life there, her parents' only child. After a suitable period of mourning, her mother pressed her to consider a second marriage.

"I am done with marriage," was Anita's firm response. "I want an education. I am going away from India to university. England. Australia. The United States."

Her parents, although well able to pay any educational expenses, were distraught. Even before her marriage, Anita's unconventional behavior was often embarrassing. She was a headstrong teenager who read too many books. She stood out in a crowd, and not just because of her beauty. To the dismay of extended family members, she had decided opinions. Strong opinions. Her entire family sighed with relief when the knot was tied and she married Raju.

But, now, Anita was a widow. Yuthi, her mother, and Uttam, her father understood their daughter's reasons for wanting to leave India and start a new life. After all, she was barely out of her teens, almost a child, and the customary husbandless and childless years that lay before her if she did not remarry were a sad and daunting prospect. A life wasted.

"Take care in deciding." Uttam presented her with a stern, unvarnished picture of reality. It was his duty as a father to reason with her. "In our community, daughter, the bold step of a young widow traveling abroad to pursue university education is rare. Many would consider it unacceptable." He paced the floor, cigarette dangling from his lips, agitated by his own argument. "Why the United States? Come, now. Kolkata is your home, Anita. *Our* home as a family."

"Please don't worry about me, Bapu," she replied, determined but respectful.

"Don't make a decision you might regret, based on a girlish whim," Uttam pleaded. "You will still be a widow when you return."

"A foreign-educated widow," her mother, Yuthi, wept. "No better than an outcast."

"Mataji, I have thought about all of that," Anita rebutted. "The prospect for any widow in India is a bleak one. And that is why I will not return to India."

Anita's firm stance met with shocked remonstrations, but by the time she announced her acceptance at Questrom School of Business, an adjunct of Boston University, both parents were resigned if not pleased. The USA. Eight thousand miles away. How dull and lonely life would be without their only child!

As it turned out, after escorting Anita to school at the start of her freshman year, and after several pleasant visits to Boston during Anita's first two years of school, they decided her choice suited the whole family. They would begin this adventure in the

United States with her, again a reunited family—the only draw-back being the bitter New England winters.

Mr. and Mrs. Chatterjee immigrated to the States, having agreed with Anita that Boston might not remain their perma-nent home. It was a wait-and-see game, dependent upon where Anita's profession might lead her. The first management position she accepted after earning her master's degree was with Sam's Club in Brookline, Massachusetts. The Chatterjee family ended up spending ten frigid winters there and lauded the virtues of thermal underwear. Then, ready for a change, having succumbed to the All-American fantasy of "heading out west," Anita accepted a similar position in Austin, Texas.

Yuthi and Uttam, grateful for the warmer climate, again set up house. Southwest Fever hit the whole family. Her father now wore cowboy boots and a felt Stetson hat with a turquoise hatband. Often, with his traditional Indian kurta. Yuthi wore a T-shirt beneath her sari, instead of a traditional sari blouse. While vacationing in New Mexico one summer, all three fell in love with its stark desert scenery. When a transfer to Sam's Club in Santa Fe became available, Anita snapped it up.

"Well, daughter," Mrs. Chatterjee stated, about six months after they settled in Santa Fe, "you may choose to move on again, but your father and I are happy here. Very happy. So if you do transfer elsewhere, we will not be going with you. We are staying put."

"No big deal," Anita reassured her. "I am staying put with you. This is a beautiful place. I love it, and I am happy."

Anita meant what she said. Her career in Human Resources was stimulating. She made friends with other single women in Santa Fe and now took golf lessons on Saturday mornings. The stifling customs of India were behind her. She was content with life.

Content? *Perhaps.* But not quite as happy as she led her mother to believe. The years were passing ever so fast, and Anita wanted a husband. Or even a boyfriend. Yet, how would her parents react to the thought of her being alone on a date? Unthinkable. Alone with a man, without them as chaperones? Impossible.

Anita was now more American than Indian, as far as acculturation was concerned. She was forty-two years old and dissatisfied with the thought of living the rest of her life with her parents. Her new friends seemed confused when she excused her apparent lack of interest in dating by saying she must look after Yuthi and Uttam. Spend time with them. Care for them. With reluctance, they accepted her explanation that America was still foreign to her parents. After all, she was their only child—blah, blah, blah.

All of this was a cover-up for what she knew was a chicken-hearted fear of leveling with her parents and letting them know she wanted to date. After all, it wasn't as if those two were ill-adjusted. They voted. They volunteered at the animal shelter. They enjoyed a movie matinee every Wednesday afternoon. Nor were they decrepit. These two sturdy sixty-two-year-olds walked three miles every day at a healthy pace.

Thus, the serendipity of Anita and Mrs. Chatterjee encountering Aaron Schuyler at Walmart on a Saturday morning in April was the most fortuitous chance imaginable.

The three Chatterjees were already familiar with Schuyler by reputation. They had been close friends with Harry Neville and Hugh Leigh for as long as they had lived in Santa Fe, having met the pair at the Santa Fe Opera. A few years later they also met Harry's sister, Clementine, when she traveled to Santa Fe to attend the opera with Harry and Hugh. The Chatterjees warmed to her at once, introduced her to Anita, and welcomed her into their family. They readily sympathized when she disclosed her fate as the mother of a no-good worthless son.

When Mrs. Yuthi Chatterjee met Schuyler that Tuesday morning at Walmart, while shopping with her daughter Anita, she was quite impressed with Schuyler's good looks. "Oh, what a handsome man," she thought to herself. Handsome enough that it was perhaps worth overlooking his unfortunate reputation. A little skepticism might prove beneficial. Mr. Schuyler was several years older than her daughter. This was not a bad thing, according to the ethic of her generation. Didn't a woman need a man with experience in life's byways to guide her? Especially in the United States with its loose interpretation of sexual mores.

Mrs. Chatterjee failed to reason that Aaron Schuyler, with his unfortunate reputation, might be an unsuitable guide in those byways. She said very little during that chance meeting in Walmart, but she observed much. The unspoken but unmistakable signals of attraction passing back and forth between this man and her daughter did not escape her notice. These told her more than words could convey. The sparkle in her daughter's eye when she smiled up at Mr. Schuyler was a welcome sight. It warmed her heart because Anita had not glowed in *that* particular way for far too many years.

But—what was this?

Mr. Schuyler seemed respectful and interested in Anita, yet Mrs. Chatterjee detected hesitation and confusion in his eye. *Hmmm.* The reason was obvious to her. This man wished to say more to her daughter—was unsure of just what to say, or how to say it since Anita was his superior at work—and certainly would say nothing at all in front of herself, Anita's mother.

Oh, yes. This was an altogether auspicious beginning.

An auspicious beginning, yes, perhaps it was. But the whole truth was unknown to Mrs. Chatterjee.

⌒

Anita Chatterjee had been attracted to Aaron Schuyler long before the day when he presented himself in her office for a job interview. Having once met him that morning she reflected for quite some time on the course of events leading up to his interview. She recalled her initial conversation with Clementine Atwater, whom she'd known as a family friend for several years.

"Why, yes, of course I remember you. It's good to hear from you, Mrs. Atwater." Anita was puzzled, caught off her guard when she received a phone call from Akron, Ohio. "It's just that I wasn't expecting to hear from you here at work."

"Anita dear, the fact that you are at work is the main reason why I chose to phone you at this time of day." Clementine's fault-less British accent forged ahead. "I have a proposal to make to you and Sam's Club, but, first, tell me how your dear parents are doing."

"Quite well, Mrs. Atwater, and let me on their behalf congratu-late you on your recent marriage. We all look forward to meeting Mr. Atwater."

"Well, let's see what we might do to bring about a visit." Having settled that, Clementine proceeded to unfold her plan of employ-ment for Schuyler, explaining at length, and in great detail, why Ms. Chatterjee must overlook her son's deficits of character. Why she must hire him despite his shabby reputation and shiftless attitude toward work.

Anita was at a loss for words. She was doubtful an employee such as Aaron Schuyler would ever become a corporate asset, and leery of how a determined no-gooder might compromise the Club's reputation.

"Well, let me see what I can do, Mrs. Atwater. I will present your suggestion to our Club manager, Alice Cordova, and just let her know a longtime friend of my family has requested a favor. We'll see what she has to say."

For nearly eight years now, Clementine had been telling tales about Schuyler's misdeeds. These were nothing new to Chatterjee, her mother, Yuthi, or her father, Uttam. And, in the interest of being impartial it happened that, as she listened to Clementine's impassioned plea, Ms. Chatterjee became more intrigued by Schuyler's imagined person and his history than concerned about whether he would be an appropriate hire for Sam's Club.

Who didn't love a "bad boy"? Weren't bad boys often the heroes of Hindi movies? These heroes always fell in love, often at first sight, with righteous Hindi women and forsook their naughty errant ways. *Forever.*

There was more than a streak of "repressed romantic" in Ms. Chatterjee.

As she came to see it, misunderstood people were often those most in need of a second chance. After all, wasn't there a little bit of good in the worst of us? She was willing to provide *this* misunderstood man with as many chances as he needed to prove that true.

And since the generous Mrs. Atwater was offering a huge donation to one of Walmart Corporation's favorite charities, what was there left to say? In her mind, that clinched the deal.

Ms. Chatterjee met with the Club's manager, Alice Cordova, and explained the bizarre request she'd received, omitting the numerous negatives about Mr. Schuyler to which she was privy. A generous sum would be donated to Miracle Network's Save the Children, in the name of the Santa Fe Sam's Club. "Oh, that will look very good to Corporate!" All they need do was hire a man who was somewhat of a reprobate and, if he didn't work out, they were free to fire him. How could they lose?

Of course, the agreement must be made with Mrs. Atwater's understanding that certain restrictions would apply. Her son must abide, to the letter, by Sam's Club associate requirements. There could be no compromise on this point.

Clementine's obtrusive request became a done deal. And if Anita Chatterjee was at first mildly attracted to Schuyler by his reputation, she soon after became enamored of the image she embroidered in her mind. She had fabricated an elaborate history for the two of them, including sexual encounters, long before he presented himself in her office for an interview.

To her credit, she had the good sense to laugh at her own silliness. *What?* At her age was she starting to act like a teenager? Revving up her hormones to no purpose at all?

Clementine's description of her son was so vague—"Well, Aaron is tall, and graying a bit around the temples. He has the Neville nose—" that Anita felt free to fantasize: "I'm sure he'll be quite tall, well-built, with a muscular physique. A bit of steel highlights in his jet-black hair. His fiery eyes bore into the most secret depths of a woman's heart—"

Grow up, she chided herself. Prepare yourself for the worst sort of ravaged, dissipated, and world-weary countenance. A neglected body. Overweight. A paunch.

When a handsome middle-aged man wearing a proper shirt, tie, sport coat, and slacks introduced himself, she was more than pleased. If she was intrigued by Schuyler's lurid past, her interest was further piqued by meeting him in person.

His mother had not lied. He was tall. His hair was brown, not jet-black, gray and curling at the temples. He had a pleasing straight nose. And if he lacked the muscular development of her imaginary hero, at least he was not flabby. His eyes were a soft brown. Anything but fiery. His eyelashes were the longest she had ever seen. And when he smiled, his mouth moved in *such* a way. She could imagine its ability to kiss.

Oh, more than anything, Chatterjee wished her conversation with Schuyler during his ill-fated job interview had not veered toward the role his mother played in landing him a job. It was as painful to her to witness his embarrassment when Clementine's meddling was revealed, as it was for him to endure the shame of having his past laid out in all its ugliness before the woman who would be his new boss. What a cock-up.

Whoops. That just slipped out. She couldn't help herself.

Her delight when she met Schuyler the very next morning in the kitchenware aisle at Walmart, having received his acceptance of employment by phone earlier that morning, was genuine. This was too good an opportunity to let slip by. Mr. Schuyler's discomfort was obvious. The man was internally squirming. Since he must be wishing himself any place other than standing in front of her and her mother, she would be as open and gracious as possible, in the hope of lessening his discomfort and welcoming him to Sam's Club.

Chatterjee knew her mother Yuthi's mind, and how that mind worked. Its primary object was to see her daughter married again. Very well, something good might come of this unexpected meeting. Serendipity was a good thing. All she need do was wait for Yuthi to pick up the ball and carry it. So to speak. Both women were pleased.

From that moment forward Anita kept her eye on Schuyler. She was aware of his constant stare during staff meetings. His scrutiny almost put her to the blush. Uncomfortable, but not unpleasant. His frequent visits to her office on the slimmest pretext were both amusing and touching. She wanted to encourage him, but how did one begin? She had no idea. This was foreign, if not forbidden territory for her. Far from an arranged and chaperoned courtship. She was not only inexperienced in flirtation, but she was his boss. *Dammit.* There were lines one didn't cross.

Dammit again. Would she ever get a break?

When the maladroit Schuyler, again visiting her office, asked her for a date she panicked. If only her savvy golf partners had been present, to whisper in her ear. They would no doubt offer a coy smile, say yes, and encourage him to keep talking. Hang on his every word and let him believe he was fascinating. It was supposed to be that easy.

Not for her.

Chatterjee was tongue-tied, had no idea how to respond, and bungled her opportunity. She felt her cheeks reddening—my God, she felt hot. Thank God, he failed to notice. She fished up an excuse from addenda relating to "Guidelines for Appropriate Interaction with Non-Salaried Staff" in the *Sam's Club Executive Handbook*. She did this not because she gave a shit about Sam's Club regulations discouraging employee fraternization, but because she had absolutely no blueprint for handling such a situation.

Fortunately for Ms. Chatterjee, Yuthi was up to the mark even if her daughter wasn't.

∽

As the months passed by after the encounter in Walmart, Mrs. Chatterjee, in a manner she assumed was both subtle and disinterested, often asked her daughter how "*Dear* Mr. Schuyler" was doing at his job. She was taken aback when Anita spat out abrupt answers designed to curtail further questioning. Her responses to her mother were so uncivil, so at odds with what Mrs. Chatterjee had observed between the two at Walmart, she could hardly believe her own ears.

After receiving this same rude retort several times, Yuthi realized it was time to point out to Anita in no uncertain terms what a good-looking, hardworking man Mr. Schuyler was. He had a college degree—a master's. Was that not so? Sam's Club was pleased with his job performance. Was that not so? His mother Clementine was worth a fortune. Was that not so?

"I do not know why you are always snapping at me like a turtle whenever I mention dear Mr. Schuyler's name! Biting your mother's head off." Mrs. Chatterjee slapped a dish towel against the bottom of a dinner plate. "You must make more of an effort, Anita. Make yourself agreeable to such an eligible man. He is welcome at our table any night of the week if you ever have the good sense to invite him!" With hands on her hips, she continued scolding.

"I'm sure I don't know what better fellow you expect to find!"

⌒

These same words of admonishment were ready to roll off Mrs. Chatterjee's tongue once again, when Anita surprised her mother by suggesting they invite Mr. Schuyler to join them for dinner on Sunday, September 10th.

Mrs. Chatterjee took a deep breath and congratulated herself on having bided her time. Sometimes it paid to bite one's tongue. She shrugged her shoulders, and with a straight face answered in an unenthusiastic, noncommittal tone.

"If that is what you would like to do, Daughter, then by all means invite the man."

The gods do work in strange ways.

CHAPTER 20

The Dinner

Schuyler went about his usual Saturday morning routine but, as the hours passed, he became more and more uneasy about the prospect of dining with Ms. Chatterjee's family the next day.

Yesterday, Friday morning, Chatterjee had slipped a note into his employee mailbox with a copy of his performance review bearing her official signature. "Dinner will be at five p.m. on Sunday but come earlier if you like. I gave you our address but forgot to include directions. Here they are."

Awesome. Schuyler had already discovered what a rabbit warren of *vias*, *avenidas*, and *calles* comprised the city map of Santa Fe, and he was grateful for the directions.

If he must be resigned to tolerating a noisome curry, while sustaining an expression of gusto and enjoyment, he would manage. Somehow. The goal was worth it. This venture required discipline and determination, and he'd been accumulating those virtues by the bucketload ever since moving to Santa Fe and starting work at Sam's Club.

These days he hardly recognized himself, so puritan pure was he. But, however hard he worked at reframing his culinary niceties, there was one stumbling block he couldn't overcome. His aversion to lamb, no matter how it was prepared, refused to give way. To avert disaster, he decided to visit Chatterjee's office and explain his disability. Once more, he tackled the steps to the Human Resources Office.

"Ms. Chatterjee is free," Janice Garcia informed him, giggling. "Please, go on in."

Chatterjee's door was open, but Schuyler hesitated and rapped on the frame before entering her office.

"Ah, Mr. Schuyler." Chatterjee looked up in some surprise. "How may I help you?"

"Might I sit down, Ms. Chatterjee? I'll only need a minute."

"Of course, of course." She gestured to a chair. "Please."

"Uh, I'm very gratified by your dinner invitation, Ms. Chatterjee, and I'm looking forward to meeting your family on Sunday," he began. "There is one thing, however, that I must mention. Uh, need to explain—"

"And, what is that?" Chatterjee raised a hand to her mouth on observing Schuyler's earnest expression.

Schuyler watched a cloud of concern descend upon her countenance. Had he spoken too hastily? "I'll manage a curry just fine," he reassured her, hoping his pending declaration of distaste wouldn't put the kibosh on her dinner plans. "But, I cannot tolerate lamb. Unfortunately I have these digestive issues. Well, that's neither here nor there, but I don't want to hurt your mother's feelings—"

"Oh, do not worry, Mr. Schuyler," interrupted Ms. Chatterjee, sagging with relief. "My parents are veg."

"*Vedge*?"

"Indeed, they are. Vegetarians." She laughed. "No meat will be served at dinner."

"Well." Schuyler echoed her laughter, and rose from his chair. "Then, that's that. Thank you for your time. I very much look forward to seeing you on Sunday."

As she nodded goodbye, he bowed himself out of her office, unable to interpret the many nuances her smile conveyed, completely oblivious to how she scrutinized his backside.

ᔐ

After feeding the dogs that Saturday, Schuyler bundled all of them into the truck. Bella's feelings were crushed if he drove off at any time without her, the only exception being when he left for work Monday through Friday. She seemed to understand the difference. On all other occasions, a dreadful whining commenced if he opened the pickup door and failed to invite her in. With the four pups now housebroken, he often took all five dogs with him.

Clementine's foresight in providing him with an extended-cab truck was commendable.

He was meeting Tom Jannssen for breakfast at the Mockingbird. After eating, they would pick up a bale of barbed wire at True Value Hardware and finish refencing Schuyler's apple orchard. The previous Saturday, they'd set the fence posts. This enclosure became necessary when the Garcia family's goats began breaking out of their pen and trampling the orchard's ancient coyote fencing.

Two weeks ago, Schuyler was sitting on the small court-yard's wall, watching the goats attack his apples. He should have listened to Hugh Leigh and begun harvesting a long time ago. The fact that goats were intelligent and often bored was news to him. Leaves, twigs, bird nests, wormy apples were all devoured. What they ate, didn't matter to them. They wanted all of it.

"You don't have to put up with this." Jannssen was paying his usual Saturday morning visit.

"What am I supposed to do? Let the dogs loose on them?"

"Might turn out bad for the dogs. I'll help you refence the orchard."

Schuyler hadn't thought of putting in a new fence. He wasn't yet an experienced country squire. The solution sounded good to him, and the fencing project was soon underway. Now, as he downed the Mockingbird special of scrambled eggs topped with carne adovada, he confessed his trepidation about the Sunday evening invitation.

"So, I'm having dinner tomorrow night with Anita Chatterjee's family," Schuyler opened with a sigh.

"Got your foot in the door, man. That's a start." Jannssen nodded. He was familiar with the tale of woe comprising Schuyler's disappointed courtship. "Know how to find their street?"

"Yeah. I checked it out last night. I didn't want to chance being late tomorrow."

"What are you taking as a hostess gift?"

"Hostess gift? *Shit.*" Schuyler looked like he'd swallowed the bale of wire. "I forgot all about that. What am I going to do? I don't have time to drive into Santa Fe and shop. I suppose I could do it tomorrow before going to the Chatterjees's."

"You might buy something at the Pojoaque drugstore. Perfume?"

"It's for her mother, man. Not for Chatterjee." Schuyler shook his head. "Perfume won't set the right tone. Too personal. Risky. Besides, I have no idea what scent to choose."

"Huh. I see your point," agreed Jannssen.

The table was silent as the men finished eating and signaled Ellen to bring their check.

"Here's an idea," Jannssen offered. "Why don't you give Mrs. Chatterjee a puppy?"

"A *dog* as a hostess gift? You're kidding. Right?"

"Why not? It isn't too personal," Jannssen argued. "It's kinda sweet. Warm and fuzzy."

"I'm not so sure." Schuyler was skeptical. "Still, who doesn't love a puppy?" In his mind he glossed over the fact that many people don't love puppies. "Yeah. Good idea. I'll give her the female. She's the smallest and much less rowdy." He left a big tip on the table, then shrugged his shoulders. "Let's go finish that fence."

∽

Schuyler was not quite easy about his choice of hostess gift, but preparing a basket with the basic resources Mrs. Chatterjee might need for puppy care relieved his qualms. After adjusting his tie for the third time and taming his graying temples—the gray hairs tended to curl in diverse directions—he donned his sport coat and gathered up the puppy supplies. A blanket, a dog bed, bowls for water and food, a rag doll toy, and a bag of puppy chow were stowed in the truck cab. The little female jumped onto the front seat.

As he backed out of the carport he heard Bella's mournful wail and wondered if he was being insensitive. Not to Mrs. Chatterjee, but to Bella. He was ripping a baby away from her mother and her brothers. The only family she knew.

The avenida he sought was located a few blocks from Rodeo Road, a major traffic artery in south Santa Fe. On the hour, at 5:00 p.m., he pulled up in front of the Chatterjee home, and parked behind another vehicle to which he paid little notice. Must belong to the family. Wrapping the puppy in the blanket, with only her head protruding, he walked through the courtyard gateway and knocked on the front door, which was opened at once.

Déjà vu.

The doorway was filled with smiling people. Must he relive the New York Chatterjee debacle all over again? Guess so. Ms. Chatterjee was wearing a knockout hot pink sari. Her mother wore a sari in shades of lime green and aqua. Schuyler assumed the older man cradling a cigarette in his hand and dressed in what looked like white cotton pajamas was Mr. Chatterjee. Another figure, obscured by the three gathered in the doorway, lurked in the background.

"Good evening." Schuyler smiled at Mrs. Chatterjee, whose mouth fell agape as she stared at the puppy. The lustrous color drained from her face and, emitting a gasp, she turned toward her daughter. Mr. Chatterjee was scowling. Schuyler was quick to read the signals. Maybe he wasn't putting his best foot forward. He might, in fact, have deliberately stepped into some really deep doo-doo. Maybe even put his head on the chopping block.

Whatever.

He needed to think beyond body parts and stop this hemorrhage of courtship opportunity, or his first chance might be his last. On impulse, he pivoted toward Ms. Chatterjee, the practiced smile never deserting him, and offered her the dog.

"My dog, Bella, became a mom about three months ago." His tone was suave, assured, his voice never quavered. "This little girl is the only female in the litter. I was wondering if you might like to give her a home."

His future happiness now lay in Ms. Chatterjee's hands. His fate rested upon whatever she decided was the proper response to his faux pas. Now desperate for salvation, he wondered if his first mistake was the heretic view that Winston Churchill was no true deity. If Winston didn't have his back, who did?

"How sweet!" gushed Ms. Chatterjee, ready to burst out laughing at his dilemma and his choice of a hostess gift, and quick to save the day as she reached for the puppy.

Schuyler, you friggin' idiot.

"Mr. Schuyler, how could you know I was so much wanting to have my very own dog?" With the puppy in her arms she hurried down a hallway, calling over her shoulder, "For now, let us put this little darling in the loo. Is she housebroken? What is her name?"

"She is housebroken, but I hadn't yet gotten around to naming her." Schuyler exhaled and his heart stopped pounding. Mr. and Mrs. Chatterjee moved aside to allow him entrance and, in so doing, unblocked his view of the figure standing behind them. *Hugh Leigh.* What the hell?

Leigh's gaze was fixed on the carpet, but Schuyler didn't miss the smirk he suppressed as he shook his head from side to side.

What the hell, indeed. How had he failed to recognize the ancient Jimmy? The very vehicle he had just parked behind.

"Nice to see you again." Biting his lip to suppress his hilarity, Leigh extended his hand.

"Likewise," Schuyler choked, reaching out with his own.

"Come in, do come in," cried Mrs. Chatterjee. Her tone was warm, although her face remained frozen in shock. "You are most welcome, Mr. Schuyler. Thank you for being so kind as to bring a gift for my daughter."

Hugh Leigh moved forward as the group separated and nudged Schuyler in the side.

"Take off your shoes," he whispered.

"What?" Schuyler spied the pairs of shoes lined up in a neat row just inside the front door. "Oh. Thanks," he whispered, sloughing off his loafers. "What are you doing here?"

"I was invited. Harry and I were old friends of the Chatterjees, you know."

"I didn't know." Schuyler nodded, inured to the far-reaching New York-New Mexico web of connections he'd been excluded from. Until now. "I should have expected as much."

Ms. Chatterjee had returned to the living room. "Oh, Mr. Schuyler, forgive my rudeness. I know you are acquainted with my mother and Mr. Leigh but, please, I would like to introduce you to my father, Uttam Chatterjee.

"Bapu"—she placed her arm around the older man's shoulders—"this is Mr. Aaron Schuyler. He works at Sam's Club on the loading dock."

"Welcome," Mr. Chatterjee's smile was a tight line. He shifted the cigarette from his right hand to his left and reached out to Schuyler with tobacco-stained fingers. His grip was strong, but not crushing. Schuyler chose to read this as encouraging rather than repellent. Mr. Chatterjee's dark skin only highlighted the intense sparkle in his coal-black eyes.

Those eyes pierced Schuyler to the core, much as had Hugh Leigh's eyes on their first meeting. He felt impelled, at once, to lay before "Bapu" the whole of his life's deeds and accept whatever judgment would be laid upon him, as long as he was allowed to court Ms. Chatterjee. He must, of course, be on his knees to do so.

"My daughter's friends are welcome in my home." The cigarette returned to Mr. Chatterjee's right hand. The piercing scrutiny abated to reveal amusement at this guest's discomfiture.

"Come," beckoned Mrs. Chatterjee from the dining room. "The dishes are hot and ready to be served. We don't want anything to overcook."

Only then did Schuyler appreciate the fragrance wafting from somewhere. The kitchen? The mix of aromas was mouthwatering. *This was curry?*

Leigh clapped a hand on his de facto nephew's shoulder and led him to the table.

"Hugh, you will sit on my right," directed Mrs. Chatterjee. "And Mr. Schuyler will sit on my left. Anita, please sit next to Mr. Schuyler."

Mr. Chatterjee sat down at the head of the table and lit another cigarette while his daughter filled his plate from various serving bowls. Schuyler noticed an ashtray placed nearby.

"We are informal tonight, Mr. Schuyler." Mrs. Chatterjee laughed. "I have served the appetizers along with the main course."

With the chance now to better observe her, Schuyler noticed what a handsome woman Mrs. Chatterjee was. Her skin was a flawless sheet of rosy tan. If she was a little plump, that was no flaw. He couldn't help wondering her age. Except for a streak of gray emerging from the peak of her forehead and ribboning over the side of her head, her hair was as dark as Ms. Chatterjee's.

"But, Yuthi." Hugh Leigh chuckled, addressing her by her given name. "We are also formal tonight. We usually dine sitting on the floor, and we eat with our fingers."

Although all four of his dinner partners laughed in appreciation, Schuyler failed to see the attraction of eating on the floor with one's fingers. At once, Mrs. Chatterjee commenced piling heaps of food onto his plate. He no sooner finished one item, before she replaced it with a second helping. As if a genie manipulated this abundance, his plate was never empty.

"Delicious!" he chimed in at intervals, as he worked his way through the dinner, asking the names of dishes whenever he wasn't chewing. Pappadums. Pakoras. Samosas. Eggplant. Potato with cauliflower. Spinach in cream sauce. Chutneys. Something called dal. Rice. Breads—chapati, poori, paratha. The list was endless. "Delicious!"

"Well, what a compliment to Mama's cooking," Ms. Chatterjee remarked more than once. "I can see your previous experience with Indian food and curries was all in restaurants. And not very good ones, at that!"

He nodded, his mouth full.

"You see, Mr. Schuyler," Mrs. Chatterjee confided, flattered by her guest's hearty appetite, "the secret to taste and flavor is in serving the dishes at once. If food lingers in the pot, there is a chance the whole will go off and turn rancid. I think this is what you encountered in New York restaurants. I don't trust those people. Home is always best."

Schuyler nodded again, although he remained a bit distracted. Throughout the meal, he had watched Mr. Chatterjee eating and smoking at the same time. He didn't want to stare, but his host's dexterity in so doing was worthy of admiration. Now, as Mrs. Chatterjee refreshed their tea and placed on the table a bowl of pistachio nuts, and a dish of what looked like squares of fudge rolled in coconut, Schuyler counted the butts in the ashtray. Six. That didn't include the cigarette hanging from Mr. Chatterjee's lips.

"You don't smoke, Mr. Leigh?" Schuyler felt the need to contribute to the conversation, and not just continue jamming food into his mouth.

"No, I never formed that nasty habit." With that said, Hugh Leigh punched Mr. Chatterjee in the ribs. Chatterjee punched Hugh's shoulder.

As he worked his way through Mrs. Chatterjee's abundance, Schuyler wondered what the hell was happening. From time to time he caught Leigh beaming at him as if he'd earned an A-plus on a math test. Instead of feeling irritated, as was so often his reaction to Clementine's officious parental approval, or her unwelcome homilies based on Winston's opinions, he was amused. He appreciated Leigh's encouragement. Everything, this evening, struck him as funny.

Was he belatedly developing a sense of humor? *Hallelujah.* Able to laugh at his own expense? *Yes.* In "getting" New Mexico, he'd come to understand that whatever afflictions he suffered were, for the most part, due to the chip on his shoulder. Whatever calamities caused him to stumble he owed to his shortsighted and sour cynicism.

How enlightening. Again—*hallelujah.*

"Well, Yuthi"—Hugh Leigh patted his stomach—"I am used to being well-fed by your kitchen, but this meal exceeds anything I've ever eaten."

Schuyler chuckled. Not so much at Leigh's comment, but at how his own perspective was shifting. Instead of directing an internal string of expletives at himself for being so naive and insensitive as to bring a dog as a hostess gift, he laughed. *Too bad you're just now learning to do that.* He'd been a jerk, a calculating leech who fed off Clementine's wealth. He'd made up every excuse in the book for his misdeeds and avoided taking the blame for anything.

Too bad you never shared a laugh with your mother . . .

"Oh, Mr. Schuyler! I can hear the puppy whining. Mataji, may I bring her to the table?" "Why not, Anita?" Mrs. Chatterjee giggled, now on her third glass of wine.

Schuyler had declined a glass, determined to keep himself in check, but even without the booze he felt like his heart was singing. Whereas, at other functions he'd often felt the need to be "on," to shine or be brilliant, he now wanted only to be himself. To be himself, and be a part of this novel company who enjoyed each other's friendship. Who were having a good time.

Had he ever had a really good time? Did he know what a good time was? Could he accomplish such enjoyment?

Yeah. He was having a good time. Just being present.

"Here is my doggie!" Anita held the black-and-white pup aloft for everyone to see.

"That's no way to hold a dog, girl." Mr. Chatterjee stubbed out his cigarette. Seven butts in the ashtray. "Give her to Hugh."

"Why me?" Leigh objected.

"Never mind, Anita. Give him the dog."

"I'm not good with dogs," Leigh growled. To the surprise of everyone at the table the pup at once settled down on Hugh Leigh's lap and fell asleep.

"There. Did I not tell you so?" Mr. Chatterjee lit up again and inhaled a deep draft. "I put it down to Hugh's mystique. His compelling air of mystery."

Schuyler sat back in his chair, relishing an unaccustomed glow of well-being. As he enjoyed their banter, he found himself regretting the price he'd paid for so many years of self-imposed exile beyond the pale. What a loss, and all due to his own arrogance. So what if Clementine forced him to accept a job at Sam's Club and he now lived with a pack of dogs. Why had he reviled, as unjust, his mother's mandate that he toe the line or be cut off from financial support? His mother was an all-knowing saint. A miracle worker.

"Mr. Schuyler? Another cup?" Mrs. Chatterjee was offering him more tea, and she had placed a dish of sliced pears and apples in front of him.

"Yes, I would. Thank you, Mrs. Chatterjee." He smiled as she refilled his cup.

"I know how it is, sir. One eats a good healthy dinner and what happens? One wants to nod off!"

"I don't think I've ever eaten a more amazing meal."

"Didn't I tell you, Mr. Schuyler"—Ms. Chatterjee bestowed one of her brilliant smiles upon him—"that mother and I would cook up something you could not resist? There are curries, and then there is *curry*!"

"I never would have thought a meal without meat could be so superb!"

Hugh Leigh laughed. "Well, Schuyler, I see in your future a round-trip ticket to Kal."

"To *Kal*?"

"Kolkata. Yes, I can guarantee you'd enjoy the adventure immensely."

As his dinnermates' conversation segued to the Chatterjees's life in Kolkata, Schuyler felt the jolt of another "ah-ha" moment. Clementine's dirty cheat of a deal in exiling him to Santa Fe was a multifaceted gift bestowed not only by his mother and Uncle Harry, but also by the good will of the people seated at this table. They were aware of his past yet, to varying degrees, they were offering him a second chance. They forgave him.

How welcome. His life had changed for the better only because he'd submitted to his mother's demands. Bring it on, Clementine.

"Mr. Schuyler?" Mrs. Chatterjee gently tugged at his sleeve. "Are you with us?"

"Oh! I'm so sorry. How rude!" he exclaimed. "I was lost in thought again."

"No worries." Mrs. Chatterjee's tinkling laugh as she poured herself another glass of Chardonnay was so like her daughter's. "Anita, why don't you show Mr. Schuyler the flowers in our garden? Bapu will help me clean the kitchen."

"What a lovely idea, Mama," exclaimed Ms. Chatterjee. "Let's take the puppy with us, Mr. Schuyler."

"I'm sure she could use a potty break," Schuyler responded, having regained his customary aplomb, liking the "let's." Both of them. Together.

He glanced around the table. The two ladies were beaming. Through a cloud of smoke, Mr. Chatterjee regarded him with a fixed stare. Hugh Leigh was shaking his head again, no doubt wondering how this lamebrain had earned his cutthroat New York City reputation. He seemed barely able to survive.

In the back yard, Ms. Chatterjee released the puppy onto the lawn, where she sniffed with relish before disappearing into a bed of day lilies.

"Your mother is very gracious. Forgiving," Schuyler apologized. "It was stupid of me to bring her a dog. I have all the supplies you'll need in my truck, but I'm also happy to take the puppy home with me if that seems best."

"Nonsense. I, for one, found the surprise amusing." Ms. Chatterjee smiled up at him. "I am keeping this little girl and naming her Lotus. What do you think of that?" She flipped the end of her hot pink sari over her shoulder.

"Lotus is a beautiful name. Your garden is beautiful, and so are—" Schuyler made a quick recovery. "And, so—uh, could tell me the names of all the flowers growing here?"

"Well, let's see. Under these aspens we have foxglove and some hen-and-chicks—"

The foliage they wandered through was vast. Schuyler would never remember half of the plant names.

"All this cultivation is my father's pride and joy."

He must be sure to compliment his host, the consummate gardener. Only, how sad—the evening light was now at that point where the balance tipped more toward shadow. He and Ms. Chatterjee were at the far end of the garden and turning, to his regret, back toward the house. It was now, or never. Did he dare?

"Ms. Chatterjee," he began, lingering beneath a catalpa tree, forcing her to slow her pace. "Next Saturday would you care to visit the Albuquerque botanical gardens? With me?"

"What a delightful invitation, Mr. Schuyler!"

Her eyes gleamed like stars in the deepening shade.

"Let me ask Mama and Bapu. We'll see if they agree."

Schuyler was puzzled. At her age did she need her parents' permission to accept a date?

"Mataji, guess what?" Ms. Chatterjee called, as soon as they re-entered the house. "Mr. Schuyler has invited us to the Botanic Garden next Saturday. I know how much you love the gardens. May we go?"

Mrs. Chatterjee, whose hands were submerged in soapsuds, glanced toward Mr. Chatterjee, who took a deep drag as he finished wiping dry a casserole dish.

"Why not?" Mrs. Chatterjee beamed. "All the asters will be blooming."

"Thank you, Mr. Schuyler," said Mr. Chatterjee. Ashes dropped onto the tiled kitchen floor. "We are *all* pleased to accept."

There was no way Schuyler could miss the "all." His invitation, he was meant to understand, must include everyone in the kitchen. Hugh Leigh, also wielding a dish towel, and ever-present in his witness role of silent Greek chorus, again grinning at his pseudo nephew's perennial discomfort, reached for another plate.

Schuyler knew what his next move must be.

"Do join us in visiting the Garden, Mr. Leigh," was his hearty if insincere invitation.

"What a pleasure. Thank you, Schuyler," was Leigh's immediate response. "I'll pick you up next Saturday at nine a.m. We can visit the Garden at leisure, and I'll treat everyone to a late lunch before we return to Santa Fe."

Well, there went his last chance of even a few minutes alone with Ms. Chatterjee. Schuyler conceded he had, once again, been managed. Even so, he was gaining ground, wasn't he? He was no longer running backward as if in a frustrating dream but heading in the right direction toward his goal.

"Thank you, Mrs. Chatterjee. The meal was divine beyond description."

"It was my pleasure. Do come again for dinner, Mr. Schuyler."

"Your garden is lovely, Mr. Chatterjee."

As the two men shook hands, Mr. Chatterjee looked oddly pleased, yet sour, at the same time. "Yes, I second the dinner invitation, Mr. Schuyler. Why not? Next time we will play some cribbage."

Hugh Leigh again clapped him on the shoulder. "I still plan to stop by and take you up on that cup of coffee."

Well, that was a significant upgrade in their relationship.

"Any time, sir. Stop by any time." Schuyler wasn't yet part of this tightly knit team but, as Ms. Chatterjee, puppy in arms, walked him to the door, he felt he was at least in the game. "I'll get the supplies out of the truck for you," he said to her.

"Thank you for being so patient, Mr. Schuyler," Ms. Chatterjee whispered, as Schuyler placed the dog chow, puppy bed, and other necessities inside the front door. "I think things are going very well. Very well, indeed."

Her words of encouragement sent Schuyler flying out the door on a carpet of euphoria.

"Say goodbye to Lotus," Ms. Chatterjee said in a much louder voice.

"Thank you again, Ms. Chatterjee. Lovely evening," he responded in the same inflated tone. Then, patting the puppy on the head—"Be a good dog"—he bounded down the walk and into his truck.

Flying, indeed.

CHAPTER 21

Days of Note

As he drove north through the inky darkness and passed by Camel Rock, Schuyler felt a heretofore unfamiliar exhilaration. Through the open window he inhaled the astringing aroma of sage and rabbitbrush—*chamisa*. Now acquainted with the shadowy shapes of landscape formations, he realized how much he'd miss life in the high desert if he had to leave it. There was a pungency not only in the native plants, but in the daily experience of being here. It smacked you right in the face. *Yeah, pungent.* Take tonight for example. The time spent with the Chatterjees and Hugh Leigh was—no lie—the best night of his life.

He'd given one of his puppies to the woman he loved and dined with her family. Although it got off to a rocky start, the evening had gone well. Every person seated at the dinner table was aware of his reprehensible history, yet they'd accepted him and seemed willing to overlook the past. One individual less than others, Schuyler decided, reviewing Mr. Chatterjee's limited range of facial expressions. Some inquisitive. Some skeptical. Some sour.

Still, he hadn't messed up too badly and next Saturday he would be part of a family visit to the Albuquerque Botanic Garden. Ms. Chatterjee's rejection of him two months prior was, perhaps, for her, the hasty action of a moment only.

Then again, perhaps not. That remained to be seen, but tonight he'd sat next to her. He'd never forget that thrill, nor would he forget how lovely she looked in her hot pink sari. Schuyler was struck once again not only by the force of Clementine's will, but by how grateful he was for her demands of him. If she'd bade him toe the line, she was not the beneficiary of that exercise. He was. For sure, if his mother had said, "I demand you move to Santa Fe because, by so doing, you'll meet the most fabulous woman

in the world," he never would have believed her. He had reaped
what she had sown, and harvested a crop—

A crop of—what? *Blessings?*

Geez. Did it have to be *that* word? Blessings. *Holy shit.* Winston
save me.

⁓

The following Saturday's visit to the Botanic Garden was a
success, as was the party's afternoon in Albuquerque's Old Town.
Schuyler was fascinated by the many shops, bakeries, and cafés.
Having had his first bite of a bizcochíto, a classic New Mexican
cookie, he bought a dozen of them and presented the gift to Mrs.
Chatterjee. From his perspective, the only drawback of the day
was the necessity of taking two cars. He drove with Hugh Leigh
in the Jimmy, and Ms. Chatterjee followed with her parents in
her own car.

"What a delightful day!" Mrs. Chatterjee had exclaimed at
lunch. "Such excellent chíle rellenos. And ah, tomorrow is
Sunday. You will be joining us for dinner at five, won't you, Mr.
Schuyler?"

All was not lost.

Schuyler dined with the Chatterjees and Hugh Leigh, for three
Sundays in a row. He was oh so happy to be there, but with his
courtship in a holding pattern his impatience was growing.
Would he never have a moment alone with Ms. Chatterjee?

He had already broached the topic of his frustration with Tom
Jannssen.

"Her parents must know we like each other, but they never
leave us alone except for that friggin' walk in the garden," he
groused, hesitant about taking the next step.

Jannssen shook his head. "Well, you're the only one who can
change that, man. Anita is too shy. It was hard enough for her to
ask you to dinner in the first place."

After this consultation in which Schuyler discovered just how
well Jannssen knew the Chatterjee family, he was still doubtful

of the outcome of his much-debated next move, but decided to forge ahead. On the Monday morning after that third Sunday night dinner he trudged up the steps to Human Resources. Janice Garcia once more informed him Ms. Chatterjee was free. He again knocked on the office door frame and, when she looked up, was greeted by her brilliant smile.

"Mr. Schuyler—do come in." In a lower tone, she added, "What a surprise! And a most welcome one. How are you?"

"To be blunt, Ms. Chatterjee," he stated, determined to be direct, "and I see no reason to be otherwise, I could be a lot better. Given what is, to me"—Schuyler cleared his throat—"the irritating circumstance of never having a conversation alone with you, would you consider dining with me tonight? Please, let me clarify. By that, I mean the two of us at a restaurant—after work and before you go home."

He had made himself plain. But if she felt they must only dine with her parents, so be it. He would submit.

"Why, of course!" she cried. "I've been expecting you to suggest the very thing for quite some time."

"You have? I mean, you will—have dinner—with me? *Alone*?"

"Indeed, yes. Why have you not asked me sooner?"

"Uhh—" Schuyler had not anticipated this response. "You asked me to your home," he said slowly, "and it seemed important to have your parents close at hand, so I thought that's how dating was done with Indian families. In a group."

"You are correct. That is how things are often done with Indian families. *In India*. Many times, also, in the States. But I see no need to forever abide by protocol."

"I'm relieved," Schuyler responded with a sigh.

"It was important to me that my parents became acquainted with you. I—" Ms. Chatterjee blushed, groping for the appropriate words. "I—you see, would very much like to get to know you better, to see where things go between us and—"

She shrugged her shoulders as if she, a modest woman, could say no more without the encouragement of knowing he understood the implications in what she had already said.

He did. He was surprised beyond any expectation and elated beyond what he could express.

"Well," Schuyler said, grinning, "perhaps the best way to start would be with a conversation over dinner. Shall we go to the India Mansion Restaurant?"

"Oh, dear God, no," she blanched. "Do not think I eat Indian food three times a day, seven days a week."

"Then, what?"

"I love Thai cooking. Why don't you go to the Lemon Grass Restaurant at five p.m. I'll follow in my car about fifteen minutes later. My parents know I often work late, so I will phone to let them know I won't be home until nine."

⌐

After Anita's first late evening, Mr. and Mrs. Chatterjee received frequent phone calls from their daughter, explaining how the eight hours of a work day were, once again, not long enough. She needed more time in which to complete her daily managerial duties. In the course of time, these phone calls came daily.

"The courtship must be going well," Mrs. Chatterjee remarked, as she and her husband relaxed on the patio after dinner. Lotus, now a much larger puppy with silky black-and-white hair, always well-brushed, was again exploring the flower garden.

"She is spending quite a bit of time with our dear Mr. Schuyler. Nearly every evening."

"I don't know why you must always refer to the man as 'dear.'" Mr. Chatterjee expelled as much smoke through his mouth, as through his nose. "I see nothing '*dear*' about him. Are we assured he is not such a loose screw as his mother painted him to be?"

"I see no evidence of that," Mrs. Chatterjee bridled. "He has been a faithful suitor, and you have seen the way he looks at her."

"Yes." Mr. Chatterjee spat tobacco from his mouth. "That is what bothers me."

"Picky, picky! Hugh Leigh reports from dear Tom Jannssen how Mr. Schuyler does nothing but work at Sam's Club, tend to his dogs, and prune his apple orchard. What more do you want?"

"'*Dear*' again." Mr. Chatterjee lit another cigarette. "Is every man 'dear' to you, woman? Yes, the fellow works at Sam's Club. On the dock. What future is that for our daughter?"

"You are ridiculous. That is not the end of the story, but only the beginning. Clementine is wealthy. Who will she leave her money to? Aaron will receive everything Harry left to her, as well. And, Mr. Smarty Pants, who do you suppose ends up with all of Hugh Leigh's property?"

"I have it on the best authority Hugh is leaving the whole caboodle to MOMA."

"Whose 'best' authority?"

"His own." Mr. Chatterjee, following the puppy's progress, choked on an inhale.

"Dammit, Yuthi! The fellow's mutt has just dug another hole in my lawn!"

↶

Schuyler and Ms. Chatterjee exchanged cell phone numbers so he wouldn't need to climb the stairs to Human Resources so often. This futile subterfuge did little to disguise their growing intimacy from the staff at Sam's Club. Janice Garcia felt no qualms about letting it be known to everyone that Ms. Chatterjee's complexion glowed in a way it never had before Mr. Schuyler became a Sam's Club associate. The dock crew were at it again, doing their best to make Schuyler's workdays as miserable as possible.

"No one is gonna believe you could snag a chick like Chatterjee," sniggered Mike Three Rivers. "You using date drugs?"

"How do you get it up, *Viéjo*?" Jesus jabbed at his ribs. "Your low pay? You must be goin' broke buying Viagra, *verdad*? Insurance don't pay for it!"

"Chatterjee gets a raw deal, old man." Ernie Daniels shook his head. "Before long she'll be pushing your wheelchair!"

These days, it was fortunate Schuyler existed in a world of heady experience. He paid no attention to the dock crew's teasing. He recalled, instead, each sweet word whispered to him by his love, while they were together. Every moment of the day he relived his dinner conversations with Anita. They were, at last, on a first-name basis.

Even his taped responses to Clementine's sinus reports took on another tone. Her latest tape for the week of October second began, "The autumn allergies have hit me hard. I'm using a neti pot and that helps some, but almost every hour I have copious amounts of stringy, thick white mucous. My nose is plugged up and my voice sounds strange, even to me. Stan thinks I should see an ENT man."

Schuyler's remarks by return tape were almost kind. "Hello, Mom, just hang in there. The neti pot is a fine solution for allergies. I know this because I asked the pharmacist in Pojoaque what was best. He said to me what I've said to you many times. 'Better out than in.' Keep blowing. You're great! Aaron."

⌒

He might be the happiest man on earth, although tormented by the dock crew's teasing, and his work hours flitted by in a daze wherein he sometimes forgot to take lunch breaks, as well as morning and afternoon breaks, but Schuyler still made frequent use of the men's room. There was no letup in the accursed IBS.

Despite his hurried jaunts to the restroom during dinner, their dates were magical. So much so that Anita and Schuyler were close to exhausting the list of Santa Fe restaurants, if such a thing were possible. Intimacy had progressed to the point where, after Schuyler kissed Chatterjee good night on their second date, they now kissed before dinner, during dinner, and long after dinner while secluded in her car with the heater going full blast.

Schuyler found these marathons disturbing for two reasons. He had decided to ask Anita to marry him, but he had severe reservations about marriage without first having sex with one's intended partner. These days, who did that?

The second reason was the physical agony he endured during these preliminaries that led nowhere. Daily, he considered asking Anita how she felt about premarital sex, but every time it came to the point of phrasing such a question, he chickened out. What did he know about this aspect of courtship customs in the Indian culture? If he asked her, might she reject him? Refuse all further contact with him? Might he never see her again?

He wasn't willing to take the chance.

One Friday evening, the two having met outside the Happy Wonton Grill at 5:30 p.m., Chatterjee balked when Schuyler held the restaurant door open for her.

"Aaron, the plain truth is, I am becoming very tired of eating in restaurants. Each meal tastes the same to me. *Boring.* Another such dinner is not something I look forward to."

"What do you want to do? See a movie? Have a bag of popcorn for dinner?"

"Here's a thought. You've been saying you'd take me to meet Bella, the mother of Lotus. We can make popcorn in your kitchen." She grew more enthusiastic. "Oh, please, Aaron. Let us do something different. Drive to Nambé. I have been wanting for so long to see the other puppies."

"If you want to"—Schuyler shrugged, conscious of the mess and disorder at home—"but I don't have any popcorn. There isn't much to eat except instant oatmeal or frozen dinners."

"Well then, we shall make a picnic with those, and enjoy them very much."

Chatterjee followed behind Schuyler's truck along the highway north, then made the turn onto County Road 503. It being late autumn, the route was no longer lush and green, the trees, bushes, and even weeds having discarded their summer foliage. Twilight had faded, and the road was dark as they turned into Schuyler's driveway.

Even before they emerged from their vehicles, the howls issuing from the apple orchard were piercing. When Schuyler opened the orchard gate, a pack of dogs streaked out into the carport, dashed around in circles, then focused their attention on Chatterjee.

"Don't worry. They won't jump up," Schuyler assured her. "But, you're a novelty."

Chatterjee was delighted with the dogs. They were silky black and white look-alikes, identical to Lotus, although larger in size.

"Enough, you hounds!" Schuyler fed the dogs, then led them away from the house and back to the apple orchard so they could pee and poop. After they charged into the fenced enclosure, he closed the gate behind them.

"Now, we'll have some peace and quiet." He ushered Chatterjee into the hallway. "I can show you the house."

After a lengthy tour of all the rooms, Schuyler lit the oven, placed two frozen dinners inside, and made a show of tidying the cluttered countertop. Chatterjee again wandered through the sitting room.

"What a lovely place!" she called out. "A genuine adobe. This is true New Mexican architecture, not like our home in Santa Fe. That's a tract house made to look like an adobe!"

Chatterjee trailed her hand over the stuccoed bancos on either side of the kiva fireplace, then gazed out toward the orchard through the old, distorted panes of the sitting room windows.

"Those dogs!" She laughed. "They're so rough with each other."

"Yeah, and it's about time to bring them in." Schuyler looked out the window from over Chatterjee's head. "They'll quiet down when I put them in the back bedroom. That's where they sleep. Our dinners are just about ready. Does the house seem warm enough?"

"A bit cool, but that's okay. While you tend to the dogs, do you mind if I look at your library?" She pulled a volume from the bookshelf.

"Be my guest."

Schuyler had already decided to follow Anita back to Santa Fe after dinner, to be sure she had no driving mishaps. That would mean a late night for him, because he'd need to drive back to

Nambé. *What the hell.* Tomorrow was Saturday and he could sleep in. Or, as late as the dogs would allow. Using Milk-Bones, he lured the pack into the house and shut them up in a bedroom near the back door. The frozen entrees should be fully warmed by now.

"Anita, the dinners are ready," he called from the kitchen.

When she did not respond, he glanced through the archway into the sitting room. *Huh.* Anita was no longer examining the bookshelf, but the bathroom light was flickering. A dying bulb? She must be washing up for dinner. The night sky out here, away from the Santa Fe lights, was pitch-black. They should eat soon and, before too long, drive back to town.

"Anita?" He walked into the bathroom but found it empty. No Anita. She might have walked outside into the smaller courtyard, so he headed in the direction of that door.

"Well, Aaron, it's about time."

Schuyler turned on his heel. Anita's voice had issued from his darkened bedroom wherein, deep within the shadows, her form was dimly defined.

Anita was sitting in his bed. Nude. At least, nude from the waist up. *Holy shit.* She held the sheet up so it covered her breasts.

"What are you doing?" he asked. The light might be low but he could see how voluptuous she was, how flawless her golden skin. Did she want what he hoped she wanted?

"What does it look like I'm doing? Are you always such a simpleton?" She laughed. "If I waited for you to make a move, we'd both be as old and gray as my parents."

"But—are you sure?" God, she was gorgeous.

"Don't be a dunce." She laughed again. "Of course I'm sure."

"I—wanted to ask you. Was afraid I'd breach some ancient Vedic code of premarital ethics." Schuyler made no attempt to veil his relief. "Never see you again. How did I know?"

"I know you want to ask me to marry you." Anita reached out toward him. "But how can you do that in this day and age, when we don't know if we'll be—compatible."

"I'll make sure we're compatible," he murmured as he kissed her. "I love you, Anita."

"Well, yes, I know that." She began unbuttoning his shirt. "I have known that for a very long time."

"Will you marry me?" He kissed her again, and slid his hand along her throat, over her shoulder, and under the protective sheet.

"Probably."

"You witch!" He laughed, urging her head onto a pillow. "Just a simple yes or no is good enough."

"I haven't yet seen the ring you're offering me," she whispered, running her fingers through the curls at his temples. "That could make or break the deal."

"And I suppose I must ask your father for your hand?"

"Not only that, but you must pay a bride price."

"No way," Schuyler shook his head. "It's the other way around. I know that much about Indian culture. If your father doesn't provide you with a sizable dowry, all bargains are off. I won't take you off his hands. You'll be a ruined woman."

"I knew that would be the case." Anita sighed. "It's not me you want, but my father's hard-earned cash. Good luck squeezing the money out of him."

CHAPTER 22

Perspectives

"My daughter did not come home last night?" Mr. Chatterjee took a deep drag on his first cigarette of the day. It didn't taste quite right. He thought he might switch to cigars.

"You're right, she did not." Mrs. Chatterjee's smile was smug. "And, don't you dare say a wrong word to Anita when she arrives home."

"I wasn't going to say anything," her husband answered in an injured tone. "You never give me the benefit of the doubt."

"And when have you deserved that?" Mrs. Chatterjee countered. "You will probably receive a visit from dear Mr. Schuyler today. Be sure to wear your best kurta. And when he asks for Anita's hand in marriage, be sure you say yes."

"What else am I going to say, woman? He has compromised my daughter."

"Oh, you are shameless." She snapped a dish towel at her husband. "To speak in such a way about our only child."

"I want to get her off my hands." He glanced out the kitchen window. "She'll take the damn dog with her and I'll be rid of that mutt. What are we having for breakfast?"

"I have to feed Lotus, first." Mrs. Chatterjee tucked a stray lock of hair into her bun. "You—go empty all your ashtrays, then scoop up the dog poop in the yard."

"Why do I always have to pick up the poop?"

"Because you do not know how to cook, wash, or sew. You only know how to smoke."

"At least I do that well."

"Get out of my kitchen. I must make a call to Clementine and break the news."

"Why can't you let that fellow phone his mother?"

"I said, out of my kitchen. *Now.*"

⤿

By the time Schuyler woke up on Saturday morning, Anita was no longer in bed, but had risen, showered, and thrown out the burnt frozen dinners he'd left in the oven.

Wearing only his shorts, he stumbled into the kitchen to apologize.

"I know it's pitiful. I'll buy more food. We'll have breakfast at the Mockingbird."

"Fair enough," agreed Anita. "But you can't eat every meal in a restaurant. That is not nourishing."

"Can't you at least say good morning?" He pulled a lopsided grin.

"Good morning, my love." She drew his head down and kissed him on the cheek. "We must get going and not waste the day. You need to speak to my father."

"Oh joy." God, he hoped he wouldn't screw this up. "You have to know I'm not looking forward to that."

"Who would? I expect he will give you a bit of a hard time. He'll see it as a game and want to be sure you understand he is the head of his household. Don't compete with him."

"Have you had other suitors besides your late husband?"

"None who mattered. And, by that I mean my father knows how much I care for you. He is delighted we met and have gotten on so well."

"I've seen no proof of his delight, Anita."

"Well, you know," she sympathized, "my parents are longtime friends with Hugh, Harry, and your mother."

"You people are always saying, 'you know,' and I know nothing of the sort. I am always in the dark until, each time, one of you chooses to enlighten me."

"That"—Anita frowned—"was, perhaps, not kind of them. But according to your mother, you made the choice to cut yourself off from your wife and children. No one else did. Is that not true?

You cut yourself off from Clementine and Harry. Isn't that the reason why you didn't know we'd all become friends?"

"What can I say?" was Schuyler's futile rebuttal. "You're right. I don't have a leg to stand on. Yet, you won't hear me say that I wish I could do it all over again because that isn't true. I don't wish that. Then I'd be a solid citizen, still married to Natalie, and would never have met you."

"Oh dear." Anita's face betrayed her conflicting emotions. "It's all so very complex."

"You're damn right it is," Schuyler agreed. "Do I wish I'd done things differently? Been a better man and not such a friggin' louse? *Yes*. But here's the catch. I only wish that because it would make me more worthy of you, not because I still want to live the A-list life in New York."

"Oh, let us not argue, Aaron," Chatterjee pleaded.

"Well, it's not pleasant to have my past thrown in my face." Schuyler's expression was dour. "I do that often enough to myself."

"Ah, well—I see your point." Anita's face softened. She lowered herself onto a chair. Schuyler sat opposite and reached across the table for her hands.

"You told me Clementine came to visit Hugh and my uncle for the opera season. Right? That's how you met my mother?"

"Harry and Hugh introduced her to us, and that was that. We loved her."

"You're a saint if you loved my mother." Schuyler grimaced.

"I'm so glad you recognize me for what I am," Anita answered in a mock serious tone. "Years before that, Uttam and Yuthi met Hugh and Harry at the opera. They shared a lot of laughs since Hugh and Harry knew what life in India was like. And, now, my dear, let's not procrastinate. Shouldn't we proceed with this wonderful day and get back to Santa Fe?"

"Yeah. Right." Schuyler exhaled heavily as he rose from his chair. He kissed the top of her head. "Let me shower. Then I'll be ready to go. But first, I do need to phone my mother."

"Yes, yes, you must speak with her," seconded Anita. "Just so you know, I expect my own mother has already spread the news."

"What the fuck," Schuyler muttered under his breath as he headed for the bathroom.

"What was that?" Anita had turned her attention to scouring the kitchen sink.

"Nothing," Schuyler flung over his shoulder. Closing the bathroom door and pulling out his cell phone, he dialed Clementine's Akron number.

"Mom!" he shouted, confused by the noise he heard in the background. "Are you okay?"

"Tip-top!" came her cheerful reply. "Sorry about the noise. I was replaying the tape I just recorded, to be sure it was accurate before I mailed it to you. Sinuses, you know."

"I can hardly wait."

"It goes in the mail tomorrow. You'll be pleased with my progress."

"Never mind that. This is important, Mom. I wanted to let you know I'm getting married."

"Yes! Brilliant! I am very happy, and so is Stan," she gushed. "Congratulations! It has all turned out quite well, hasn't it? I was telling Stan earlier how I prayed to Winston and asked him if I should give you another chance. His reply was rather oblique, but I hope I understand his phraseology by now, and how he works his magic."

"Mom, please. Let me get a word in—"

"Convoluted. Winston is always convoluted. But, he said I should at least make the effort, and I'm so glad I did. I suppose you will want to give Anita the ruby engagement ring?"

"Uh—no. I think the sapphire ring will look better with her skin tone," Schuyler replied. You still have it, don't you?"

"Of course, dear boy. It's part of your inheritance. What would I be doing? Giving it away to someone on the street?"

Schuyler wouldn't have put it past her, if Winston suggested she do so.

"How soon can you send it to me?"

"Stan will ship it FedEx from his office today. You will have it overnight, or Monday at the latest. And—I'll tell you what! Why don't I include my tape in the package?"

"Splendid, Mom! Simply splendid!" He mocked her British accent. "Whatever."

Schuyler stopped short, sickened by his surly response. Sickened by his deliberate intent to hurt his mother. *Whatever.*

Too often, that was his flippant comment to Clementine, with her annoying quirks. Too often that had been his reply to Natalie, desperate for love, aching from the wrongs she suffered at his hands. To his kids—daring to want more from him than the money he shelled out for cars and new clothes.

Whatever.

"I'm sorry, Mom," he said at once. "What I said was very rude. I apologize."

Clementine made no response, but Schuyler knew she was deeply hurt and only pretending to ignore his sarcasm. What a shit he was. *Whatever.* Hadn't such dismissal of his family, of their wants and needs, been the guiding principle of his adult life? The impact of his selfish arrogance, his complete absorption with his own pleasure, was shattering to all of them. Just like his last snide remark to Clementine. He choked on that damning realization.

How soon would his commitment to Anita be relegated to *whatever* status?

"I love you, Mom," Schuyler whispered into the phone. He couldn't remember the last time he'd told Clementine he loved her. Perhaps he never had. "I love you very much. Thanks for everything, Mom. I'm happy."

Schuyler was sure Clementine heard the catch in his voice. He'd given away more than he wanted. Damn it, she never missed a thing. It was his own fault she questioned the veracity of not only his statement of happiness, but of his regard for her. She deserved better. He sincerely hoped his mother received reassurance from Winston that her son loved her. Whether or not the PM believed his own words was another matter altogether.

"Are you, dear boy?"

"I do love you—" he repeated. *Geez, Schuyler*—how are you going to convince her of that? You've done a rotten job showing it so far. "And I wish I'd done better with my kids. I miss them, don't really know them. It hurts inside. What an ass I've been."

"Ah, yes. The children," murmured Clementine.

CHAPTER 23

Plain Speaking

To Schuyler's relief, Tom Jannssen wasn't having breakfast at the Mockingbird. That eliminated the chance of delaying their return to Santa Fe with endless comments and sidebars about who in New York knew whom in New Mexico. Tom, well-acquainted with Hugh Leigh, the Chatterjees, and Anita, already knew Schuyler's intentions. He'd have plenty to say if he saw them breakfasting together on a Saturday morning in Pojoaque. It was annoying enough with Ellen the waitress smirking and jerking her head toward Anita.

When they reached the Chatterjee home, Anita pressed his hand for encouragement.

"If Bapuji sinks his teeth in, you're done for, Aaron. Don't let him get the upper hand."

"Stop with the advice, Anita. Right now." Schuyler's clipped tone bordered on irritation. "You sound like my mother and Hugh Leigh."

"Is that a bad thing?"

"No." He heaved a sigh. "It's not a bad thing. It's just me acting like I don't ever again want to act." He planted a kiss on her cheek and knocked on the door of Mr. Chatterjee's study.

"Come in," was uttered with a barking cough, and Schuyler entered the hazy room. Didn't anyone in this family ever open a window?

"Good morning, sir."

"Is it?" Mr. Chatterjee was wearing a sky-blue kurta. He rose from his chair and bent over the desk to shake Schuyler's hand. "Please, sit down."

"I imagine you know why I've asked to see you," Schuyler began.

"To paraphrase Winston Churchill, responding to a similar prompt, 'I haven't the slightest idea.' Do you smoke?"

"I do not."

"Pity. What man doesn't light up on occasion?"

"Are you an admirer of Churchill, sir?" Schuyler asked, seeking to establish a bond of amicability with his future father-in-law.

"Absolutely not!" choked Mr. Chatterjee. "Why would I be? Churchill was an advocate of empire, man. My good father was posted to Burma with the British Fourteenth. Barely survived the ordeal." With a pause and a sharp inhale, he sat down. "I will only say I am *grateful* for the PM's maintenance of morale during those dark times."

"My own mother is a strong admirer of Churchill," offered Schuyler, grateful for the massive desk separating him from his host.

"I know that. And many, many times I've bitten my tongue in her presence. Churchill a deity. *Indeed.* How can such a brilliant woman be so deluded?" Chatterjee stubbed out his half-smoked cigarette.

"Come now, sir. It isn't that bad a failing," replied Schuyler. *Imagine.* Here he was, defending Winston. And Clementine. Was she brilliant?

"Agreed. We all have our blind spots, do we not? I cannot tell you how much I admire your mother's sacrifice and devotion to a worthless—"

Schuyler saw what he was up against. It was all too easy to guess what almost tumbled out from between Mr. Chatterjee's clenched teeth. A British Indian Army brat sat opposite him, and the desktop was their no-man's-land. Could he rebuff the challenge? He was ready to wage an uphill fight if need be, ready to make a stand, but this mustn't become a losing battle.

"Mr. Chatterjee, your opinion of me is irrelevant. For the moment, let's leave it out of the conversation."

"I might be happy to do that if you had not so insulted my wife." Mr. Chatterjee twitched his head sideways in an effort to contain his ire, perplexing to Schuyler. "And—myself."

"I never did!" exclaimed Schuyler. "That's an outright lie."

"It. Is. No. Lie." Mr. Chatterjee ground the words out between his teeth. "Furthermore, I'll wager you have no memory of the incident."

"Well, you're right, although I doubt there ever was such an 'incident.'"

"Think back to the reception line at Harry Neville's funeral," Mr. Chatterjee prompted Schuyler, his lips gripping a cigarette.

"I'm there—but you weren't. Neither was Mrs. Chatterjee."

"Wrong on both counts. Think again. My wife and I passed through that line and offered you our condolences. Where your mind was, I cannot say." Mr. Chatterjee's smile was not pleasant. "But, then—I've wondered that on more than one occasion since meeting you."

"Oh, come now. You talk about insults!" Schuyler retorted. "I have no idea what you're talking about."

"And that is your problem. That day you saw only dark faces. *Our dark faces*. You looked right through us, and said to me, 'Congratulations on getting your green card!'"

Schuyler took a deep breath. His mind raced back to the monotony of the endless reception line, his mixed emotions on learning Harry was gay. His snap decision to exaggerate and overplay the role of a bereaved but stalwart and cordial host. To show off. To shine. To be witty. The very non-virtues Stan Atwater had complimented him upon.

Had he missed his mark yet again?

"I—I don't remember you being there."

He recalled his confusion after discovering Harry's secret life, but what kind of excuse was that? Yes, he'd been aware of some dark faces among the stream of mourners offering condolences but couldn't zero in on recognizable features. What an unfortunate, thoughtless, and painful comment to make. That crude blunder went a long way in explaining Mr. Chatterjee's lack of warmth.

"It—was a long morning, sir. All I can do now is apologize. I'm sorry."

Mr. Chatterjee lit up again. His frown as he inhaled was indicative of a deep internal struggle. He stubbed out his cigarette in the overflowing ashtray, his basilisk glare softening, and nodded his head. "I accept your apology on my wife's behalf, as well as my own."

"Sir, if I could relive that moment I would do so in a heartbeat, and I would do better. I would not be heedless of others. So negligent. But, right now, I'm choosing to live in the present and not in the past." A vision of last night's passion shared with Anita loomed before him, reminding him why he must tolerate this interview. "I haven't come here to annoy you, but to ask a specific question. I love your daughter. Will you grant me permission to marry her?"

Schuyler's question was met with silence. A mellowing of Mr. Chatterjee's features as he lit up again, held the hint of a smile. It was, by no means, an encouraging smile.

"And, if I refuse? Will you go away and never return?" Mr. Chatterjee shifted his seat in the capacious leather chair.

"Certainly not. Look—can we stop playing games? This is serious."

"I never play games. I never had the knack for deception that some people have." Mr. Chatterjee spat out the words and picked some stray threads of tobacco off his tongue. "Did you think I had no inkling of your sordid history? Tales of your shenanigans have been repeated to me for years. Am I to be blamed for this foreknowledge of which you were unaware?"

At this moment the door to the study opened a crack and then at once snapped closed, almost upon the tail of Lotus, who bounded into the room.

"Am I to be blamed for seeking a worthier man than you to be my daughter's husband?"

Lotus jumped onto Mr. Chatterjee's lap. "Off, you damn dog!"

Schuyler lost all hope of détente. His future father-in-law no doubt hated Lotus.

"Anita has already suffered tragedy with the death of her first spouse." Mr. Chatterjee began scratching the dog's ears. "And *he* was a good man. Forgive me if I fail to see how this marriage will enhance her happiness."

It was Schuyler's turn to be silent. The right words to justify his pretensions to Anita's hand weren't forthcoming. He couldn't blame himself for being bereft of speech when the justice of Mr. Chatterjee's comment was beyond challenge. He could, however, blame himself for the deeds underlying the objections thrown at him. Was he the right husband for his beloved? He had his own qualms about that.

"Maybe another man, a better man than me, should stand next to her at the altar and repeat those everlasting vows. I can't justify a life like the one I've led. Every step of the way I made the worst possible choices," he admitted.

Lotus lay curled in contentment on Mr. Chatterjee's lap, even as Schuyler squirmed. The clock on the bookshelf ticked away. Louder and louder. Ticking away all hope for the hand of his beloved. Life with Anita now seemed beyond his reach. His only chance lay in an aggressive advance. Utter frankness was required but—did he know himself well enough to be that honest?

"Don't worry. I won't waste your time trying to exonerate myself," he began. "The life I've led hasn't been well spent. You already know that, and I won't argue otherwise. But, will you allow me a few minutes to explain what I've learned since moving to Santa Fe?"

Mr. Chatterjee scratched his companion's ears, then looked up. "Continue."

"As I see it, my time in Santa Fe has been an endless string of humiliating circumstances, one after the other, including this conversation. And I admit I deserved every bit of it.

"My mother made me a take-it-or-leave-it offer—move to New Mexico or be set adrift. Penniless. That wasn't an option I relished." Schuyler breathed heavily beneath the weight of his mixed emotions. "Despite my level of education, or maybe because of it, she demanded I apply for a job at Sam's Club. Upon doing so, I discovered the corporation only agreed to interview me because she made a hefty contribution to the Children's

Miracle Network. A Sam's Club charity. A worthy cause, but I wasn't given a chance to stand on my own merits, however few those might be."

"From what I gather, those merits are very few, indeed," was his host's caustic rejoinder. Lotus was now fast asleep. Mr. Chatterjee's cigarette had burned away to nothing in the ashtray.

"You know, I enjoy working on the dock," continued Schuyler, ignoring the provocation. "What with that, walking my dogs, and maintaining my apple orchard, I'm in better shape than I've ever been. I never was a smoker—"

"Pity," Mr. Chatterjee inserted once again.

"—And I no longer drink. I've learned to drive a manual-shift truck, clean out a well housing, put up a barbed wire fence, drive a leveler/stacker, and light a gas oven. If these tasks sound like slight accomplishments, then remember that, in New York, I had no need to know any of these things. I've been on a fast learning curve.

"It's been galling, saddening, to learn how long your family has known my mother and Uncle Harry. To realize Clementine has known Anita for years. I never suspected Harry was gay and that he had a partner. I never even knew Hugh Leigh existed until my uncle died. I never knew Harry and Hugh circumambulated Mount Kailash and published a book about their journey. I've lived my life in ignorance of the people who were most dear to my mother."

"Ah, yes, Mount Kailash," interjected Mr. Chatterjee. "I accompanied them, you know."

"Of course, you did." Schuyler sighed resignedly. "No, Mr. Chatterjee, I didn't know."

"I was the photographer, you see."

A memory jolted Schuyler like a thunderbolt. The photographer. Only the initials "U.C." in Harry's book had identified the Mount Kailash photographer. *Uttam Chatterjee.*

"In saying that, you proved my point, sir. For my whole life I've been ignorant of the web of connections linking this group of people who loved each other. In all honesty, I can't say I loved my children. Or, my wife. I certainly never acted like it." Viewing Mr. Chatterjee's stern countenance Schuyler realized his was a lost cause. "My mother and Harry were the only people I ever loved. And, in saying that I have to add I didn't know, myself, how much I loved them until I moved to New Mexico."

In a near whisper, and as he rubbed his graying temples, he continued. "They probably never knew. How could they? I never told them."

He raised his head to meet Mr. Chatterjee's piercing stare. His host continued scratching Lotus's ears but remained silent.

"Now, I've met other people I've come to love. Anita, of course, is foremost. I thought I'd collapse on the floor when I first laid eyes on her. I was speechless. Tom Jannssen is my best friend. I never had a best friend before Tom. Hugh Leigh tolerates me. He thinks I'm always good for a laugh. I like the guys I work with on the dock. There's Mrs. Chatterjee. There's—"

"Stop right there, Schuyler!" Mr. Chatterjee slapped the desk top. Lotus woke with a start. "Don't you dare say you love me!"

"I don't love you. Why should I? I was going to say I love all my dogs."

"That's better, because I don't love you."

"Big deal. Who cares? All I want from you is your permission to marry Anita, so she will be happy. Then, we can get on with our life together."

"And, if I refuse to give it?"

"I could care less if you refuse. It was Anita's idea to ask your permission, not mine. We will still get married, but she will be unhappy."

"Well—that would be a shame." As Mr. Chatterjee lit his third—or was it his fourth?—cigarette Schuyler realized his opponent hadn't smoked for fifteen minutes. "If you must have her, then I suppose I cannot refuse. Anita no longer has even the shred of a reputation left."

"Don't be so dramatic. This is the twenty-first century."

"And since I will be paying for this travesty, I will also dictate the terms."

"Meaning I must sign some kind of premarital agreement? With *you*? Not with Anita?"

"Here's the deal, and you better take it." Chatterjee tightened his hold on Lotus. "I will pay all your wedding expenses, but I will also choose the site of the ceremony and the officiant. Not negotiable. And the dog stays here. Also not negotiable."

"*What*? But you don't even like Lotus."

"I never said I dislike the dog. I have only said I dislike what the dog does to my lawn."

"I gave the dog to Anita. Lotus is her dog. Not yours."

"Let us be clear. Your original intention, until you caved like a coward, was to give the dog to Mrs. Chatterjee. My wife. As I understand it, you have dogs of your own, Mr. Schuyler."

"I have Bella and the other three pups."

"They shall have to suffice. Make your choice. Take my daughter or the dog."

"I don't know how I'll explain that to Anita," growled Schuyler.

"Tell her you got off easier than you expected. Tell her you're committed to lifelong fidelity as a husband." Mr. Chatterjee ushered Lotus off his lap with a harsh laugh. "I have work to do. Will you please leave?" He rose from his chair, laughing again as he extended his hand.

That laugh was something Schuyler could live without.

CHAPTER 24

Reflections

Plans for the wedding went forward at a rapid pace. Anita and Schuyler set the date for the Sunday following Thanksgiving Day, November 26th. The six-week lead time would give East Coast friends, as well as guests traveling from India, time to get a good fare. Schuyler pretended to listen to Anita's endless conversation about wedding details. It was all she ever talked about.

"Sweetheart, will you agree to something?" he said at last. "Something that would make me very happy?"

"And what would that be?" she asked. "Have I chosen the wrong flavor for the cake?"

"All your choices are perfect. But, for the next three weeks I'm making it a rule that we only talk about the wedding on Tuesday, Thursday, and Saturday. On the other four days we will not once mention the word 'wedding,' nor will we talk about wedding plans."

"Well, what a spoilsport you have turned out to be," she said, laughing. "Perhaps I will surprise you by wearing a flannel night-gown on our wedding night. Or—should I insist we sleep in separate bedrooms for the rest of our lives? That used to be quite a common custom, you know."

"If I thought you were serious, I'd call the whole thing off and transfer to Sam's Club in Anchorage. Maybe I'll do that, anyway. I'm getting pretty tired of goats jumping the orchard fence, and coyotes eating the dogs' kibble."

After lengthy ruminations, and ready to accept a curt refusal, Schuyler took the bold step of asking Hugh Leigh to be his best man.

Leigh shrugged and said, "I wish I could oblige you, old man, but I can't. Sorry."

"Why not? I thought you would be pleased?" Schuyler hadn't missed the fact that Leigh now referred to him as "old man" and not as "boy."

"Under any other circumstances, I would be pleased," Leigh agreed. "But, you see, I'm your officiant. If I'm performing the ceremony I can't be bouncing back and forth between two roles, can I? Guiding you in your vows, and then sliding over to stand beside you and hand you the ring? That would look ridiculous."

"I had no idea you were a minister. What faith?"

"The Church of Hallah's Divinity," answered Leigh.

"Never heard of it."

"Most people haven't."

⤶

Schuyler asked Tom Jannssen to be best man.

"You sure about that, dude?" asked Jannssen, fighting a furious blush and not at all bothered by being his friend's second choice.

"I'm sure. I can't wait to see you wearing a tux. Better yet, Jannssen, don't bother with a tux. Wear whatever you'd wear for a Santa Clara dance."

"It's your call. I'm honored you asked. But I don't know how the old man will take it."

"I don't give a shit how the old man takes it. After the way he raked me over the coals I could care less."

With the flurry of recent events and the pressure of wedding plans, Schuyler was more prone to stress. That meant intestinal problems. IBS was now a daily aggravation. A good part of the reason behind Schuyler's exacerbated bowel symptoms was his pensive mood. Having proposed to Anita, been grilled by Mr. Chatterjee, secured Jannssen as his best man, and removed all the worm-eaten apples from beneath the trees in the orchard, severely repressed memories from his past life surged to the surface. His thoughts turned toward his three children, Nora, Sandy, and Nate. Overwhelmed by guilt he admitted how little their welfare and security had meant to him. How little love he had given them.

Funny. They were still at the bottom of his list of priorities.

Not so funny.

A long-neglected, long-overdue examination of his paternal performance underlay these ruminations. His yearning for a "take number two" in fathering had begun during his road trip to New Mexico and intensified with Harry's death. The happier he now became as the date of his marriage to Anita approached, the more he regretted the loss of those child-rearing years when he should have been more than a disinterested and occasional parent.

Of course, there was no such thing as take number two. He wasn't going to get a second chance to be with his kids, day after day, and year after year. But—*what if?* He wasn't certain of the exact extent of his alienation from them. Since he'd checked out as a father almost from the get-go at Nate's birth, his three children seemed little more than strangers to him. He knew nothing about their hopes, their dreams, or what made them happy.

Could he do anything to redress that regrettable state of affairs? Was there any way to make amends? Was there even a slim chance he might tweak the script of their life together as a family? Do a bit of editing. Was there any chance at all he could rewrite the past and become a decent dad? Be the facsimile of a hero to them, if not the real thing?

The root of this surge in parental nostalgia was his current view of himself as the luckiest man in the world. If guilt due to his role as absentee father was a festering sore still flaming beneath its toughened scab then maybe, just maybe, sharing the happy news of his upcoming marriage with his children might right some of the wrongs he'd done them. His need to reestablish those connections became a powerful urge and Schuyler decided to test the waters. He'd phone his mother and see what she thought about inviting Nate and the girls to his wedding.

"I had an inkling you might want to do that," Clementine began. "You see, Winston—knowing you—hinted the question could crop up. I straightaway asked what he thought of the idea."

"And what did Winston think of the idea?"

"I quote: 'How much more insensitive does Aaron wish to be? Can he name the dates on which his daughters were married? Has he any notion how many grandchildren he has? Has he ever inquired? He'd best prepare himself to go to ground,'" Clementine stated. "I'm not at all sure what comprises the scope of his answer, or what foxhole he was referring to."

"Nora and Sandy are married? *Go to ground*? Could you have misunderstood him?"

"An unlikely chance, Aaron." Clementine cleared her throat. "If I were you, and I intended to proceed with this ill-begotten plan, I'd steel myself to expect the worst. Stiff upper lip, and all that. Otherwise, scrap the project. Why would those young people consider your marriage anything but another insult to their mother?"

Winston's opinion, and Clementine's commentary on said opinion, were discouraging. Daunting, in fact. But, after all, Nate, Nora, and Sandy were his children and not Winston's. *Right?* As their father, he knew them best. Oblivious to the fallacy in his argument he phoned Nate at a number that he hoped was still current.

"Hey, Nate!" he opened cheerily. "How's everything going, son?"

"*Dad*? Oh, my God. Wow. We haven't talked in a long time. Ages."

"I know. I'm sorry. Things just pile up and I should have phoned you. Are you okay?"

"Yeah. Sure. I'm okay—I guess. I'm not sure what you mean—what's up?"

"Well, I wanted to let you know I'm getting married at the end of November. It would be just great if you and the girls could come out to Santa Fe for the wedding." Schuyler waited expectantly for Nate's response, which was as slow as a snail in coming.

"Grandma Clementine told me you had moved to Santa Fe." Nate appeared to choose his words with care. "She also mentioned the wedding, and that you might ask us."

"So, what do you think? Could you make it out here?" enthused Schuyler. The weighty silence that followed was not only unexpected, but uncomfortable.

"I—I don't think so, Dad," faltered Ned. "Thanks for the invitation, but there's so much going on. You know. Like you said, things pile up. Making a trip to Santa Fe doesn't fly."

Schuyler swallowed hard. Doesn't fly. The lump was back in his throat again.

"Yeah. Life, huh? How've you been, son?" He stepped off the end of the plank and asked, "What's new?"

"What's *new*? Well—where to begin?" Nate gave a short harsh laugh. "I'm doing great. I've been great. I'm part of a cardiology practice in Patterson now. Doing okay. Look—I know how busy you are, Dad—"

Schuyler took the hint. Attempts at intimacy were unwelcome. The book of Nate's life was closed to him.

"Great. That's great, son. I'm proud of you," Schuyler added softly. "Maybe I'll ask Nora and Sandy. That is—if you have their cell numbers."

Again, Nate paused.

"I wouldn't do that, Dad. Honestly, I wouldn't do that if I were you. Not that I can't give you their numbers. But, just saying—"

Schuyler struggled to stifle the quiver his voice would betray if he tried to speak. He held his breath as the silence lengthened, but Nate spoke no more.

"Well—" Schuyler exhaled at last. "Thanks. I understand. Thanks for the input. Well—I guess, let's try to talk soon. Call me sometime, Nate."

"Will do, Dad."

Schuyler waited a long time with the phone to his ear. If he could even hear Nate breathing into the phone, that would mean something. He didn't want to be the one to sign off first. Finally, he powered off his cell to forestall any incoming calls. If Anita tried to reach him now, he didn't know how he'd handle their conversation. Would it help if he screamed with rage? *At himself.* Could he ever rid himself of this emptiness, this loss wrenching his heart? Would it help if he broke everything in sight that was breakable?

What had he done? What had he done. What had he done to his children, and himself? To his ex-wife? To his mother. He wanted to scream, to shout, to rage away the guilt and sorrow relentlessly squeezing his lungs and heart in a vise.

This last part, he could do. Schuyler opened the door leading to the small courtyard and walked outside. He stared at the apple orchard filled with barren trees, their empty branches uplifted to heaven like open hands in supplication, empathizing with him. *How could they help?* What might they do to help him?

It was useless trying to control his ragged breathing or the pain in his chest. It was useless trying to control his wild emotions. Instead of screaming, Schuyler collapsed onto the seat of one of the plastic chairs and broke down and let it all out. Crying. Bella and her pups huddled close to his feet and stared up at him, wide-eyed, and wailed in unison with his wracking sobs.

CHAPTER 25

The Big Day

The remaining prewedding weeks flew by. Schuyler, his anticipation now bittersweet following the traumatic conversation with Nate, ordered a tux. Mourning the loss of his three children had become a full-time job, yet life wasn't a total waste. As he thought long and hard about the lurid swamp of his past decisions, the light dawned. He discovered the value of assessing his many stumbles, the little cruelties, his constant negligence of others. By recognizing how he could have avoided each misstep, he could apologize. He learned to beat himself up in a less violent manner. It still hurt like hell but what a breakthrough.

He could cope. The cultivation of a proper mode of life wasn't a question of intelligence, but of decency and sensitivity to the feelings of others. *Duh.* Imagine that.

He now did his best to recall that singular moment every time he conversed or interacted with anyone at all. No matter who. Even Mr. Chatterjee.

❧

The day of the wedding arrived, with the ceremony scheduled to begin at four in the afternoon. Chatterjee relatives arrived from Kolkata, London, and the East Coast. Stan and Clementine Atwater were staying at the Plaza Hotel downtown. Mr. Chatterjee, enamored of his abundant late autumn chrysanthemums, decided Anita and Schuyler would be married in the sun room of his home, with baskets of deep gold and russet blooms hanging from a vast wedding canopy. The two spare bedrooms were bursting with family and cots were set up in his study. With no hideaway to call his own, he moved a chair, a small table, and an ashtray into a corner of the garage. Wearing a down jacket and a woolen cap he spent hours at a time there with Lotus, near a portable heater.

"Kicked out of my home," he grumbled to his wife the night before the wedding. "Kicked out of my own study."

"Well, I don't know what else you expected, Uttam," she hissed. "These people have spent thousands of dollars traveling to Santa Fe for Anita's wedding!" Exhausted, strands of sweaty hair plastered to her forehead after cooking dinner for twenty-five people, Mrs. Chatterjee had joined her husband in the garage. Their guests were asleep, the kitchen was once again clean, and now it was time for a final review of Sunday's festive schedule.

"The least you can do is pretend you are happy."

"I have no use for pretense," Mr. Chatterjee snarled through a smoky fog, "and the wedding kurta you ordered for me set me back one thousand dollars. Is that something to be happy about?"

"Oh, you are impossible. Your daughter is getting married tomorrow, and you should be the happiest man in the world."

"I fail to see how those two points are either logical or connected. The one does not follow the other."

⌐

Schuyler, at home in Nambé, donned his tux in no time—he was accustomed to this routine from his funeral-scrounging days—and locked the dogs inside the house. A nearby neighbor had volunteered to feed them, give them potty breaks, and let them run around in the orchard during the day. Schuyler was concerned about his gurgling intestines. Today they were more active than usual, but what the hell. His intestines gurgled most of the time, and he was anxious to be on his way. It was time to pick up Tom Jannssen, and he had a ten-mile drive to Santa Clara Pueblo. From there they'd head toward Santa Fe and the Chatterjee home.

With his foot pressed to the gas pedal—and his mind occupied with a myriad of pre-wedding details—he failed to check his rear-view mirror. He didn't see the light flashing atop the

Explorer behind him and was unaware of pursuit until a siren pierced the air.

That friggin' cop.

He pulled over, fidgeting, more than ever aware of being on the verge of a big mess.

"Mr. Schuyler? How've you been?" grinned Officer Gomez.

"Just fine," was his victim's curt reply. "Look, Officer, if I was going a bit fast—"

"A bit over forty miles per hour in a twenty-five zone."

"You see, I'm heading into Santa Fe for my wedding—look how I'm dressed, if you don't believe me." He gestured toward his gray vest, the boutonniere in a tidy box, and a tux jacket draped over the passenger seat. "I have to pick up my best man in Santa Clara and we're running out of time."

"Then you should have left home earlier," cackled Gomez. "But, congratulations, sir. There's nothing like marriage. I'm on my fourth."

He returned to his car, filled out a citation report, then walked back to Schuyler's car.

"If you're not more careful, your insurance is gonna go way up. Sign here." He handed the clipboard to Schuyler. "You might want to notice I only gave you a warning. Wedding gift." He retrieved the clipboard, ripped out Schuyler's copy of the citation and handed it to him.

"See you next time!" Gomez touched the brim of his cap.

"Thank you, Officer!" Schuyler shouted out the window as he started his truck and proceeded down 503 at a crawl. After what seemed an age he reached Highway 84 and the light turned green. But he no sooner crossed the intersection when the pressure in his abdomen tightened like a fist and his intestines expelled a flood. *Whoosh.*

"Oh, Christ!" He didn't dare exceed the speed limit, but he teased the edge of it as he hurried toward Jannssen's home. Once there, he pressed the horn and kept honking until Tom emerged.

"What the hell, Schuyler! You're early and I'm not dressed."

"I had an accident in my pants. It's that damned Gomez who lurks along 503. He got me again and I pooped."

"You don't have to tell me. I can smell it for myself."

"Funny. Really funny," Schuyler replied hotly. "I'll need to wear your tux pants and you can wear jeans under your jacket."

"I don't have a tux, man. Remember? You wanted me to wear a dancing outfit."

"Holy shit! What am I going to do?" Schuyler screeched. "As it is, we'll just make it to Santa Fe by four o'clock."

"Come on in. Get yourself cleaned up. Wear my jeans with your jacket and you'll be fine. No one will notice and we'll drive my truck into town."

Bowlegged, protecting Jannssen's floors with a bath towel between his pants legs, Schuyler limped into the bathroom. He did his best to wash up but wasn't all that sure he'd done an efficient job. Did he still smell? What was he going to tell Anita?

Struggling to stuff himself into Jannssen's best pair of skinny jeans, hauling on his vest and tux jacket over them and adjusting his boutonniere, he rushed out of the bathroom.

"Let's go, man," said Jannssen, jingling the keys to his own truck.

"You've got the ring?" panted Schuyler.

"I've got the ring. You're in good hands."

At 3:30 p.m. Jannssen jammed on the brakes in front of the Chatterjee residence. He and Schuyler jumped out of the truck and raced up the walk to the front door. The street was lined with trucks, sedans, and SUVs. An odd cacophony issued from the backyard. From his vantage point Schuyler discerned a string quartet tuning their instruments. A quartet overwhelmed by fierce competition from sitars wailing an aggressive raga.

The door opened as Schuyler rang the bell. Before him stood Mrs. Chatterjee, resplendent in a pink sari encrusted with silver embroidery. Mr. Chatterjee, attired in a white silk kurta heavily embroidered with gold, gave her a run for her money. Peering over Chatterjee's shoulder was Hugh Leigh wearing what looked like a saffron-hued Buddhist monk's robe. *Holy hell.*

The tiers of people behind them included Clementine and Stan Atwater, and what looked to Schuyler like Mr. and Mrs. Amit Chatterjee of the Bronx. *Déjà vu*. Again, Schuyler's worst nightmare. In the flesh.

The eager smiles adorning the faces of all these people faded in horror at first sight of Schuyler and Tom Jannssen.

"Good God, man, what are you wearing?" exploded Mr. Chatterjee.

Mrs. Chatterjee gave a shriek, then covered her mouth. "Mr. Schuyler! *Jeans*! Oh, no!" spilled out as she recovered her power of speech. "Not even in Santa Fe!"

"Hey, Lone Goose. Good to see you," said Hugh Leigh, raising his saffron-robed arms in confusion. "But why are you dressed for an eagle dance?"

Only then did Schuyler realize what a sight the two of them presented. Absorbed as he was in shedding his soiled clothes and putting on Tom's jeans, he hadn't taken a good look at Jannssen's cream-colored chamois top and leggings with fringed sleeve and leg seams. Or, at Tom's resplendent moccasins bearing thousands of beads. Personally, he felt it was a gorgeous outfit. Just the touch of local color he'd hoped to add to an uptight ceremony.

The Chatterjees plainly thought otherwise, and Schuyler had given up trying to fathom Hugh Leigh's thinking. Unprepared for what happened next, a flush seared his cheeks as Mr. Amit Chatterjee squeezed Yuthi Chatterjee's arm.

"Yuthi!" Amit Chatterjee cried. "That is the fellow! Remember what I told you? This is bad. Too bad! I tell you, that is the fellow from New York!"

Mrs. Chatterjee stamped on her relative's instep with a strength Schuyler hadn't imagined her capable of. "Oh, do come in, Mr. Schuyler! Come in before someone sees you!" She grabbed her future son-in-law's tux sleeve and jerked him over the threshold.

"You've added more beads to your sleeves," Leigh commented to Jannssen. "Nice touch. It really defines the fringe."

"Who cares!" Mrs. Chatterjee shrieked again. "What are we going to do?"

Everyone stared as if expecting her to provide the answer to her own question. When had Yuthi Chatterjee never had the solution to a problem? A door down the hall suddenly opened and Anita appeared in all the magnificent glory of her wedding clothes, a gold-embroidered crimson-red sari with matching blouse.

"Go!" Mrs. Chatterjee commanded, waving her arms in an attempt to herd her daughter back into the bedroom. "Go! Your face is uncovered. He mustn't see you before the ceremony!"

"Someone please tell me what all this noise is about?" Anita asked, ignoring her mother's distress. "Aaron, where are your tux slacks?"

"That is what we would all like to know!" seconded Mrs. Chatterjee. "Where are your tux slacks, Mr. Schuyler? Why are you wearing those jeans that are too tight for you?"

"Upon my word, Aaron," chimed in Clementine. "What *has* happened to your slacks? And don't give us one of your dodgy stories!"

"Can we please have some privacy?" Schuyler shouted to Anita over the crowd gathered in the entry. "This concerns only you and me. Maybe your parents, at the outside."

"Not Stan and myself?" asked Clementine, gesturing toward Atwater.

"Later, Mom."

"Follow me." Beckoning to Schuyler, Anita walked back toward her bedroom. Schuyler, following upon her heels, shut the door behind him. "Speak to me, Aaron."

"This isn't easy to say," he began. "But you know about my troubles with IBS. That damn cop on 503 stopped me again and I shit my pants. Tom lent me these jeans. End of story."

"Well, I don't see what is so very bad about that. And this fix will be easy to remedy." Anita opened the bedroom door. "Mataji! Bapu! Please will you join us?"

Mr. and Mrs. Chatterjee having entered her room, she again closed the door. "Simply put, and don't ask any questions, Aaron

had an accident. Now, we cannot let him stand through the ceremony wearing a pair of Tom Jannssen's ill-fitting jeans."

"I agree," stated Mrs. Chatterjee. "But what are we to do,
Anita?"

"Bapu," Anita turned toward her father. "You must let Aaron
have this wedding kurta you are wearing. It is suitable for a
groom as well as a bride's father."

"Absolutely not." Mr. Chatterjee glanced around for an ashtray.
Not finding one, he flicked the extinguished ashes into the palm
of his hand.

"Bapu, put out that cigarette. I do not wish to have smoke
residue in my bedroom."

"Well, I don't imagine you will be sleeping here tonight, nor
ever again, so what does it matter?"

"Very well, Bapu, but you must let Aaron wear this kurta.
Today is my wedding day and I want everything to be perfect!
You can wear your sky-blue kurta instead." Anita was pleading
now, tears welling up in her eyes.

Schuyler felt helpless. He had no choice but to shut up and
pray. *Show me what you've got, Winston.* If he dared back up
Anita's request, the old tiger would fly off the handle for sure.

"Not on your life, daughter!" Mr. Chatterjee thrust out a hand
to thwart Anita. "This kurta set me back a thousand dollars—and
let *him* wear it? Again, I say no!"

"Come, Uttam!" urged Mrs. Chatterjee. "We are out of time. Is
that such a big deal?"

"Oh, Bapu! *Please*—" With a graceful swish of her sari, Anita
sank to her knees at his feet, her hennaed hands clasped together
in a prayerful posture.

"Up, girl! What are you doing? You will ruin that sari! Do you
have any idea what those six feet of fabric cost me?"

"Uttam! Never tell her!" Mrs. Chatterjee slapped his arm. "Oh,
how shameful!"

"Five thousand dollars! What do you think of that?"

Simultaneously, both Anita and Schuyler perceived a shift in
the atmosphere of the room. This was a now or never moment.

This was their moment. Anita lowered her carefully coiffed head to the floor just as Schuyler stepped forward and gently took her arm, helping her to rise.

"Come, my dear," he urged. "You had best obey your father. I don't mind wearing this old pair of jeans. The only important thing is that we get married."

"Oh, what a charade this is!" Mr. Chatterjee threw up his hands, spewing sparks and ashes from his cigarette onto the carpet. "Enough! Let him wear the damn kurta. What does it matter if the sky-blue one I must wear has a hole in the knee?"

"A cigarette burn!" challenged Mrs. Chatterjee. "And whose fault is that?"

"You—you women! Leave the room!" Mr. Chatterjee ordered. "We don't need you. Bring me the other kurta. I will help him put on this one."

As Anita and her mother scurried out, Chatterjee crushed his cigarette into the carpet. "I never liked this color. Rose. You— Schuyler. Take off everything but your underwear."

"I don't have any. It got soiled."

"Ooojjyy!" Mr. Chatterjee thrust his glance toward the ceiling, jerked open the bedroom door, and called down the hallway. "Bring me a pair of jockeys!"

The bedroom door opened a crack and Mrs. Chatterjee handed in the sky-blue kurta and underwear. The two men changed garments and Schuyler brushed back his hair. He pinned his boutonniere onto the kurta jacket and ventured a comment.

"You do look good in the blue, Mr. Chatterjee. Quite distinguished."

"Just remember what that kurta cost me," Chatterjee growled. "And don't let the damned dog jump on you."

"Sir." Schuyler cleared his throat. "You can have no idea what this day means to me. No idea how—" Unable to speak further, he clenched his jaw, closed his eyes, and shook his head.

Mr. Chatterjee clapped him on the shoulder and extended his hand.

CHAPTER 26

Just Married

As Schuyler and Mr. Chatterjee approached the sun room, Schuyler was startled to see the entire room blanketed, wall-to-wall, by chairs packed with chattering guests. He stopped abruptly on viewing this scene. At the far end stood the massive wedding canopy bedecked with Mr. Chatterjee's prize chrysanthemums. The guest chairs were arranged in two phalanxes with a narrow aisle separating them. This aisle, which would soon deliver his bride to him, must first be traversed by him in order to arrive at the canopy.

"Well, go on!" hissed Mr. Chatterjee, giving Schuyler a sharp shove. "Get up there. It's something we all have to go through."

"Don't push me."

"Then get going. I have to get back to Anita."

Beneath the canopy stood Tom Jannssen, glaring at Schuyler who, with a heavy exhale, strode up the silk-carpeted aisle. Why was this so difficult? After all, his only task was to stand next to Tom and give the correct response when prompted to do so. He was acutely aware of all the eyes fastened upon him as he took his place near the best man.

"I've been standing here for twenty minutes," whispered Jannssen. "What took you so long? They're all staring at me. Are we ready to start?"

"God, I hope so," answered Schuyler, wiping a few drops from his forehead. Beset by flashbacks to his first wedding some thirty years ago, he clutched at Jannssen's arm.

"You okay, man?" Jannssen asked. "You don't look so good. Remind me never to do what you're about to do."

"I'm fine. Maybe a little nervous. You got the ring?"

"Here in my pocket. Like I said, no worries."

Schuyler scanned the first two rows of guests and fixed upon Stan Atwater and Clementine. His mother was resplendent in a pink two-piece outfit. No doubt an Alexander McQueen original. When Clementine caught his eye and waved a handkerchief, Schuyler squinted. *What the hell—?*

Not a handkerchief. Clementine was waving a mini British flag. A cheap copy from some National Trust shop. Must have been Winston's idea.

Stan Atwater's mouth was a thin grim line. No surprise there. His piercing glance was a clear warning that the groom better not fuck this up. No more chances. Still, Schuyler mused, as this signal joined the whirl of impressions cruising through his mind, in all fairness, Atwater wasn't a bad guy. If you didn't cross him.

Behind the Atwaters, the rows of chairs were filled with guests as well-dressed as Clementine. Most of them were his mother's New York cronies. Bishop Martin Euless took pride of place next to the Anglican Church Guild members, the country club members, rowing team members, and Neville family members from Leeds, Chichester, and Hay-on-Wye. Schuyler was delighted to see several former staff members from Novel Ideas on that side of the aisle. When he waved, they waved back.

On the other side of the aisle, sitting behind Mrs. Chatterjee, he spotted Mike Three Rivers, Ernie, and Jesús all dressed in sport coats and creased slacks. *Way to go, guys.* Schuyler thrust both arms straight up into the air. Until tonight he'd never seen them wear anything but their work clothes and associates' vests. "Happy to Help." The three high-fived one another then, as one, raised their fists. What? Was this some kind of Pueblo-Hispanic code?

The rows behind the dock crew were filled with saris and kurtas in every imaginable hue and color. A magnificent sight. *Uh-oh.* Two rows behind his future mother-in-law sat Amit Chatterjee and his wife, flanked by their three children, now much older. Mr. Chatterjee greeted his nod of acknowledgment with a scowl. His wife again seemed confused, and Schuyler saw no reason to keep looking in their direction. He was jittery enough without that negative feedback.

Sensitivity to others. Remember, Schuyler? Decency. He owed Amit Chatterjee an explanation and a sincere apology, if not a down-on-his-knees grovel. Yes, that would happen before this day came to an end, but first he had to get married.

As the string quartet ended their soft rendition of "I can't help falling in love with you" and the sitar trio commenced a slow-paced raga, Schuyler glanced back down the aisle. Behind two toddler girls bearing baskets of rose petals stood Mr. Chatterjee with Anita. His mouth fell open as he stared. He had never seen her look more radiant, even with the glow of sex upon her. Aware of his gaze, she slowly lowered the transparent red silk veil over her eyes. Mr. Chatterjee placed Anita's hand on his arm and the two paced down the aisle behind the toddlers, now occupied with strewing rose petals and bumping into one another. Cute.

At last Anita and her father reached the canopy. As Mr. Chatterjee placed Anita's right hand in Schuyler's, he fixed a meaningful stare upon the bridegroom and gripped his sleeve. *Shit.* That wasn't part of the rehearsal.

"Go, Uttam," spoke a voice from behind Schuyler. He glanced over his shoulder to see Hugh Leigh standing but a foot away in his saffron robe. When had he appeared upon the scene?

"Let go of Aaron's sleeve, Uttam, and take your seat." Leigh whispered again, urging Mr. Chatterjee away from the canopy to where Yuthi awaited him in the first row.

With a fierce and baleful look Mrs. Chatterjee patted the seat next to her. "Here, Uttam!" She beckoned toward him with a pack of Wills Navy Cut cigarettes. "Here!"

Schuyler breathed with relief when his sleeve was released and Mr. Chatterjee plopped down in his assigned chair and lit up. From beneath his seat he extracted an ashtray.

Anita's smile was brilliant. Clementine's smile was brilliant. Stan Atwater fidgeted and looked bored. In his book, no doubt the best wedding was one over and done with. Schuyler, sweating as he observed his stepfather, couldn't agree more. *Right there with you, buddy.*

In a daze, he listened to Hugh Leigh's homily about the joys of marriage and wondered why he had failed so abysmally to experience these in his first marriage. He smiled down at Anita. A fixed, plastered-on smile. *Marriage.* He'd fucked it up the first time around through sheer selfishness and self-absorption. Was there any guarantee he wouldn't do that again? With Anita—whom he worshiped as a goddess?

"And do you, Aaron Daniel Schuyler, take this woman to be your lawful wife, to have and to hold, from this day forward?"

What if he wasn't cut out for taking vows?

Schuyler heard the words spoken by Hugh Leigh, but only as if he, himself, were a witness at someone else's wedding. That avowal surely wasn't meant for him. Surely, those words didn't require his agreement. His commitment. His body and soul. He took a deep breath but all he inhaled was the smoke from Mr. Chatterjee's cigarette and the odor of Nag Champa incense drifting toward him.

He choked.

"Aaron! Are you okay?" Anita whispered. Her bridegroom's vacant expression was anything but reassuring.

Schuyler choked again and gulped down a second breath. Maybe he should have run this marriage proposition past Winston and asked him if it was a good idea. It's true, he'd never put much store in the PM's advice, but was it too late to start now? Hadn't he always been a late bloomer? *Better late than never.*

"Aaron! What is happening?" Anita queried as she tugged at his sleeve.

"Bloody hell, Aaron!" hissed Clementine, leaning forward from her first-row chair. "Hugh asked you a question! Answer the man! Winston says it's a go!"

"I do!" Schuyler ejaculated in a less assured tone than he would have wished his future wife to hear. *Damn.*

Anita's response, delivered as Hugh Leigh opened his mouth to speak her cue, was curt.

"I *do!*"

Schuyler's breathing relaxed. He straightened his slumped shoulders and glanced toward Hugh Leigh who was pronouncing Anita and himself "man and wife."

"Well done, old man!" Leigh's familiar, almost-invisible smirk appeared, then disappeared as he clapped Schuyler's shoulder. "Best move you've ever made in your life."

"Fuckin' right!"

"Aaron—!" Anita gasped, casting a swift glance at the congregation.

"What—?" Schuyler answered as he bent to kiss her, smearing her lipstick as he did so, delighted to see Anita's shocked expression morph into a wicked grin.

"Fuckin' right!" she echoed.

With Schuyler's arm wrapped tight around Anita's shoulder, followed by Tom Jannssen, Hugh Leigh, and the flower girls, the newlyweds paced back down the aisle to the strains of Bach's Great Fugue in G minor—*whose play list was this?*—challenged by the raga now raging at an ear-splitting volume and dizzying tempo. They failed to see Hugh stop near Clementine's chair and share a fist bump with her.

Foremost among Schuyler's memories when he later had time to reflect back upon his marriage and sort out what mattered from the blur of cigarette smoke, rose petals, champagne, incense, carrot cake, and a spoken mix of Hindi with English, were three things. He was married to his beloved Anita. He'd taken Amit Chatterjee aside and offered him a heartfelt apology. This was accepted with a graciousness Schuyler felt he didn't deserve and had no right to receive.

"Ah well, Mr. Schuyler, we all have our peccadillos and inglorious moments, you know." Amit Chatterjee's head listed gently from side to side. "May Ganesh bless your household with happiness and many children."

Schuyler reached out to shake Amit Chatterjee's hand.

"Anita tells me that, for some reason, no room in your home has draperies or curtains," Amit Chatterjee began with an expression of concern. "It makes me very happy to tell you she is buying from me styles so elegant they are beyond belief. Styles for every room. What excellent taste she has!" Chatterjee accepted the handshake. "I know you will approve her choices. Such taste she has! So highly refined, but expensive, you know. Very expensive."

Schuyler grimaced, hesitated, then nodded. He knew when he'd been had.

If that memory stood out in his mind, it was no competition at all for the third thing that mattered most to him. His waltz with Clementine for the traditional mother-bridegroom, father-bride wedding dance. This was the first time Schuyler had put his arm around his mother and danced with her. The first time ever. Again—his loss. He'd been skeptical about what to expect as they circled the sun room, all chairs having been removed. Would she chide him for his hesitation at the altar? Would Winston read him the riot act?

The string quartet was playing Tom Petty's "Wildflowers" and, as it turned out, Clementine said nothing at all. Her grip on his shoulder was numbing. Her hand, held by his own, was rigid. Her shoulders were shaking, and every now and then a tear escaped and rolled down her cheek.

"Rise above, Mom," Schuyler whispered into her ear. "Rise above."

CHAPTER 27

The Last Diary Entry

Under a shower of imported marigold blossoms rained down upon them by the wedding guests lining the front lawn walkway, Anita and Schuyler made their way toward Tom Jannssen's waiting pickup. Jannssen had loaned it to the newlyweds for their honeymoon drive to Big Sur on the Central California coast. He would drive Anita's Prius back to Santa Clara Pueblo and use it while they were away. Always generous, he also offered to clean up the mess in Schuyler's truck as a wedding gift.

After spending their wedding night in Nambé, the Schuylers loaded Bella and her three pups, dog care equipment, and luggage into the pickup on Monday and headed west. They reached their lodging five days later after visiting the Grand Canyon, Santa Barbara, and Pismo Beach. An internet search turned up a Big Sur motel with kenneling facilities to meet their needs.

Both Anita and Schuyler were worn out by the time they ate dinner and settled into the rooms they'd occupy for a week. The fireplace with logs stacked next to it was a welcome sight. They hadn't stopped to think that the sunny California coast would be cold and windy in early December. They unpacked their clothes, checked on the dogs one last time, and, exhausted, fell into bed.

Schuyler lay there, thinking, unable to sleep despite his fatigue. There was something he needed to do, must do, and it made no sense to postpone doing it.

Careful not to waken Anita, he slipped out of bed, pulled on a sweatshirt, retrieved his Diary, and an envelope he had picked up from the motel reception desk, and tiptoed out of the bedroom. In the sitting room area, he sat down on a couch with a view of the shoreline and ocean. It was too dark to see the waves, but he could distinguish the dull roar of the surf and its accompanying crash onto the rocky beach. Turning on a small lamp, assured the light wouldn't disturb Anita, he flipped the pages of the diary until he found a blank one, then started writing. When he finished the entry he carefully tore the pages from the diary. *Wow.* He'd often threatened to remove incriminating pages, but the diary was so sacrosanct he'd never actually done that. First time for everything. He folded the pages into the envelope, sealed it, addressed it, turned off the lamp, and returned to bed.

⌒

Clementine and Stan Atwater stayed on in Santa Fe for a few days after the wedding, visiting with Yuthi and Uttam and Hugh Leigh and reliving highlights of the festivities. Stan, who viewed himself as a rugged individualist, was enthralled with the Southwest. He bought a four-hundred-dollar pair of Tony Lama boots and was reluctant to return to Ohio. Once back home, he asked Clementine if she'd like to sell the Akron mansion, buy a spread near Santa Fe, and raise some cattle. They weren't that old, he argued, and it was never too late to start over.

"What do you think, dear?"

"Sorry, love! Give me a moment." Clementine had received a letter postmarked Monterey, California. The embossed return address on the envelope stated, "Big Sur Lodge."

"How odd. I think this is from Aaron." She slit open the envelope and saw, revealed, the strangest missive she'd ever received.

"Oh!" With a gasp, she collapsed onto the silk-upholstered sofa and began to read.

Dear Diary,

I guess the best way to start is to tell you how around the beginning of autumn, maybe it was the middle of September, not sure about that, I started having an epiphany. Anyway, that's what I call it. Well, no—I take that back. *Not* the epiphany, but the timing. Let's go back to June 23rd. I'd been in love with Anita Chatterjee from the very first moment I saw her, but on June 23rd I thought everything was hopeless between us because when I asked her for a date, she said no. You know from other things I've written, how down and frustrated I was, thinking I'd *never* have the chance to tell her what was in my heart.

Then, about three months later everything was turned around and upside down. That was when Anita first asked me to have dinner with her family and we started dating. It turns out she was as much in love with me, as I was with her. This I found hard to believe then and, at times, often, really, still do.

Looking back, I remember how nervous I felt, how worried about an episode of IBS when I went to their home for dinner. *Hugh Leigh* was also there. I didn't say a lot that night, wasn't the most voluble guest, but there was a lot going through my mind. Up till then I'd thought Leigh was a crusty old fart. Of course, he was far from finished mourning Uncle Harry, and I knew that. But while we ate I watched him watching me and I could see his opinion of me was changing for the better. *Not* that he said so. I knew he was glad I was there, part of the company, and having dinner with them.

Diary, you *can't imagine* how much I enjoyed that evening. It made me wonder if I had ever enjoyed anything ever before in my life. It left me wondering if, at last, all the countless chips *had fallen off* my shoulder. It hit me in the face, and I finally understood that whatever misfortune I'd suffered, whatever ill luck came my way, was always the result of my *poor* choices. I thought to myself, *Hallelujah*.

Is it in the bible that someone says the scales fell from their eyes? I don't know what kind of scales those are, but I know what it feels like to have them gone. My perspective changed. I didn't feel angry or humiliated because I'd been such a moron as to bring a dog to Mrs. Chatterjee as a hostess gift. I laughed, and I realized how much better off I'd have been if I'd laughed more often. Laughed with Clementine, instead of laughing at her.

This is almost tragic but, you know, I don't think I've ever had a good laugh with my mother and I know she has an outrageous, beyond good sense of humor. *My loss.* Instead of enjoying her for what she is, absolutely fantastic, I kept taking advantage of her and acting like an adolescent, making up excuses for doing so. A rotter, in her terms.

I was so comfortable with those people sitting around the table. Yeah, I didn't say much, and that was probably all to the good, but I was happy to be with them. I was enjoying myself. I was having fun, not to mention the fact that I was sitting next to Anita.

In some ways it was better to be a listener. Here was a group of people, people my mother knew, but I hadn't known they knew each other. They valued and respected my mother. I couldn't pat myself on the back and say I'd done the same.

I felt pulled apart. Sad. I could have belonged to this group a lot earlier on if I'd lived my life in a different way. In a *better* way. And if I'd chosen differently I would have seen my mother as the Chatterjee family and Hugh Leigh saw her. As an incredible woman who got stuck with a son who was almost worthless. I know *she never* stopped loving me and trying to do her best by me. If only I had done the same for her, and better understood her relationship with my father. How she protected me as a child.

I made myself my own victim. What moron does that, and chooses to hurt himself, to *shut out* all those who really love him?

My mother gave me the greatest gift in the world when she gave me one more chance, sent me to Santa Fe and forced me to work at Sam's Club. She planned the whole thing out, down to the last detail, even knowing I'd meet Tom Jannssen, who knew her, and that she could depend on Tom to take me under his wing. She knew when I walked up those steps to the Human Resources Office that I'd fall in love with Anita.

How could I help myself? *She gave me Anita.*

I phoned my mother on October 31st, about a month before our wedding, to wish her a happy Halloween. Her favorite holiday. She started talking at once about Winston's latest communication, his views on every possible subject under the sun. Something was triggered in me as I listened to her.

You see, my mother is a most fortunate woman. Right then, I yearned to believe in something—*anything at all*—with the same passion, fervor, and faith she offered to her god. Winston. It was a real *ah-hah* moment. I'd always wondered what that term meant, and now I understand. If I was speaking to her right now, I'd say thank you and I'd say I love you, Mom. Very much. I always have.

December 1, 2018

Clementine was still seated on the sofa lost in thought, her lips parted as if she was about to say something. There she sat, bolt upright, staring straight ahead, her eyes glazed over and unblinking. She still held the diary pages in her hand. Her form was so rigid Stan wondered if she was having a seizure but he wasn't sure what a seizure looked like. As far as he could recall, there was nothing of the sort in her medical history, but you never know. At their age it could happen.

She slowly sagged off the sofa and with a soft thud landed on her knees. Reverently placing the pages from Aaron's diary on the carpet in front of her and smoothing them out as if they were a map to hidden treasure or celestial riches, she clasped her hands together.

"What is it, darling?" Atwater was agitated. "Tell me. Please tell me."

"Stan, love, hold me for a moment," Clementine whispered. "My every prayer has been answered. If only you knew how much—oh, if only Harry was here to share this moment with us. I'm so grateful for *you*, Stan!"

Atwater knelt beside her and clasped her clasped hands in his.

"I knew neither of them would fail us. Neither Aaron nor Churchill. I knew Aaron wasn't a lost cause. That wasn't even possible. Just hold me, and let us give thanks to Winston!"

ABOUT THE AUTHOR

Photo: Susan Levin

Rhenna St. Clair, a Portland, Oregon, native, arrived in New Mexico in 1992. Fascinated by the beauty of the land and its history, the archaeological sites and the mix of cultures, she can't imagine living anywhere else. A licensed acupuncturist and practitioner of Chinese medicine, St. Clair has traveled in China as well as in India and other parts of Asia. She now practices Chinese medicine and acupuncture in northern New Mexico. Her poetry has been published in *Perspective(s) Magazine*, the literary journal of San Juan College. *Getting New Mexico* is her first book.